THE BINDING OF BLOOM MOUNTAIN

DEFINITIVE EDITION

VESPER DOOM

PRAISE FOR THE BINDING OF BLOOM MOUNTAIN

WINNER OF THE 2023 QUEER INDIE AWARD FOR BEST ADVENTURE

A love letter to nature and an unsettling adventure into the Appalachian occult.

— CRAIG MONTGOMERY, AUTHOR OF *A CIRCLE OF STARS*

A comforting hug concealing treacherous shadows, a warm cup of tea that soothes the reader while terrors are getting dangerously close. A cozy horror masterpiece that traps pure magic in its pages.

— FREDDIE A. CLARK, AUTHOR OF *UMBRA: TALES OF A SHADOW*

The OwnVoices Autism representation was phenomenal.

— KARA @BOOKS.AND.SALT, BOOK REVIEWER

There is something so entrancing about the storytelling. Vesper really spins us into the narrative of the binding of the mountain.

— CHAOTIC WITCH AUNT, YOUTUBER AND FOLK MAGIC PRACTITIONER

A cozy mix of folk horror, personal discovery, and sweet sapphic romance.

— DANI FINN, AUTHOR AND BLOGGER

What a lovely, dark, chilling, and magical book.

— AZALEA FORREST, AUTHOR OF *THE WITCH OF EMELLE* SERIES

The Binding of Bloom Mountain is a true book. More than a story, more than a work of fictional entertainment, it winds its roots into the soul of Virginia and blossoms with native fervor. Doom has done something magical here.

— BELLAMY SCOTT, AUTHOR OF *A KIND VOICE IN HELL*

Bloom Mountain is the definition of cozy.

— S. S. GENESEE, AUTHOR OF *ALL TOMORROW'S PHOTOS* DUOLOGY

Reminiscent of both Jean Craighead George and Jeff Vandermeer, *The Binding of Bloom Mountain* is a beautifully haunting read and a hell of a good yarn.

— GABRIEL HARGRAVE, AUTHOR OF *THE ORCHID AND THE LION*

"A wonderful refresh that dives this modern, dark, folklore-inspired tale and leaves me wanting more of this liminal universe."

— CARA NOX, AUTHOR OF *TRICK* AND *THE THIRTEENTH KEY* SERIES

"Doom builds a tense, yet cozy story full of excitement and tenderness. Her deft hand at world building offers a vivid backdrop for the wilderness drama that unfolds. You won't want to leave Bloom Mountain once you've begun."

— SARAH L HAWTHORN, AUTHOR OF 2025 DEBUT *THE DROWNED COAST*

"Cozy and creepy aren't two things I usually see meshed together but somehow Vesper Doom brilliantly pulls this off with a delicate, eerie build to some wild twists all with a dash of romance thrown in."

— MN BENNET, AUTHOR OF THE *BRANCHES OF PAST AND FUTURE* SERIES

"The Binding of Bloom Mountain is an atmospheric tale with the perfect mix of Appalachian folk horror, sapphic sweetness, and self-discovery."

— KARA JORGENSEN, AUTHOR OF *THE REANIMATOR MYSTERIES SERIES*

This one is still for me.

For the past me who needed help.
For the present me who is still here.
For the future me and all the books I'll write.

It is good to have an end to journey toward; but it is the journey that matters, in the end.

— URSULA K. LE GUIN, THE LEFT HAND OF
DARKNESS

CONTENTS

FOREWORD

This is a book about an autistic woman. As an autistic afab person, it was important to me to show the different ways that autism can manifest. No two autistic people experience it the same way, so if Celeste doesn't act the way you expect, please keep your mind open.

CONTENT WARNINGS

This book contains the discussion or description of content that might be triggering. Please read the following before deciding to read this book:

- autistic shutdowns, meltdowns, overstimulation
- vomiting
- drowning
- death: of children, of animals (both off-page)
- alcohol use
- swearing
- family traumas, family secrets
- mental and emotional manipulation
- body horror
- illness: cancer, unspecified wasting illness

1

ADVENTURER WANTED

It was a beautiful Friday afternoon in late August when Celeste Foster's life imploded.

Celeste had just come back from lunch when her manager called her into his office. It had the same look as every other US Government office in the building: cold, uncomfortable, impersonal. A couple photos of his wife and their daughter dotted the desk and filing cabinets, but there was only so much that could be done.

"Foster," he greeted her, gesturing to one of the chairs by his desk.

Celeste sat down and waited. The tone of his voice worried her. She always noticed when someone she knew well acted differently, whether they intended for her to notice or not.

Her manager, Evan Moore, was a tall, broad guy; former military who'd successfully transitioned to a civilian government job with the US Forestry Service. He had a crop of dark hair trimmed short over watery blue eyes and an angular, but aging, face. His suit was tighter across the middle than it had been when he'd taken the job five years earlier.

"Everything okay? Did one of those reports go missing?"

Moore shook his head. "As you know, *Congress* has reduced the budget further." He sounded annoyed, resigned, more like himself. "Your name was put up by one of my managers for a reduction in force and the orders came in today"

Celeste, uncertain how to process what she'd just been told, blinked at him for several moments while she formulated a response. "Did I do something wrong?"

"No, just unlucky this time." He stood and handed the papers to Celeste, but she didn't want to look at them. She'd been lucky in past *reductions in force* and her luck must have run out.

Celeste worried about what would come next. A break would do her good, providing that it didn't last too long. Two months was as long as she could manage to fend for herself.

Her manager cleared his throat. "We'll get you back soon or into a field job in Colorado or Arizona."

Celeste nodded and stood. "I'll get my stuff."

"Celeste?" His voice pulled her attention back into the room. He stood beside his desk, an unreadable emotion on his face. "It'll all work out. I promise."

Looking to the floor, Celeste failed to keep herself from tearing up. She fled before she started crying.

Celeste left the building and stepped out into the kind of day in DC where the summer sun bakes you into a cheerful lassitude and the Potomac whispers promises of cooling water activities. She didn't really enjoy watersports, but she did like to read by the banks of the Potomac. When it wasn't on fire.

She took her time going home, enjoying the walk more than

she had in a long time. Fewer people crowded the sidewalks this time of day, and her favorite coffee shop was in a lull when she stopped by. It was pleasant, but it threw off her inner schedule in a way that was worrying for the future.

"You're off early today," the pretty barista commented as she made Celeste's usual decaf latte. "You got a date or vacation?"

Shaking her head, Celeste watched her hands move from tamp to machine to cup. "Got laid off." She'd always been a little terse with the barista, knowing that if she wasn't, if she let her guard down, she'd make a fool of herself and have to find another shop for her morning and evening brews.

"Really?"

Celeste shrugged. "Yeah, no warning either."

"Fuck." Her nose scrunched when she swore. Celeste liked that about her. "I'm sorry."

Celeste looked up at the barista and registered that she was looking at her with sympathy, and perhaps something more. They'd had the same routine for two years now: Celeste getting a big coffee in the morning, a smaller decaf one in the afternoon. The barista knew or could guess which seasonal flavors Celeste liked, and changed them with only a heads up.

Celeste grabbed the cup, avoiding her hand. She definitely didn't need to get entangled with someone right now. "Thanks. I'll still be here in the mornings." The vanilla latte soothed her aching throat as it went down. "Dunno about the evenings, though."

"Well, if you need company, let me know." She slid a napkin across the counter with her name and number, and Celeste pocketed it before heading home.

AT FIRST CELESTE FOUND THE TIME OFF FREEING. THE FIRST week was spent getting caught up on sleep and reading. She gently flirted with Agatha in the mornings, but didn't text her. The evenings were filled with job applications, chores, and measured pours of her favorite Virginia brandy.

She had enough money to last her six more weeks, and more in savings that she'd rather not touch. And though she called people she knew, she never heard back from anyone about a job. Which made her increasingly anxious and unsettled.

That anxiety mixed with anger at the whole situation, and by the middle of the second week, Celeste started drinking. A lot.

The measured pours of brandy turned to walking to the local bars and drinking until she couldn't think or feel anymore. Some nights she stumbled home in a drunken haze and slept through most of the next day, only to go out and do it again. She stopped caring for herself, the routines and rituals she used to keep her system in check abandoned.

By the third week, Celeste dwelled on every little mistake that might have affected her professional life. Every time she took too long to process a conversation, every page of messily filled paperwork, every field trip ended with her not quite having fulfilled what was asked of her. She hadn't heard back from anyone; those she knew, those she called and emailed. She couldn't help but think that her disability was the reason.

Autism was a part of her life—had always been a part of her—and she always wondered if it would one day it would affect her work too much. She had no idea if it was protected under the Americans with Disabilities Act, but she wasn't hopeful. There were plenty of jobs that would take on less qualified candidates over a disabled one.

One morning in mid-September, when it was almost late

enough to be afternoon, Celeste lay curled up in bed, hungover, crying and frustrated with life. Her bank account had taken a big hit and she felt like absolute shit from the constant drinking. Her limbs were swollen, muscles ached, and stomach constantly churned.

I gotta do something. I gotta get my shit together and act like an adult. What would Elise say if she saw me like this? Nothing I'd want to hear, that's for sure. Damned big sisters and their advice.

After crying for what felt like an hour, Celeste found a sense of clarity she hadn't felt in weeks. She had to get up and do *something*, anything, or she would rot in her bed for another three weeks. In the mirror, her olive skin was puffy and red from malnutrition and poor sleep, her long hair tangled. It took ten minutes to detangle before she slipped into the shower for the first time in a week or more.

She felt better after she'd washed her hair twice and scrubbed her body with the most abrasive loofah she owned. It hurt and she hated the texture, but it worked. She was still bloated, hungry, dehydrated, and angry, but at least she was clean once more.

The last clean clothes she had were sweats, but it felt good to be out of the house with the sun kissing her skin once more.

"You good?" the barista asked as a croissant sandwich joined her usual latte. Her eyes told Celeste not to argue with her over the free food.

"I'm okay."

The barista at the coffee shop only gave her a worried and wary look, and Celeste was glad to return to the comfortable distance they'd shared before. Anything closer would make things more difficult for Celeste.

A handful of local newspapers and art magazines dotted the only empty table in the shop, and Celeste waded through them while she absently ate her sandwich and drank her latte. She didn't taste them so much as savor having real food and coffee for the first time in days. She skimmed pages of the magazines, not paying any attention to the words.

Until she saw the ad:

ADVENTURER WANTED FOR OVERNIGHT HIKE
Inquire at Milton City Hall, I-81 S, VA exit 257W.
Accommodations and equipment provided.
Compensation upon completion.

The ad was crammed in a corner at the bottom of the page, a one- by two-inch rectangle that she shouldn't have noticed. But she did. And now that she had noticed it, she couldn't help but fixate on it.

What kind of hike is it? Why do they need to advertise *for a hike?*

Celeste reread it over and over while she finished the dregs of her lunch, then pulled out her phone. The ad was in a small paper from some tiny town in the mountains to the west. The exit was a little north of Harrisonburg, Virginia, and it would only take a few hours to drive out there and check out the job.

Celeste thought it over.

Can I afford to drive out there? Can I afford not to try? If nothing else, I can get away from DC for a while.

With that decided, Celeste went home and tried to piece herself back together.

2

GAS STATION ATTENDANTS

DESPERATION LEADS PEOPLE TO STRANGE FRONTIERS... THE WORDS materialized in Celeste's head as the traffic around her loosened and sped up.

Beyond the reaches of DC, the drive was enjoyable. Suburban sprawl gave way to flat farmland and forests, then up into hillier terrain where towns grew farther apart and a dark shadow grew on the horizon. As she approached, it loomed larger and more ominous, until finally it resolved into the eastern edge of the Blue Ridge Mountains.

Around noon Celeste stopped at a combination coffee and bike repair shop to stretch and finally eat something. Locals loitered at the tables, eating steaming bowls of soup and paninis despite the summer heat. Celeste got an iced brown sugar latte and a half sandwich and chips.

Celeste pulled off I-66 at a scenic overlook to eat. The half-sandwich was a caprese panini with thick slices of purple-brown heirloom tomatoes, fragrant basil, and gouda cheese. Fresh bread was toasted to perfection, and mozzarella had melted into the sweet tomato slices. She sipped the latte—the brown sugar syrup mellowed out the acidic espresso and mixed well with the milk.

Around the car, the mountains sat quiet, peaceful. Oak, maple, hickory, pine, sycamore, and birch trees covered the mountains from root to peak, with only outcroppings of pale grey stone breaking through the variegated green. Small patches of wildflowers grew along the highway and in the meadow below the overlook.

But it was also quiet, unnaturally so–there hadn't even been birdsong to accompany Celeste's meal. It didn't help the uncertainty that she still felt.

What now? I've already left and I can't really go back…I don't have any other leads to follow unless I call someone up and ask for help.

She hadn't told anyone about losing her job. Not her family, friends, or roommates: just the one flirty barista. She had nothing to fear from asking for help; her family and friends were supportive. But there was a small part of her brain that whispered in the dead of night that Celeste had only gotten where she was by their connections, their good graces.

Because of that, she'd always tried to fix things on her own first. She desperately needed to get herself out of this wretched mess, but she also needed to let someone know where she was going.

Just in case.

She called her sister, Elise, but it rang through to voicemail. Celeste paused a moment before deciding to leave a message.

"Hey Elise, been a while, right? Well…I lost my job. Fucking Congress reduced the budget again. Anyways, I saw an ad for a job, but it's in the mountains somewhere out by where Mom's folks are from and I wanted to tell someone where I was going…just in case, you know? And can you tell Mom about everything? I know she worries about me…Well…

thanks Ellie, love you." She hung up and waited a few minutes to see if her sister would text or call back.

But she didn't. Celeste hadn't heard from anyone that morning, but she hoped it was just a coincidence.

She got out to stretch again, uncertain how much longer it would be until she reached Milton. She looked out over the meadow below the overlook, thick with goldenrod and black-eyed Susans, and she realized that it was only as she'd been talking that she knew something of the area around Milton. That she'd *heard* of Milton before, even if she didn't really know where it was.

Her memories were hazy, at best, but she'd spent a long time with her grandparents every summer. There were trips to the mountains to see the animals, learning how to farm and turn berries into jam from her Grandaddy. Learning to press leaves and flowers from her Grandma. And a lake—but it was fuzzier than the rest, and pulled a pang of fear from Celeste's core, so she turned her attention back to the scenery.

There was something to the quality of the air and the trees on the mountains, like some great invisible being was watching her. Celeste had the strange sense that she was close to the edge of the world, far from anyone she knew and everything she'd experienced. She was on a precipice, looking out over a new world of uncertainty.

A COUPLE HOURS LATER, CELESTE APPROACHED EXIT 257W off of I-81 S.

To her left, a ridge of mountains carved its way through the Shenandoah Valley, towering over the rolling farmlands and forests that the highway cut through. Brown signs for historic locations dotted the sides of the roads, advertising houses, schools, and battlefields. Many of them rested half destroyed because their upkeep was more than they could reasonably collect for entrance.

To her right, the Appalachians loomed, much closer than their Blue Ridge siblings. Stretching for a hundred miles or more to the east and more from north to south, they towered over her even at a distance. Ridge after ridge of ancient, rounded mountains full of secrets and hidden wisdom. Like the Blue Ridge, they were covered in forested land where civilization was scarce and ruins more common than anything else.

Celeste had spent time in the Appalachians during college, but most of her forestry experience had been out west where the forests stretched for an age and felt untouched by the taint of man. There the mountains were steep and sharp, showing bare rock to the stars above. Few places could compare to the redwood forests of California, the dense pines growing at elevation in Arizona and Colorado, the red rock of Utah, or the sheer, dizzying heights of the Rockies.

Here, though, the woods felt like they closed in around you, blocking the sun. The bone-white limbs of birch and sycamore reached out of the darkness between oak and maple and pine. The mountains, ancient and watchful remnants of a forgotten eon, waited to catch the lost or unworthy off-guard.

Several miles of sparsely populated countryside separated the exit from a small town. To be careful, Celeste pulled into the first gas station she saw and filled up. There was no telling how far she was going to have to drive through the mountains, or where the next gas station was likely to be. But there was a very real chance she would end up in the ass-end of nowhere with less than a quarter tank of gas to her name and no gas stations for fifty miles.

Remember, mountain miles take more gas than highway miles. You don't want to get stranded like on the drive from the Very Large Array to Holbrook, do you? Elise has only just let you live that one down.

She pulled out her phone and searched for Milton in the maps app. She hadn't needed it before now—it had all been easy highway driving with large interstate signs—the mountain roads were a different bag altogether. There was no guarantee that there were signs for Milton on the backroads, and less of a guarantee that she could read them through a multitude of bullet holes and scraped paint.

The app thought for one moment, then another, then told her that there was no such town anywhere nearby, and suggested a town far north in New York.

"Piece of shit," she sighed, then slipped the phone back in her pocket.

Celeste looked around.

She was on the outskirts of a town that had the run-down look that a lot of small, rural towns picked up as they aged. She could see the smoke stacks of some factory or power plant in the distance but there were no other buildings of any size and no signs for an historic downtown—practically a requirement in any Virginia town. The gas station boasted two pumps that could serve four cars at a time, and a short line had formed behind her and the Camry. She pulled alongside the ice bag cooler and an air pump that only took coins.

Inside, a mishmash of groceries, car parts, medicine, and junk food stocked two aisles and one wall of refrigerators. A woman with deep, dark circles under her eyes greeted Celeste with a falsely cheerful, "Mornin'! What can I do for you, hon?" Her accent was thick, but was still easy to understand. There were parts of the state where Celeste couldn't catch one word in five from the locals.

You got this. You can ask for directions.

"I'm, uh, looking for a town called Milton? My phone said I should be headed towards New York, not West Virginia."

Narrowed, piercing eyes sized Celeste up before responding. "That's a fair drive through the mountains. Ya sure that's where ya want to go?"

Celeste shrugged and held out the ad. "That's what it says here."

Why would you ask otherwise? The way the conversation was going made Celeste want to chew her nails, but that wasn't polite so she refrained.

The woman took the ad between two long, beautifully manicured nails, the paper not touching skin. She read through it twice and let it fall to the counter before heading to the back wall.

She called over her shoulder. "We don't get many folks through here looking for Milton, but they always say the same thing: *It don't show up on the map*. It got real tiresome, so we made up some directions for y'all."

What the actual fuck is this lady going on about?

She handed Celeste a half sheet of directions printed in large, bold letters that would make it easy to consult while driving.

"Thanks." Celeste felt a little wary of the woman, of the way she looked at Celeste, the tone of her voice. Wouldn't it just be easier to hand her a map and clarify any questions?

The woman grabbed her arm as Celeste went to retrieve the ad. "You be careful, ya hear? Things in Milton ain't like you're used to in the city." The bags under her bright eyes gave her a manic, almost crazed look.

Please stop touching me. Celeste shook her arm out of the woman's clutches and backed away. "Nothing's like DC."

The woman shook her head. "That's not what I mean." And they stared at each other a moment longer.

"Thanks, I'll be careful."

"I hope so. 'Cause I sure as hell ain't gonna be there to tell you 'I told ya so.'" The woman turned to the counter behind her, her duty apparently done.

Celeste returned to her car and attached the directions to the dashboard where she could see them. She was still uneasy, still felt that intense gaze on her as she pulled out of the gas station.

Getting out of town was easy. All she had to do was go to the first light and turn left and follow that road. It seemed simple enough.

The town was nothing much to look at as she crawled along the streets. Half the houses were run down, condemned, or up for sale. There were a few dollar stores and a discount grocery store, and one additional gas station at the other end of town.

I prefer the city to this. It may be overwhelming even on the best days, but least it isn't depressing.

A short stretch of road separated the first town from an even smaller, more depressing one. It didn't even have a stoplight, just two stop signs and a gradual thinning out of buildings as she drove out into the foothills of the Appalachians. Signs thinned, just as the buildings, and soon there was nothing to tell her how far she'd gone or where the next town would be.

The road, which had been a four-lane separated highway, narrowed down to two lanes and the quality of the paving deteriorated. She passed farmland full to bursting with crops ready for harvest and pastures for cattle and sheep on both sides of the road. The traffic dwindled until Celeste saw no other cars for long minutes at a time.

The lady had said it was a "fair drive" to Milton, but Celeste had no idea if that meant thirty minutes or three hours, and the directions weren't any clearer.

She followed the road through the foothills and then up into the mountains, until Celeste breached the Appalachians and was consumed by them.

3
THRESHOLD

Appalachia felt different from anywhere else in the U.S. The mountains held their ancient secrets close, divulging them only to those who dug deep and ventured far from the cities; those who counted the stars in pollution-free skies; those who respected the enormity of age and experience; those who respected Nature, and her rage.

Here the colors were subtly different from the Blue Ridge. Autumn had already begun her descent into summer—red and orange, and brown punctuated fading green. Summer heat still reached the forest floor, but the wind had a crispness to it that only came with cooling weather. Soon the animals would forage in earnest, just as the farmers would bring in their harvests. Man and animal alike prepared for the coming winter.

Celeste drove into a hollow ringed on three sides by old pine trees, leading to an antique covered bridge. Not many of those were still in use in this part of the country. She parked the Camry and got out. The rush and splash of a river greeted her as she approached the bridge.

Time had not been kind to it.

Its exterior was once painted a vibrant red, but now only flakes remained on the weather and age-stained wood. The interior was water stained around the large cutouts. Moss grew between the steel-reinforced beams that made up the floor.

"I hope you'll hold the ol' girl," Celeste told the bridge conversationally. "I don't really like the idea of losing the Camry after everything else, especially all the way out here. Wherever here is."

The wood and steel did not reply. But beneath her feet, the creek rushed over rocks, around boulders and a half-submerged tree trunk while the splashes of a waterfall echoed from upstream. The foamy rapids gurgled and giggled, echoing around her like ghostly children or nymphs.

Okay, I don't like this anymore.

Light faded; the breeze picked up. Shadows danced under tree and rock, taunting her with unnatural movement while the spirits taunted her with their mirth. Shivers ran up Celeste's spine. A lump clogged her throat.

The wood creaked under her feet as she scurried off the bridge, towards the safety of the bank and the familiarity of the Camry. She turned back and watched as the bridge took on a ghoulish cast. The shadows made its old wood look like greying skin flaked with fire or blood. It hunched over the creek, a great gargoyle that waited for her to dare attempt the crossing.

"What the fuck?"

Back beside the Camry, Celeste finally took a deep, gasping breath. Her heart pounded in her chest, her hearing muffled by the rush of blood. She considered turning around and going back to DC. But there wasn't enough room. The pines stood too tall and close to the road.

And if she went back now, she'd have to tell someone else about losing her job. She'd have to undergo the mortifying ordeal of asking–begging–for help. That was worse than a haunted bridge.

A gust of wind blasted the hollow. The Camry shook under her hand, pine boughs and branches from other trees whipped around her, and shingles shook loose off the gargoyle bridge's roof. It battered her, ripped her hair from its braid, sang a haunting song directly against her skin. The shadows swayed as though they heard it too.

Then it was over.

The wind died as suddenly as it'd risen, and took with it the shadows and giggling specters that haunted the hollow. Everything was as before: shadows behaved as expected; the creek bubbled peacefully; the bridge stood tall and straight, no longer grotesque.

Celeste's heart still hammered, but she felt her resolve return.

"I can't go back," she told the Camry. "I drove all the way out here and was spooked by a fucking bridge." She slapped the hood to emphasize the point. "I *need* to make it to Milton." Around her everything paused a moment, as if listening. "I *will* make it to Milton," she declared.

Celeste had no idea what she'd mentally signed herself up for, but it felt like her best option right now. Hopefully the job was still available and would bring in enough money to ease her worries a little longer. She returned to her seat slightly more hopeful than before, but wary after the experience she had.

The Camry crept forward onto the bridge, wood creaking and groaning, but holding. She crossed one beam after another; the *thunk* as tires moved from beam to beam felt like rumble strips. She dismissed the shadows playing on the hood and an odd shimmering effect in the sunlight, focusing on the other side.

After what felt like an eternity, the Camry rolled off the bridge onto the far bank. Celeste hit the brakes before it could go any further, and looked over her shoulder.

A shimmering pearlescent veil hung over the bridge, undulating in a rainbow of colors reflecting off spray from the creek. She'd never seen anything like it before. It lasted only a moment before another gust of wind rushed down the creek, dislodging leaves and branches as it went. Celeste reflexively ground her foot into the brake pedal and cowered against the steering wheel, expecting some reprisal from the haunted bride.

But nothing happened. When the wind dissipated, Celeste put the car in park and emerged.

Outside, green leaves and pine needles littered the moss-covered ground, the pure air filled with their earthy scent and the freshness of the bubbling stream. Celeste took a deep breath, only to cough and choke. Taking a deep breath after living in a polluted city for so long hurt.

Sweat rolled off her forehead and down her back as she took step after cautious step back to the bridge. The creek giggled still, but in a light, airy way that she expected.

The bridge itself was drenched in late summer sunlight. The flaking paint was quaint and pretty now, the interior bright and cheerful. Everything gave off an aura of strength and respectable old age.

A thread of something squirmed in her chest, but Celeste wasn't certain if it was anxiety or caution or joy. All around her the sounds of the forest trumpeted: birds and insects cried out, wind whistled through the trees, branches dropped and crunched the moldering underbrush.

She felt a moment of shame for being afraid of the bridge. She'd been so caught up in her worries that her imagination had run wild with the unfamiliar scenery. But now everything was as it should be. There were no ghosts under the bridge, no menace in its wood and steel and paint, no shimmering veil descending from the trees.

Celeste sighed out the last of her rogue emotions, returned to the Camry, and started up the road. It climbed uphill and twisted through the forest, far from any signs of civilization. She followed it for an hour or more—time had no meaning here—until she emerged from the shadows of the forest onto a bright mountainside.

The road wound around to her left, but ahead was a large gravel pull-off protected by guard rail. She stopped to admire the scenery.

Below her, the mountain plunged into a valley—a valley so like the one she'd just crossed that she wondered if she'd gone in a circle.

In the distance a small town lay nestled at the foot of a tall mountain. Wispy clouds hid the peak. To one side, a large tree cloaked in red overlooked the town. It was the only tree ready for autumn, standing out from the multitudes of green.

A wide, lazy river twisted through the forests, town, and around the mountain before disappearing out of sight.

Everything was so familiar, yet Celeste wasn't sure that it was the Shenandoah Valley that she'd crossed earlier in the day.

A battered wooden sign just down the hill from the pull off stated: MILTON – 3. With no other direction to go, Celeste started down the mountain towards Milton.

The Camry sped downhill and hit a sharp curve, nearly sending itself and Celeste into an overgrown yard. The derelict tractors and pickup trucks on cinder blocks would've stopped her eventually, but then she'd be in a different world of issues. She slammed on the brakes and took control back from her over-eager car.

Farmhouses with pastures of cows and chickens and sheep, and small fields of corn or wheat graced the sides of the road before she reached the first of the neighborhoods. Small brick homes squatted in neat flower gardens with bright white fences. Old wooden company houses broke up the pleasing red and brown, but grew more common closer to town, and Celeste wondered how long ago the local mines closed. She couldn't imagine it pulled in enough to bring any wealth to the town.

A brightly painted sign welcomed Celeste to "Milton, established 1772." Beyond it were old estate houses with more yard than an entire block in DC.

While the outskirts had felt lived in and loved, the town itself felt *off*.

On the surface, everything was normal. The road was clear of litter. Large houses with well-maintained gardens each took up a comfortable amount of space. The sidewalks were clean and flat. It seemed too nice, too pristine, for a town as old as Milton claimed to be. There were no obvious signs of age, outside of the style of architecture.

Celeste drove through one stoplight, stopped at the next, and finally realized why it felt so wrong.

Here she saw the first people in hours: a well-dressed middle-aged couple waiting to cross the road to Celeste's right. And they were staring at her.

Celeste nodded to them, hoping that would put them off, but they continued . She felt their eyes penetrating the depths of her soul. It was unsettling being the center of such intense attention when she hadn't seen a soul since leaving the gas station.

Maybe I should've stayed in DC after all...

When the light changed, she continued down the street, looking for City Hall. She crawled through another intersection, seeing the people she'd expect in any town: a gaggle of small children toddling after their minders, patrons at a small café, people passing on the street. Everything was right and normal—except they all stared at her too.

Milton might be small enough for everyone to know everyone else, but Celeste felt like a neon sign was lit over her head, alerting everyone that she was from somewhere else.

Calm down. It's okay. Maybe they just don't see DC license plates out here that often.

Eventually Celeste found a sign directing her toward the historic downtown area and City Hall. Here, no one loitered on the street to stare at her. But a weight settled itself between her shoulders as she parked next to a sign for coffee.

Celeste felt that something incredibly strange had happened to her at the bridge. Like she had passed through the mountains and ended up not in Appalachia, but somewhere else entirely.

4

WITCH PEAK BREWS

THE SCENT OF COFFEE BEANS, SPICES, AND BUTTER HIT Celeste as soon as she exited the Camry. She would've been drawn to the shop by the scent alone, but a cauldron-shaped sign over the door that said WITCH PEAK BREWS intrigued her. A smaller sign on the door read: MARTA FINCH, APOTHECARY.

The plaster-sided exterior was painted pastel grey and orange, and on the door hung a wreath of dried wheat stalks, pinecones, and dried leaves in autumnal shades. Multicolored pumpkins and carved jack-o'-lanterns framed a welcome mat with little black cats and cartoon witches.

The savory smells of roasted coffee and cheese surrounded her as soon as she opened the front door. The interior had the same witchy, Halloween vibe as the outside: baskets of colorful, palm-sized squash flanked the register, old metal lanterns with flameless candles hung high on painted chains, and antiques decorated wooden shelves set into the old plaster walls. Each piece stood out on its own, yet coordinated with the rest.

Ads for local events dotted a cork board next to the door. The largest was a block print poster in orange, red, and brown for CIDERFEST, starting on the first Friday in October. It advertised hayrides, apple picking, corn mazes, farmer's markets, the ambiguously ominous OTHER AMUSE-MENTS, and special guest The Harvestman.

The aged oak counter, stained from heavy use, contained an inset bake case holding a variety of pastries. A thin fridge with bottles of cold brew, kombucha, and freshly pressed juices sat between the counter and the wall. Shelves full of glass jars lined the right-hand wall behind the counter.

A small hand-written sign on the bake case stated: Potions available by appointment and prescription.

That's weird. I guess it fits the witchy theme.

Three women worked behind the counter, dressed in varying amounts of black clothing. Each wore a mini crocheted witch's hat set at a jaunty angle on her head.

Celeste chuckled. *They look ready to celebrate Halloween already.*

Soft folk music filled the room, a song that Celeste recognized but couldn't remember. A man sang of losing his love and dueling a devil for his lover's soul. It was a bit like that popular Charlie Daniels Band song, but slower, sadder. It was closer to a lament for love lost and not regained than triumph over evil, though the singer got his lover back in the end.

"What can I get you?"

Celeste panicked; she had been so distracted by the music that she hadn't looked at the menu. It hung from the ceiling and the only thing that readily stood out was that their house coffee was called the Cauldron Blend.

Celeste looked at the barista and swallowed hard. She was pretty, a gothic witch with a pointed hat in yellow to orange ombre. "W-what do you suggest?"

The barista looked up at the menu board and pursed her black-painted lips. She was tall and pale with a long black bob. There was a gentle wave to her hair that framed her small, round face. She wore glasses with thin round frames that partially hid bright brown eyes and thin, pointed eyeliner. Her name tag said MARTA with little stars drawn around it.

Marta *hmm'd* a bit before answering. "We're still making maple drinks till the end of the month, but pumpkin is the new seasonal flavor. We make the drinks with house roasted pumpkin puree and brown sugar syrup." She flipped long fingers through her hair, twirling the ends around her pointer. "Chai lattes are pretty popular this week. We had that chill on Tuesday and *everyone* has been ordering them." She sighed in a theatrical way, shoulders heaving and eyes rolling.

"The chai goes well with the cinnamon roll bread." She pointed at the bake case.

The cinnamon roll bread was displayed in a tray and covered with icing. Beside them was a half dozen different flavors of muffins with only one or two left of each and a large plate of crispy scones. More conventional pastries like croissants, cookies, brownies were long gone, though their tags remained.

"Today's scones are cheddar and chive."

Celeste salivated when her sight returned to the cinnamon roll bread. Her stomach growled loud enough for Marta to hear her. She smothered a giggle while heat rose to Celeste's cheeks.

Come on, Celeste, you can order a damn drink.

"Uhh…" Celeste cleared her constricted throat. "Can you do the chai with almond milk?"

Marta nodded and held up a paper cup. "This size good?" Their eyes met and she winked.

Celeste nodded without really registering the cup and

looked back at the bake case. It was easier to talk to that than the pretty barista when she'd made a fool of herself. "Can I get a scone and a piece of the cinnamon roll bread, too?"

Celeste was getting more and more flustered as she spoke.

Marta rang her up, handed over the pastries, and pointed towards a curtained opening. "Find a spot to sit in there, I'll bring out your chai when it's done."

Celeste nodded her thanks, not quite trusting herself to speak coherently.

Black lace and gauze curtains hung from the frame in lieu of a door. Inside, a dozen round tables filled the room, each with cozy armchairs and an antique lamp or lantern on the table. Golden stars painted on velvet black wallpaper stretched from floor to ceiling, and silver lines connected constellations. A door on the far side of the room led out onto a patio.

Half the tables were occupied and Celeste claimed one against the far wall, near enough to the door to escape quickly if necessary.

Celeste pulled the cinnamon roll bread out. It was a fat square of dense coffee cake that smelled faintly of cardamom, cloves, allspice and cinnamon. The icing was sweet enough to make her teeth hurt, which was just how she liked her pastries. She shoveled fork after fork into her mouth, wondering why she was so hungry.

If only I could unroll this like a regular cinnamon roll.

Marta appeared through the curtain, deftly carrying a large ceramic cup and saucer. Setting it down before Celeste, she slid into the second chair.

Celeste's face flushed as she pulled the cauldron-shaped mug from its saucer. "Um, hi?"

"I wanted to talk some more."

Marta's hands trembled as they rested on the table, but Celeste couldn't tell if nerves or pent up energy were the cause.

Her voice, which was low and rich, was more serious than before.

"I'm sorry I made things awkward. Can't really help it."

Marta cocked her head to one side. "You might be a little shy, but it wasn't awkward."

Celeste sipped the tea: mellow and sweet with the underlying black tea almost tasteless. It wasn't as spicy as chai lattes she'd had before, but it was comforting. She didn't want to word vomit at Marta, so she changed the subject.

"Is this your café?" Celeste felt a little stupid for asking. But just because her name was on the door didn't mean that Marta *owned* the store.

Marta shook herself a little, black hair silky in the dim light. "Yeah, Witch Peak is mine and Samone's. She does the baking, I do the potions, and Anna does coffee and smoothies."

"Seems like it's a popular place." Celeste weighed the mug in her hands between sips. It felt more like cast iron than ceramic.

"It's grown on the community," Marta said with a smile. "I needed something to do when I moved here to look after my aunt. And this must've been the only town in the Valley that didn't have a coffee shop..." She trailed off and held up a hand. "I appreciate your interest, but that's not why I came over to chat." She sounded genuinely disappointed that they couldn't just talk. "I wanted to ask if you were here about the ad."

Hot milk burned the roof of Celeste's mouth and throat. "Yeah," she managed between muffled coughs.

Does everyone know something I don't?

Marta nodded once. "I thought so. We don't get many *outsiders* here, and when they do come, it's always about the ad." The way she emphasized "outsiders" made Celeste pause.

This town is really fucking weird.

"Anyways, you'll be looking for City Hall." It wasn't a question.

Celeste gripped the coffee cup tightly between her hands.

"When you exit from the front door, go left down the alley and right on Broad Street. City Hall is three blocks down on the left side of the street. You can't miss it." She paused for a moment, then continued in a lower, more ominous tone. "I expect someone will be waiting there for you."

She brightened up after that, her voice returning to normal.

"Come back if you need any help. I can direct you to a mostly pest-free hotel." Marta slid out of the chair with a wink, crossed the room, and passed through the gauzy curtains.

Celeste blinked away confusion. The way Marta was suddenly here and then gone sat in the pit of her stomach, fizzling away. Something left in her wake prickled Celeste's skin and crawled up her spine. And Marta hadn't seemed to act out of the ordinary.

Except knowing why I am here.

Celeste turned her attention back to the half-drunk latte that was cooling. She finished it, deposited her cup into a bin, and slid out the back door into a sweltering summer afternoon.

5
THE BELLS

There's something weird about this town, Celeste told herself again. With each repetition it felt more and more like an understatement. There was definitely something *different* about this town, even compared to other rural, mountain towns. Something in the atmosphere or maybe the water. She couldn't quite put her finger on it.

Celeste found herself on a wide, wooden patio with a newly built pergola. Moonflowers grew up the supports, new blooms preparing to unveil themselves once the sun set and dusk settled on the valley.

From here, Celeste could see the mountain that towered over town. Even in the sunlight, it was an ominous presence. It was the largest mountain in the valley and seemed to crouch over Milton, oppressing the town with just its existence. She felt in her core that the mountain was *the mountain* she would be hiking up. And though she was still determined to see this through, nausea crept up her esophagus and anxiety shook in her limbs.

This is already more than I bargained for.

Celeste left the patio and walked around to the front of the shop to orient herself.

The alley was a single-lane road going one way with no sidewalks. Celeste followed it towards Broad Street. At the corner, Celeste stepped aside and observed what must have been Milton's historic downtown. To her left were shops and cafés, some with chalkboard signs proclaiming new menus or sales. A few people entered and exited as she watched, each stopping to stare at Celeste before moving on.

To the right, it was quiet.

Celeste crossed the street and turned right, following Marta's directions. The first block was empty storefronts, boarded up and locked against any intruders. A few had signs saying that the building was FOR LEASE or that a shop was COMING SOON, but they were as grimy as the storefronts. The sidewalk cracked and crumbled in places, the gutters littered with trash.

It feels like a different town, Celeste thought. *This one is slowly rotting while the other still has life left in it.*

The area around City Hall was better maintained, but still had an edge of grime. There was something in the air that Celeste couldn't place—some acrid scent, some whiff of dread that had settled on the town and the people here.

City Hall was a red brick rotunda capped in white with a golden statue. Mulched flower beds punctuated a wide lawn of smooth green grass where a matching brick path led around a stone statue. Upon closer inspection it was a cloaked woman holding a book and up to the building's red door. There was no plaque to tell Celeste who the woman was.

Celeste turned away from the statue. A group of townsfolk stood at the edges of the lawn, watching her. Thirty or forty had assembled and more were joining at the periphery. As she watched, the crowd grew until the whole square was surrounded. No one spoke or moved, just stared. The only sound was the bright tweeting of a bird and the gentle undulation of grass and flowers in the wind.

What the fuck?

Celeste swallowed down her anxiety as it peaked.

One woman stood out from the rest. She was almost a head taller than the next tallest, with bronze skin and a long dark braid over one shoulder. Brown leggings tucked into calf-high boots and a flowing blouse of the deepest blue adorned her. She watched Celeste with an intensity to her dark eyes that almost hurt.

Celeste pulled herself away from the woman's gaze and walked up to the building. The doors opened before she reached the steps and three people stood at the top, looking down on her. A middle-aged woman dressed in a very sharp suit stood with another, dressed more casually, who supported an ancient man with milky cataracts covering his eyes.

The woman in the suit had an air of unquestionable authority about her. "You have come about the ad."

Celeste shuffled backwards. She wanted to be further from the trio, while still not close enough to the crowd. "Yes."

Beside her, the old man swayed from side to side like a tree branch in the wind. His head faced towards the sky, but Celeste felt his concentration on her. He swayed, never coming close to falling with the older woman's firm grip on his arm and a steadying hand on his back. His lips opened and he spoke, his aid leaned in and listened to his murmurs.

Around her, the silent crowd was a palpable presence. After being stared at on her way in and being questioned by the pretty barista, Celeste didn't think she could be rattled again. But she was wrong. The people around her made her want to hide, to run screaming back to DC. Their presence said 'you do not belong here, girl' and Celeste was hard-pressed to argue with them.

But before she could retreat, the older woman nodded.

Suits turned back to Celeste. "It seems you have what it takes. The payment for successful completion is $20,000 in cash. Do you accept?"

Are you fucking kidding me?

Celeste stared at the woman, chin halfway to her chest. She never imagined such a large amount. It would be more than enough to pay her bills for several months while she looked for a new job. Maybe she could move out west to take a permanent job in one of the big national forests or parks. Elise would visit her when she had time, and Celeste would welcome the silence and solitude of Nature after being in the city for so long.

Something was wrong with Milton, and something told her that there was more to this bargain than what it seemed.

Do I care?

Celeste held her breath to make her choice.

Not at all.

"I accept."

DONG!

Deep, resonant tones rippled over the town, as if a massive church bell rang for a funeral. They were close enough to drown out everything, but far enough away that Celeste couldn't pinpoint their location. The ground rumbled in response, almost knocking her off her feet.

Silence reigned after a moment.

Then the bell rang once more.

DONG!

Seven times the bells tolled, and then the sound was gone. There was a crackling in the air around Celeste, as if lightning were about to strike. It wasn't unlike what she'd felt around Marta, but magnified a thousand fold.

It felt like a spell had been cast, a pact sealed by Celeste's agreement. Whatever she'd just agreed to went further than a mere hike, but just how far did the secrets of Milton go?

The suited woman smiled, tight and unimpressed. "Selena will give you directions and the items you require for the *Binding*. She lives in a cottage just outside of town at 356 Well Street. Go there, tell her you are here to attempt the Binding and she will help you."

She held out an arm and assisted the other woman in taking the old man back inside. The door closed behind them with a soft metallic catch.

When Celeste turned around, the crowds had dispersed again, the stragglers quickly disappearing around the buildings that lined the grassy area. Gone as quietly and quickly as they'd arrived. She dug in her bag for her phone, but she had no signal and consequently, no way of finding her way to Selena's house.

Standing there alone, without a way to contact anyone she knew, Celeste felt a rush of loneliness she hadn't experienced since her ex-girlfriend left years before. She hadn't heard from any of her friends, or her roommates, and even her sister hadn't responded to her. She didn't need them with her, but she wanted to be able to talk to someone, to make sure she wasn't going crazy.

Wait…

Celeste's eyes went wide. She was alone in the sense that she didn't know anyone in Milton. But that didn't mean she couldn't get help from someone new. Celeste walked back down Broad Street and up the alley to Witch Peak Brews.

She entered by the side door, where the dining room was mysteriously empty. In the main room a blonde woman cleaned the espresso machine while Marta and a Black woman with a pale pink afro packed pastries into colorful paper bags.

"I see you're still around," Marta called from behind her spot in the back.

"Did you think I'd already left?" Celeste tried to keep her tone light and jovial, but it sounded forced to her ears.

Marta nodded to the Black woman and approached, leaning on the wooden counter. "It's always hard to tell. A lot of potential binders just leave town after meeting with the mayor."

"Miss Moss is an intimidating woman," the blonde said, her voice muffled by water.

"True, but we haven't had a successful binding in oh…ten years, was it, Samone?" She turned and shared a look with Samone.

"Binding? What do you mean by binding?" Celeste's voice was too soft to carry.

The Black woman, Samone, arched one eyebrow at Marta and spared Celeste a brief, searching look. Then she turned back to packing croissants, cinnamon bread, and scones into paper bags decorated with colorful doodles.

"Don't ask me, it's your aunt doing the binding." Her voice carried well, though her back was to Celeste. "Or did the binding anyway. I just work here."

Marta rolled her eyes. "You've been in Milton like, twice as long as me, and you know my aunt. I know your mom nursed her after she broke her hip."

Celeste enjoyed the show they were putting on, but wished she understood half of what she'd seen since she encountered that covered bridge.

Samone finished with the bags and piled them into boxes. Her hat was bright pink and purple, matching her afro and glasses. "I guess we had some close calls at the start, some people from The Valley came and tried. But we never saw the signs, and the mountain remained unbound."

Celeste sighed.

There's a lot going on here and I don't know what they mean by binding or signs.

The door opened and two young Mennonite women entered. They wore modest dresses in muted blue, and one wore a small mesh cap over her tight bun.

"Sarah, Hannah, you're a little early today!" Samone called from her table at the back.

The one with the cap responded, "There was a *commotion* earlier and our charges were taken home to pray with their families. We took the opportunity to stop by early." She had a warm smile and a twinkle in her eye as she talked.

Celeste moved out of the way while Samone and the woman with the cap spoke. The other woman stared at Celeste in her corner. Her dark eyes narrowed and her head cocked to the side in thought.

"Sarah," she called to her companion, "this is the woman who has come to bind the mountain."

Sarah turned her attention from the boxes on the counter to Celeste. She had the same dark eyes as Hannah. They both had small, slightly pointed faces with thin mouths and narrow cheekbones. Sarah appeared a year or two older than Hannah; there was a spark of experience in her eyes that Hannah didn't have yet.

"Yes, she has come to bind the mountain." There was a curious tone to Sarah's voice when she spoke, something that rang like tinnitus for one long second and then dissipated. Celeste's eyes went wide as she felt a rush of vertigo.

Sarah turned to Marta. "You must lend her aid, Marta Finch. She is like a newborn lamb, vulnerable and ignorant of our world. Without you, she will perish."

Marta nodded. "I understand."

Something passed over Sarah's eyes. Then she shuddered

and a weight that had settled over the room lifted. Celeste badly wanted the two women to leave.

This town has gone from weird to fucking creepy real quick.

Celeste watched as if from a distance while Sarah took one box and Hannah the other. "Thank you Samone, Marta, Anna. As always, the children appreciate their treats."

Hannah nodded at Celeste as she passed. "Be careful, Outsider. Things here are not always what they appear to be."

That's what the lady at the gas station said...

Celeste watched them leave and then continued to stare at the door, almost expecting the two to return with more dire predictions and ominously worded guidance.

"Hey? Are you okay?"

Someone shook Celeste out of the strange fugue state. Her eyes had unfocused, and she'd been standing staring at nothing, thinking about nothing except how strange the day had become. She shook her head, trying to rid herself of *whatever* had caused that.

Marta was standing in front of her, concern heavy in her eyes.

"What?" Celeste saw Samone and Anna halfway around the counter, staring at her as well. "Did I say something?"

"You went blank and started trembling," Samone responded.

The barista, Anna, nodded in agreement. "You okay now?"

"Yeah, I-I didn't even realize that happened." Celeste rubbed her forehead with the fingers of her left hand, relieving some residual tension that had built up. She was going to have a monster of a breakdown when the time came.

"Did you come back for something?" Marta asked beside her, one hand on Celeste's arm.

Her hands are so warm. It must be from the pastries...

"Oh, um, I need to get to Selena's house? On Well Street?"

A remnant of the fugue remained and Celeste wasn't certain what she was supposed to do next. "My phone doesn't have signal, and no one gave me any directions. So I came back here?"

She sounded small and pathetic, and babbled longer than she intended to, but she didn't really care. This trip was already overwhelming, and she'd just agreed to do a *binding* instead of a hike.

The creases between Marta's eyes softened. "Is that all? I can write out some directions for you. Where'd you park?"

"Just outside the shop." Celeste pointed at the door, as if they didn't know where it was. As if she wasn't sure that it was really there.

Marta went back behind the bar, retrieved a pad of paper and a bright red pen, and scribbled for a minute. She pulled the sheet off the pad, wrote a little more at the bottom, and then folded the paper up. "These will help you find Selena. She's at home today and is probably expecting you by now."

Celeste took the proffered slip of paper. "Thanks." She paused a second to read the paper without actually reading it before continuing. "For the coffee and help."

Marta smiled and shrugged. "Always willing to aid Outsiders, especially if they are here to do the binding."

They stood for a moment, staring at each other without saying anything. Celeste smiled and turned around.

"If you come back tomorrow, there'll be a new scone flavor," Marta called as she reached the door.

Celeste looked back. That felt so normal it was the strangest thing anyone had said to her all day.

Then she left Witch Peak Brews.

6

THE BLOOM FAMILY CURSE

The strangeness of the encounter with Sarah and Hannah stuck with Celeste as she navigated the narrow streets out of Downtown Milton. The look in the Sarah's eyes and the hollow distance in her voice would haunt Celeste's dreams.

As she stopped at lights, Celeste watched as people crossed the streets and loitered outside of homes and shops. A few stared at the passing cars, but none seemed to focus on Celeste in particular. It felt like her earlier experiences were a byproduct of stress and the lingering effects of drinking every day for multiple weeks. And by the time she parked the Camry in front of a small stone cottage, Celeste still felt on edge, but not as acutely as before.

Celeste studied the cottage while she stretched. It was for show, since she had spent most of the last hour standing, but she wanted a few more moments to herself. She had no idea what was next, so there was no way to mentally prepare herself.

Nothing has been normal today. I shouldn't assume that trend is going to change now.

The cottage was one story with a covered front porch and immaculately maintained flowerbeds and bushes. Their fragrance wafted sweet in the stifling air. Large, flat stones led from the sidewalk to the single step up to the porch. The neighboring houses were all close enough for comfort, but not so close as to crowd.

Celeste heard the gentle, rhythmic creaking of a rocking chair from behind one of the flowering bushes. It mixed with the chatter of birds and the rhythmic sound of insects in the woods that loomed behind the house.

She stopped at the stone path when a voice came from the porch. "Come up here, child, so I can get a good look at you."

Celeste stepped onto the porch but strayed no further. In the far-right corner an old woman sat in the rocking chair. She had that lean, muscular look of a life in motion that had softened with age. A round face slightly wrinkled and framed with wild grey hair that escaped its bun met Celeste. She wore a white blouse, narrow crimson skirt, and a soft purple sweater despite the heat. There was something vaguely familiar about her that Celeste couldn't place.

Selena eyed Celeste over her knitting, her eyes a penetrating green. She alternated her gaze between her stitches and Celeste.

"You got the look of the mountains about you girl." She spoke slowly, with a slight drawl. "You ever been out these ways?"

Celeste blinked, unprepared for that question. "Uh, my mom's family is from *somewhere* around here, I think. I'm not really sure…"

What a strange way to start a conversation. What is the 'look of the mountains' that she's talking about?

"Not that, *child*." Her drawl came out more with irritation, it seemed. "I meant the way you stand and hold yourself. You ain't unfamiliar with being out in the woods."

"Oh." *That.* "I spent several years out west doing forestry work in the national forests." Celeste cleared her throat. "I was told to come here to get directions for *the hike*?"

Selena nodded in time with the movement of her chair. She finished a line in her knitting, set it on the bench beside her, and leaned forward. She held Celeste's gaze for several moments before nodding once and relaxing.

"You have what it takes, it's true, but this ain't gonna be easy. We best go in and get comfortable while I tell you the story."

"What is this *it* that I have?" Celeste let her frustration out.

What could I have that they need? Other than experience being outdoors. What do I need other than hiking and rock climbing experience?

Selena didn't answer. She rocked on her feet as she pushed up out of the rocking chair. "Damned hip," she muttered. "It's the reason I need to keep putting ads out there. Broke it ten years past and now I can't do the *binding* myself." She looked up at Celeste with a twinkle in her eye. "Excuse me, I can't do the *hike* myself."

What am I missing? What's this binding? What is going on in this gods-forsaken town?

Celeste stepped ahead of Selena, held the storm door open, and eyed the knitting on the bench. "Want me to grab your knitting?"

"What? Oh, sure. That'll give me something to keep my hands busy."

Celeste waited for Selena to enter and then picked up the project. The yarn was a pretty sage green, but she couldn't make heads or tails of what it was supposed to be.

She followed Selena into the cottage. The ceiling slanted

upwards with dark brown beams crossing from front to back. Pale wood floors ran throughout and a motley mix of furniture gave the cottage a cozy, lived-in feel. The remnants of beautifully hand-painted wallpaper clung to the walls beneath paintings, prints, and decorative gilt mirrors. They were almost art in and of themselves.

Selena settled herself in a large, plush armchair in a corner near the fireplace on the far side of the room.

Celeste navigated around a small dining table and the surprisingly modern kitchen to stand near Selena, uncertain where she should sit, or if she should sit at all. She handed the knitting over.

"Oh dear, pull up the dark chair from the table."

Celeste did and sat down across the fireplace from Selena. Two cats slunk out from a room on the far side of the kitchen; a large white Persian hopped gracefully into Selena's lap while the other, a sleek Siamese, crept towards Celeste and sniffed the hand she offered. Once she was deemed not a threat, the Siamese rubbed itself against Celeste's legs and meowed for attention.

"These two get more spoilt every year," Selena said with a depth of affection. She scratched the Persian between its ears. "What's your name?"

"Celeste Foster."

"Foster? There were some Fosters who lived over Blue Mountain way. That's the big one on the other side of Lighthouse Lake. Ol' Foster had a cattle farm once, but it got to be too much and they sold off the cows and rented the fields." Selena thought for a moment. "My friend, Abigail Foster, died of some disease years and years ago. Not sure what happened to her husband, Abner, though."

A lump grew in Celeste's throat, threatening to choke her.

Her grandparent's' names had been Abigail and Abner.

Celeste couldn't remember anything around the farm, but the names were the same. It couldn't be a coincidence. It'd been so long since she'd last seen them, her memories were hazy.

She remembered a lake and her grandmother's soft hands as they walked along the shoreline and splashes as Elise ran through the shallows. Then there had been an *incident*, and they hadn't visited again.

Then the worst happened.

"It was cancer." Celeste's voice was surprisingly clear, despite the lump and rising emotions.

Selena paused whatever she had been saying and looked at Celeste. "What was that, dear?"

Just breathe.

"Abigail Foster. She died from ovarian cancer."

Selena nodded. "That's right. 'Twas a shame. We were friends growing up, but she got married and I took up the binding." Her eyes were wide, wet when she looked back at Celeste. "At my age, you get used to people dying and being the only one left. Are you related to Abigail?"

Bile burned in Celeste's throat, and anxiety shook in her fingers. "She was my grandmother."

It's been so long and I was so young. Can I even remember her face? Granddaddy's face? The farmhouse with its garden of blue flowers? Those sun-drenched days under trees so tall it felt like they touched the stars?

Grandaddy always said that the meeting of trees and stars was me and Elise.

Celeste pulled herself away from her memories, not wanting to burst into tears in Selena's living room.

"Well, where shall I start?" Selena thought for a moment. "The beginning would be best, but I don't know the beginning of this story. I'll tell you what I know.

"Now, you need to understand that the mountain has

always been an uncanny place. Strange things happen on its slopes and in the shadows it casts during the day. Sometimes those strange things touch Milton, but the mountain is wary of hurting us."

"What kinds of things?" *Mountains can be wary?*

"Lights burn bright on the slopes at night and shadows didn't always act proper. Creatures move strange—disappear and reappear elsewhere. Things like that." She waved a hand as if this was all common knowledge, not worth repeating. Or, perhaps, not worth invoking.

"People have been in Yuback Valley longer than recorded history. The Indigenous tribes lived alongside the big mountain and there was a respectful relationship between the two. The mountain protected the tribes and the tribes revered the mountain in return. But, eventually, the tribes were pushed out when Europeans discovered The Valley. Then *trouble* started brewing around the mountain."

Selena opened her mouth to continue, but reconsidered. She focused on her knitting, counting stitches and holding the project up at various angles, for a long moment before continuing. With her lips pressed together she reminded Celeste of the cat in her lap.

"Back in the 1670s or so, a man and his wife came from *Outside* and settled on the slopes of the mountain. His family name was Bloom. Since they were the only ones who lived on the slopes, the mountain started to carry their name. No one asked why they came, and it didn't really matter.

"After a while the Blooms tried to find someone to help keep the mountain in check, but no one knew what the Indigenous tribes had done before their lands were stolen. So they had to improvise, had to adapt some rituals to ease the mountain, else it would grow too big for its bounds."

Selena sighed heavily.

"The family grew and prospered after the rituals started. But then the Great War happened and everything got worse. All their young men went off to fight. Only one came back and he wasn't *right* anymore."

The atmosphere in the room was stifling. Celeste adjusted in the uncomfortable seat, but didn't want to appear rude.

"Soon, there were disappearances in town, farm animals were found slaughtered, and strange tracks led from town to the mountain. The wise were consulted, but no known creature made them. Then a few years on, when I was young, the family started dying off. A wasting sickness sucked the life from them, left them husks. Some of us witches were called in to try and save them, but well–"

"Witches, really?" Celeste couldn't keep the disbelief from her voice. Selena told a good story, strange and fascinating, but Celeste was wary about taking her at her word.

Who really believes in witches and potions and curses? Is it something in the water, in the soil? What happened to this town to make it so fucking strange?

Selena gave Celeste a look, filled with emotions that she couldn't decipher. "I meant what I said, young Foster. And you should understand it quite well, for all the years you've lived *Outside.*"

Selena gently pushed the Persian out of her lap and adjusted her position.

"Anyways, four of us *witches* were called to the farm to help, but only the Bloom man and his two teenaged children were still alive. Rest had withered away where they'd fallen and died. It wasn't a pretty sight, all those corpses strewn about the farmhouse and barn. I can still see the faces in my dreams."

Selena shook her head and wiped a lone tear from her left eye.

"The boy died soon after we got there. It was terrifying

how quickly it happened. We couldn't do anything, just watch as his body dried up. It was like all the water and blood and organs had been sucked out of him. His hair fell out and his nails fell off. It was *horrible*. Ain't never seen anything like it since."

"What about the other child?"

"She lived, for a while. Stayed out of the farmhouse and kept to the barn with the animals. She had a bit more life in her than her brother, and the sickness didn't touch her as deeply as the rest. Some magic and aggressive medical treatments kept her going and she lasted out the year.

"But then the old pear tree fell on the house and started a small fire, killing her and her father. The last of the Blooms snuffed out like a candle." Selena snapped her fingers as she finished.

"Don't really know what the Blooms did to deserve such punishment. But several people got it into their heads that the Blooms were cursed. Whatever happened to the father in the war changed him. He kept too much to himself; the lights on the mountain were brighter; the drumming in the deep forest stronger. All the animals fled to the woods, abandoning the farm. What crops they grew withered in the soil. The curse touched the town too, putting strange dreams in our minds and an unnatural fog rose from the Nomini. Then they died and everything returned to normal.

"Well…" She paused and smiled. "As normal as things get around here. Animals still avoid the farm and only the toughest weeds grow there now. The earth started taking the farmstead back and no one wanted to get in the way."

Selena sighed and lapsed into silence.

Celeste thought on the story for a while, wondering what really had happened to the Bloom family. Surely the curse was just a local legend to explain why no one lived on Bloom Mountain anymore?

"Where do I come into this? What does the hike have to do with the Blooms?"

Selena rolled her eyes but her voice deepened as she replied. "It's been eleven years since Bloom Mountain was last bound. The rituals have worn off and the magic has run wild. If it ain't contained soon, then the whole of Milton will be cursed like the Bloom family."

Oh gods, she's serious.

"The ad didn't mention any rituals or binding or curses. Just a hike…" Celeste was drowning. Too much had piled on top of her and she sank into it, wondering when she'd hit the bottom.

"Silly girl, the hike *is* the ritual. D'you think we'd've gotten someone by saying we needed a curse bound? D'you think a magazine or newspaper from *Outside* woulda run that?"

Selena ground her feet into the floor, clutched her skirt in her fists. "No, we lie and trick people to have any hope. If you don't do it, we're all as good as dead. But, if you complete the ritual we will be safe from the mountain. And the mountain will be content with us."

She sighed and slumped over, the fire gone out of her. "Bloom Mountain is wary of harming us, but I don't know how much longer that'll last."

Celeste opened her mouth to respond, but she had no idea what to say. "I…I don't understand…" Something in Celeste's stomach unlatched and roiled around.

Selena smiled at her, weak in the afternoon sunlight. "I know, child. It's going to be rough this first time, but I'll tell you everything. You only get one chance to complete the ritual: two days and one night. If you need more than that, you'll find yourself in a world of trouble." She paused a moment. "You won't be the same woman when you come down that mountain, but, Celeste, you *can* do this. Even if you don't realize it yet. Especially if you don't believe it yet.

"Just remember that you'll know when you're doing it right. *The mountain will respond.*"

A knock on the door interrupted Celeste's attempt at a response; a protest that this was not what she'd signed up for. But she remembered the tolling of the bells after she said *I accept*, the strange feeling that something had changed, Sarah's strange words to Marta in the coffee shop. And Celeste realized that no matter what her intentions were, she had already agreed to do this ritual.

The hike.

The *Binding*.

Celeste had agreed to bind Bloom Mountain. She'd agreed to climb a cursed mountain, to do a ritual of some sort to save Milton. The strange feeling of a spell being cast on Celeste tightened its grip around her mind, her heart. She felt in her core that there was nothing she could do to back out of this deal, so she'd have to do her best.

Celeste asked for directions to the bathroom and hurried off before she got sick all over the floor. She heard the door open as she slammed the bathroom door shut and rushed to the toilet.

7
FEVER DREAM

Celeste was rarely sick to her stomach. There had been a few cases of food poisoning when she was a child, but nothing since. Smells didn't bother her, and neither did seeing the remains of animals out in the woods. But she knelt before an old woman's toilet, gagging and coughing out the last of the bile that had overwhelmed her.

She flushed and rinsed her mouth, wiped the sweat and fear from her face. She sat back down and leaned against the side of the tub. The porcelain was cold and felt wonderful against her burning skin.

She waited a minute, five minutes, an age to see if she would be sick again. But the nausea passed, and she was left with the aching feeling that she had been played. And played very well.

Everything had been orchestrated so beautifully by some cosmic force. The day started out so normal and then gradually got stranger and stranger. She wouldn't have come out here if she'd not been desperate, if those numbers in her bank account had stayed stable, if she'd not been so lost. Maybe she'd still be in DC. Maybe she would have found a new job by now.

But instead, she sat in the bathroom of a cottage belonging to a woman who claimed to be a witch. In a town close to where she'd spent the happiest summers of her childhood. A place supposedly so full of magic that mountains could be cursed and families could have the life sucked out of them for no discernible reason.

There was a knock on the door and a soft voice called out, "Are you okay in there?"

The door opened slowly and Marta poked her head inside the room. Her small face was covered in worry lines.

"Why are you here?" Then it hit Celeste. "Selena's your aunt, isn't she?"

She should've seen it before. She knew Selena looked familiar, but she assumed it was someone back home, or someone she had met as a child. Not the woman she'd met only a few hours ago.

Marta smiled. "I wondered if you picked up on that at the shop, from what Samone said. But I think Sarah's *sight* put you off."

Celeste felt a pang of fear and a return of the nausea. "Is that what you call it?" She immediately regretted speaking. Her tone was off.

Marta's smile faltered and her response was sad. "There's no need to be harsh with me. We are all limited in what we can say about the mountain and the ritual."

She rallied a bit and smiled again. "I'm here to help you, just as Sarah suggested, and I *promised*." She held out a hand and Celeste used it to pull herself to her feet.

As they stood together, hands clasped, Celeste noticed that they were probably the same age. Marta was a little taller than her, with brown eyes flaked with fire and honey, and tiny freckles dotted her forehead and left cheek.

Celeste let go of Marta, stepped back, and wiped her hand on her pant leg. "Thanks, and sorry. I'm a little out of my depth here."

"Outsiders usually are when they first come here. You'll get used to it, hopefully." She opened the door and stepped out. "I've given Aunt Selena her afternoon pills."

They reentered the living room and Selena sat comfortably tucked in to her chair with a footstool and a quilt.

She smiled at Celeste. "Come back tomorrow evening and I'll be ready to tell you the steps to the ritual. Marta will take care of you until then, won't you, dearest?"

"Of course, Aunt." Marta kissed Selena's forehead. "Be sure to take your night meds and call Alexandra if you need any help."

As Celeste and Marta approached the door, Selena called out from her chair, her voice low and soft with fatigue. "Do try and believe, Celeste. It'll be easier for you that way."

Once outside, Celeste felt like she could breathe again. It was a hot afternoon, but a breeze carried with it the promise of autumn, and relief from the unrelenting heat of summer. She took deep breath after deep breath.

Marta stood by the step, watching Celeste. She wore shorts, thin tights, a black t-shirt with the Witch Peak Brews logo, and calf-high boots. The shorts emphasized the swell of her hips and the length of her legs. Expertly applied black makeup hadn't smeared during her shift at the coffee shop. She was stunning, even standing stiff as a board with her arms pressed against her ribcage.

"What now?" Celeste asked, trying to direct her thoughts elsewhere.

Marta loosened up. "That's up to you. Aunt Selena has asked me to show you around Milton. And get you acquainted with the locals and differences here in the Valley."

"So…this isn't some sort of fever dream? You guys do believe in magic and curses and all that shit?"

Marta took one of Celeste's hands in her own and a faint electric spark passed between them. "We don't just believe in it, Celeste, we live it. Magic and curses and monsters are a part of life in the Valley. I know it's hard for you Outsiders to understand. But please, you must try."

Bile in Celeste's throat threatened to make her sick again. The hand that Marta wasn't holding clenched, nails digging into the soft flesh of her palm as she took several steadying breaths.

"I'll try," Celeste managed to get out. They stood there for one long, tense moment before Marta smiled and let go of Celeste's hand.

"You hungry? There's a good diner in town. We can eat and I'll answer any questions you've got."

Celeste nodded. "That sounds nice." She wasn't hungry, didn't think she could eat after being sick, but she didn't mind spending more time with Marta. If nothing else, she could learn more about what she'd stumbled into.

Marta started towards their cars. "You can grab your stuff and leave your car here. I'll drive you around."

Celeste grabbed two bags from the Camry and took them over to Marta's beat up Ford Explorer.

As she climbed in and buckled herself up, Celeste wondered what would happen over the next few days.

Would she be returning home? What would happen during this *ritual* she'd agreed to perform? If she didn't come back down the mountain, who would tell her family? What would Elise think of her wayward little sister if Celeste did come back down the mountain? What kind of story would she have to tell then?

Those questions and more rolled around in Celeste's head as Marta pulled away from the cottage and headed back into town.

8

THE FRENCH SILK PIE PERSUASION

Half an hour after leaving Selena's place, Celeste and Marta settled into a corner booth at a retro-style diner close to downtown. They hadn't said much on the drive, but Marta pointed out local attractions and her favorite shops. They'd passed by a new-and-used bookshop located in an old mill, an alchemist's shop that sold skincare and haircare products, and a candlemaker who worked from their historic farmhouse. Milton was brighter and livelier than its downtown suggested.

Maybe rent is just out of control here, like back in DC.

Jed's Kitchen looked like it was brand new out of the '50s with a chrome plated exterior, checkerboard tile floor, and stiff, cherry-red vinyl seats. The servers weren't required to dress up similarly, which was a relief. Half of the booths and all the stools at the bar were filled with early dinner patrons.

One staff member stood at a large dessert case at the end of the bar. It was filled with homemade pies: key lime and French silk, both topped with a thick layer of whipped cream; pecan; various fruit pies; sweet potato and pumpkin lined up on one shelf all their own; and more pies that Celeste couldn't identify. The sheer number of pies was astounding.

Celeste watched as some customers went directly to the pie counter and got little plastic containers to go. Others loitered outside, peeking in at the stools near the bar, and ran for a spot when one was vacated. Again, no one stared at Celeste, which should have set her at ease, but the experiences of the day had made her paranoid.

A waitress approached with water and menus for them. "Hey, Marta, how's the coffee shop?"

Marta looked up as she spoke. "Emilia, didn't know you were working today." She gave the waitress a tight smile.

"I'll be back in a few," Emilia said, and then sauntered away.

Marta sighed and slid the laminated menu over to Celeste. "Milkshakes and pie are the best things here, but you can't go wrong with the sandwiches." Her hands shook a little as she distributed water, straws, and silverware.

"You okay?" Celeste was more curious than worried.

Marta pursed her lips and stared out the window behind Celeste. She seemed to shrink into herself. "Emilia and I were together for about two years. She cheated on me and we broke up. Been able to avoid her the last six months…" She shrugged, as if she was trying to rid a weight that had settled on her. She turned and waved at someone behind the bar.

"Oh…should we go somewhere else?" Celeste was thinking about the pie counter more than anything else. She didn't know how to comfort a near stranger when seeing their ex, especially when her own had been a constant presence in her mind the last three weeks.

"No, I'm hoping Jed will take care of us now. And this really is the best place to eat in town if you don't want something fancy."

A tall, gaunt-faced man approached with his arms wide and a wide, toothy smile. He was older, at least in his mid-60s, with a long apron starched stiff and brilliantly white tied around his waist. "Marta, my dear, you are as radiant as the moon today." He slid into the booth next to Marta and gave her a one-armed hug.

Marta brightened up and returned the hug. "Jed here is Selena's younger brother and my great uncle."

"Nice to meet you," Celeste muttered.

Jed turned eyes the color of young maple leaves to Celeste. She'd never seen eyes that bright a green before. "Aha! The *Outsider* makes her way here to me for pie. As all visitors do." He squinted and raised a hand at a passing server.

"Jakob, could you get a slice of pie for our new friend here?" He waved a hand at Celeste. "I think sweet pot–no. No, no, no, our friend here is definitely of the French silk pie persuasion. Extra whip on the side, and make sure it's from the fresh batch that Sadie made this morning." Jakob slipped off and returned a moment later with a large slice of chocolate pie.

"That's on the house, *Outsider*." Jed winked at her.

"Uh, thanks…" Celeste hesitated.

She wasn't really of the pie persuasion, no matter what Jed thought. She definitely preferred savory over sweet, and cake over pie. But uncle and niece watched her, waiting for her to try it so Celeste shoveled a forkful of the pie into her mouth. It was silky, chocolatey heaven; sweet and rich, but not too far in either direction. The whipped cream was fresh and had cinnamon sprinkled on it. Thick spirals of dark chocolate decorated the top.

"Wow," was all that Celeste could say before scooping up another forkful.

"You were right, as always," Marta was saying to Jed. She rolled her eyes in mock anger.

"It's a gift!" Jed stretched his arms back behind his head. "No one else can tell which pie someone needs at any given time." His tone was part boasting and part joy. "And I am never wrong."

Celeste snort-giggled and covered her mouth with her hand.

"Ahh, and that's what I really wanted. You are far too serious for us, Miss. But I gotta get back to the grill." Jed slid out of the booth. "I'll send Jakob by to get your orders. You take care of this one, Marta, I think we need her."

Celeste watched Jed as he walked off to the kitchen, waving to patrons as he went.

"Your uncle is…interesting."

"He's always been that way. He took over the diner from the previous owner and renovated it. Sadie is his wife." Marta pointed to a plump woman with bright orange hair, a rosy complexion, and one of those silly chef's hats, who was whipping up a pot of chocolate over a double boiler. "She's a marvelous baker. Samone took classes from her for several years before we set up Witch Peak."

Celeste picked up the menu and absently scanned it while she finished the remnants of chocolate pie. There was the usual fare that she expected from a diner like Jed's: meatloaf, lasagna, burgers, chicken tenders, all-day breakfast. But, as Marta had mentioned, they also had a large selection of specialty sandwiches: chicken with bacon and avocado, four cheese grilled cheese with add-ons available, open-faced caprese sandwich on toasted baguette, meatball subs—the list went on.

Jakob returned while Celeste was mulling over the list.

"What can I get for you ladies today?" He was the epitome of an early-20s waiter, complete with bored expression and voice that only just masked internal screaming.

"The bacon grilled cheese with fries and a lemonade, please." Marta ordered with the same customer service voice and smile she had used at the café.

Jakob wrote that down and turned to Celeste.

"The meatball sub, please."

"Okay, sorry, but we just ran out of the fresh mozzarella." He smiled, but it didn't touch his eyes.

"Oh, then the chicken, bacon, and avocado sandwich."

"Fries good for the side? And any other drink?"

"Fries are good and no, water is fine. Thanks."

Jakob noted that down and slid off without another word.

Marta and Celeste looked at each other and then away. Celeste had a growing number of questions and concerns but she wasn't really sure where to start.

How is there magic here?

Where is here?

How do they know I am an Outsider?

And what does that even mean?

"So, uh, is your aunt really a witch?"

Marta stared for a moment and then started laughing.

Celeste felt herself flush in response.

"I'm sorry," Marta wheezed as she got the laughter under control. "I just didn't expect you to come out swinging like that." She took another moment to control herself. "Okay, I really am sorry to laugh at you. Yes, Selena is a witch. Most people who live in The Valley have some sort of magical ability or gift."

"Do you have any?"

Marta nodded soberly. "I brew potions. Healing kind of runs in the family. Aunt Selena can do magical healing and I make potions and salves to help speed up the healing process. All this is in addition to *modern medicine*, of course. Magic and medicine go hand-in-hand."

"Is this something that you studied or...?" Celeste knew she sounded very skeptical. *Remember, you promised to try and understand.*

"Yes, there is a university up in Springfield, the big city to the north, and they teach magical arts there. Anyone can study potion making, but to make the really good ones you have to have an inborn talent for it. My dad does it, too."

"And Selena? How did she go from magical healing to mountain duty?"

"Mostly she did healing when she was young, as I'm sure she told you. But then she took over the binding of the mountain from the previous woman when she got married."

Celeste blinked rapidly in response to all the information being rattled off so casually. "So this binding thing, it's like a tradition?"

Marta sobered. "Yes, a very important tradition." She pointed out the window behind Celeste. The sun was starting to set, the dark shadow of the mountain blocking out vast swathes of the red-orange sky. "That is Bloom Mountain, our Mother, our protector; and our doom if the magic isn't bound soon."

"I saw it from the overlook when I came through the mountains."

Marta nodded. "You can see Bloom Mountain from anywhere within Yuback Valley. There is a little road that leads around the base to the other side, and from there you can get to the town of Birch Branch, Blue Mountain, and Lighthouse Lake. But those are considered a part of a different area of The Valley, not really a part of Bloom Mountain's domain."

"So, what is this binding?"

Marta shrugged. "I don't know. I asked Aunt Selena once, when she was mostly recovered from breaking her hip. But she shook her head at me and told me that I couldn't take over for her. I don't have the right *whatever* to do it." She waved a hand through the air to emphasize her point. "Which is why I opened a coffee shop instead."

Then why me? If someone who has inborn magic can't do the binding, what do I have to offer?

Their sandwiches arrived as she finished speaking.

Celeste's chicken, bacon, and avocado sandwich could have fed a small family and would have cost at least $20 back in DC. It was delicious, with crisp lettuce, fresh avocado, tangy ranch, and melted gouda. The fries were crispy on the outside, soft on the inside, and sprinkled with fine-crystal sea salt.

"I might move here for the food," Celeste commented after she had eaten the first half.

Once they were done, Marta ordered pie for both of them.

"Why did you answer the ad?"

Celeste considered making up a reason, but only for a minute. A fake story would be harder to maintain than the somewhat embarrassing truth. "I lost my job. And then had a breakdown."

"What was your job?"

"I worked for the U.S. Forestry Service, doing what we call silviculture."

"What-culture? That doesn't sound like English to me."

"Silviculture is the process by which we maintain and adapt the forests to meet the needs of the environment. So, like, doing prescribed burning to try and prevent forest fires, helping reforest privately owned land, harvesting and replanting native plants, monitoring the local biodiversity, things like that."

Marta blinked at her, long ebony lashes fluttering against her alabaster cheek. Celeste looked away, avoiding thoughts that strayed too close to the structure of Marta's face, the shimmering black of her hair, the way the shorts she wore fit. It was too much, too soon, especially after the day she'd had.

"It was what I always wanted to do, since I was a little girl. My granddaddy taught me how to distinguish between different trees and my grandma taught me about wildflowers."

"Why did you lose the job you always wanted?"

Celeste shrugged. The conversation felt like a job interview, but she didn't mind it too much. It was easier to answer questions than try to offer up the important information herself. She'd always had issues knowing what was the right or appropriate thing to say in any given situation. Questions made it easier.

"Congress reduced the budget. My department was considered bloated, and the higher-ups selected me for a reduction in force."

God, that sounds so pathetic. Way to impress her, Celeste.

Marta frowned but didn't respond.

"Honestly? I was devastated. I'm not good with change. I drank too much for two weeks. Then a few days ago I saw the ad in an arts journal or something. I thought about it while I drank my coffee, then said *fuck it* and came out here." She paused and considered one question she'd had since she'd driven up into the mountains.

"Where is *here*, anyway? I thought I was going towards West Virginia, up into Appalachia, but this looks like Shenandoah, but I don't think it is…" Celeste trailed off and shrugged.

And there you go, talking too much again. You never know when to stop.

The second round of pie came then, and Celeste waited while Marta took a few bites. Her own pie she left untouched and thought about taking it for later.

"You're right that it looks like Shenandoah, but it isn't. We call it *The Valley* and it's…special, different. It's next to, but not a part of, Shenandoah and greater Appalachia. Kind of like a parallel universe, but not really. I can't explain it any other way." She took another bite. "There are other regions like it, all over the world, with a sort of highway system between them. All hidden from *your* world for protection."

"Really? Are they all weird too?"

Marta snorted. "I call your world weird, Celeste. It's so quiet and predictable and boring."

Celeste nodded. "I can see why you might think that, I guess, if you're used to witchy stuff. But there really are other places like here? All over the world? What makes them really different?"

"Oh yes. In theory there is a whole extra Earth in this parallel world, but I think it's hard to map out the Lands Between. They shift according to rules and whims that we don't understand. But you were asking about the Liminal Words, not the whole cosmos."

I don't know what the difference is, if there is one. Or if I should take this literally or not.

"There are a lot here in North America. I know that there are at least two in Mexico, and one that covers most of the Southwest." Marta tapped her nose in thought with the hand that didn't hold a forkful of pie. "Then there are ones in Colorado, Minnesota, Vermont, and one that covers a lot of the Pacific Northwest up into Canada and Alaska. There are probably others too, I'm not an expert and I haven't visited many of them."

Celeste was shocked and a little impressed. "And they just, what, don't register to people? Like half the country is magical and the majority of us don't see it?"

Marta nodded. "Basically. The normal parts are there too, but if you know the way or are lucky, you can stumble into those special areas like The Valley."

Celeste started picking at her pie while she thought some more about what Marta was saying, about what Selena had told her earlier.

I wonder if I knew some of this when I was a kid, but just forgot. But how can you forget magic? And have I even seen any magic so far? Should I tell her about the lighthouse on the lake? About the last memories I have here?

Celeste felt a swell of fear in her chest. Something about that last memory still terrified her, occasionally woke her up in the middle of the night from dreams filled with nameless, faceless horrors.

No, you don't want to invoke those nightmares.

"I came out here a lot when I was a kid," she admitted.

"Oh, really?" Marta sounded noncommittal, uninterested, but there was a bright spark in her eyes like she had suspicions confirmed.

"Yeah, I didn't know it was out here, but I guess my mom's family is from over by Blue Mountain. Your aunt mentioned the Fosters who lived there on an old cattle farm. Those were my grandparents. My sister and I came out here every summer."

Marta raised an eyebrow at Celeste's confession. "I've heard about *them* from Aunt Selena. Did your dad take your mom's name?" Something about the way she said them piqued Celeste's curiosity. Selena hadn't pressed Celeste to say anything about them either.

"No, they just agreed to give Mom's surname to my sister and me; any boys would have taken Dad's name." Other people had pointed out how odd it was, but it was just normal for Celeste and her family.

"So…how did you come here so often and not know about The Valley or the magic or anything?" She sounded skeptical.

"There was a falling out when I was like…nine or ten.

Something to do with my older sister, Elise, and I never saw them again. They sent us letters and presents and called us every week, but our parents never let us visit their farm again." Celeste felt a pang of longing for them, felt a rush of emotions that she hadn't felt since she was little and getting used to not being *allowed* to see her grandparents again. And now that Celeste was in her 30s, she didn't really remember anything about the visits to the farm by Blue Mountain. Just brief flashes of happy memories, and those dark dreams that occasionally resurfaced.

"I'm sorry. I know that doesn't really help, but it's hard to lose family." There was a softness, a pain to Marta's voice as she spoke that tugged at Celeste's heart. Made it ache in a familiar, terrifying way.

Marta slid out of the booth and went to pay the bill while Celeste waited. Dusk was falling when they left Jed's Kitchen and headed across the gravel parking lot to Marta's car.

"So, about that mostly pest-free hotel?" Celeste was tired and not expecting to get a lot of sleep once she started on the hike, or the *binding*. But how would she get there and back? She'd left the Camry at Selena's. Would Marta just drop her off and pick her up, leaving her without any means of getting around and no way to contact anyone?

Marta laughed. "That would be my apartment. Aunt Selena asked specifically if I could take you in." She sobered a little. "I expect she is trying to set us up." She shook her head. "She can't leave well enough alone, but I don't hold it against her. She's gotten sentimental in her old age, and—well, never mind that."

Celeste stopped in her tracks for a moment and then continued walking, hoping that Marta hadn't noticed. "Bit much of her to ask me to fix a cursed mountain and get a girlfriend all in one trip," Celeste said when she caught back up.

They got into Marta's car and Celeste saw her roll her eyes. "She's been like this since Emilia and I broke up. She had basically made all the wedding plans and we weren't even talking about marriage before I found out about the cheating."

"You seem to have gotten over it pretty well."

"I'm still angry at her, but I'm not crying about it anymore, if that makes sense."

Celeste understood. Marta pulled away from the curb as they lapsed into a comfortable silence.

9
MATCHES

Marta's apartment was in an old, four-level brick building, weather stained but well maintained. Her apartment was on the second floor, at the back of the building.

Celeste followed Marta up the stairs and down a carpeted hallway, marveling at how clean and modern the building was inside. The exterior was from the late 19th or early 20th century and the interior was almost brand new.

"When was this place retrofitted?"

"Maybe 10 years ago. It was an old warehouse and the owners got permission from the town to turn it into apartments. There's been a bit of a migration into The Valley over the last two or three years, so the extra housing has been very useful." She stopped and set a bag down outside her door. "Watch out for Matches. She can be feisty when I get home late."

Celeste didn't have time to ask who or what Matches was before the door opened and a grey fur-ball slunk out into the hall, meowing as loud as she could.

Marta reached down and picked up the undersized cat,

cooing at her and scratching between her tiny ears. Matches appeared content with the apology and turned her large amber eyes to Celeste. She watched as Marta and Celeste piled into the entryway.

The apartment was small, but very comfortable, with real wood floors, a nicely designed kitchen, and a large living and dining area. There was a door to the left of the kitchen and a doorway flanked by heavy curtains was in the right wall of the living room. Marta carried Matches into the kitchen and rummaged in the fridge for a half-empty can of wet food.

"Are you happy now, little chonker?" Marta's voice was fond as she watched Matches settle in for her dinner. "Alright, let me give you the tour."

Marta pointed to a door at the far end of the kitchen. "Bathroom and laundry are in there. There's another door that leads into my closet. Also, Matches's litter box is in there, so don't shut her out."

Marta ushered Celeste through the curtains into a small, cozy study. Inside was a sofa, a large desk, and built-in book-cases. Glass-topped end tables flanked the sofa. Loose papers, antique books, and writing utensils covered the desktop, while a vintage style lantern hung from the wall.

"This is my study. I put up the curtains to keep it dark in here."

"Does the dark help?"

Marta turned the key on the lantern, and warm LED light filled the room. She smiled, coy and mysterious. "I like the dark. It helps me think."

She started pulling pillows and cushions off the sofa. Celeste positioned herself to take them from Marta and sat them in a neat pile against the wall.

"Did the apartment come furnished?"

"Yep, it did. Part of the reason I wanted this place and not a refurbed farmhouse." She pulled out the sofa into a bed and settled the mattress. "Plus, there is a much higher chance that an old farmhouse is haunted."

Celeste's eyes went wide at that.

Ghosts too? But Celeste reasoned that if they believed in curses and witches and potion making, then they would also believe in ghosts.

And so far, nothing too strange has happened…

If you exclude the Mennonite woman, and everyone staring at me as I drove into town, and the old man, and that tall lady with eyes that bored into my soul. Celeste smiled a little rueful smile. *Okay, there has been a lot of human weirdness that has happened today, but beyond that? The bridge? Well, you were jumping at shadows again. You've spent too much time in the city the last five years. You've forgotten the wilds, how they feel and sound and smell, and the eyes in the woods.*

Celeste shivered and recovered before Marta noticed that she was once again lost in thought. *Get a hold of yourself.*

Marta handed her one side of a fitted sheet and they made the bed. Celeste was surprised how nice and fat the mattress felt. Usually pull-out beds were thin and uncomfortable.

"I don't know where the landlord found this sofa, but it's the best one I've ever slept on."

Marta walked back and forth between the study and somewhere else in the apartment, bringing sheets, a selection of pillows, and several handmade quilts for Celeste. Then she went into the kitchen and left Celeste to make her own bed. It was just 8 PM according to Celeste's dying phone when she finished.

"Uh, Marta?" she called. "Do you know why my phone doesn't work?"

Marta returned, holding two steaming mugs. "Is it one of those fancy phones y'all seem to not be able to live without?"

She cocked an eyebrow like she'd made a joke and drawled the sentence with an affected southern accent.

"Sorry, I'm not poking fun at you maliciously. This is strange for me, too." She sat herself down in the chair at the desk. Matches followed her into the study and leapt onto the bed and made herself comfortable in the quilts.

Marta held out one of the mugs and Celeste took it. She settled on the couch next to Matches, who was gracious enough to allow Celeste to pet her.

Celeste took a sip; it was honeyed herbal tea of some sort. Sweet, but kind of tart.

"It's elderberry tea. Good for your immune system." Marta sipped her own and set the mug down. "As for your phone… you won't be able to get any signal out here."

"Do you not have the internet? Or smart phones?"

"No, we have them, but they only work within the confines of The Valley, maybe some of the other areas too. I think you can get SIM cards for your phone up in Springfield, but there's no point if you are only going to be here for another couple days. And there's no signal on the mountain."

"Guess I won't be calling for an evac then."

Marta snorted but didn't say anything.

Celeste kicked off her shoes and pulled her legs up against her chest. She was getting tired and had a headache trying to reconcile her life against everything that she'd heard today. Matches curled up next to her feet.

"This is all so surreal. I don't even know that I really believe you guys…like…I know I said earlier that I would try, but this is all so…" Celeste trailed off, realized that she had just said exactly the wrong thing. She sat her mug down and looked up at Marta, hoping that she appeared apologetic.

Marta pursed her lips. Her voice was full of emotion when she spoke. "My aunt is dying, Celeste. She's got cancer and probably won't make it through the year. You are her last hope, and if you don't start believing what's in front of you, then you're going to taint her legacy." She turned to look at the wall. "And you'll doom us all." Her voice was barely above a whisper.

Celeste's eyes were wide and she felt her face flushing. "I-I'm sorry…I didn't know…" *Great job, Celeste, really stellar work. You've alienated the only friend you had.*

Marta stood, still facing away from Celeste. She heard a sniff that might have been from tears. "Tomorrow I will take you around town, show you the destruction that the unbound mountain has wrought on us over the last decade. I hope that will be enough to convince you to believe."

"Don't you have to work?"

She shook her head and wiped her cheek. "Anna and Samone can handle Witch Peak tomorrow. After that, well, we don't work when someone is binding the mountain. It can cause…complications."

"What sort of complications?"

Marta avoided the question. She looked back at Celeste, her pale cheeks flushed and damp with tears.

Yep, you fucked up good.

"Goodnight, Celeste," she said, and walked out. There was a coldness to her voice that Celeste hadn't heard before and it filled her with anger and dread and shame.

Celeste waited until she heard Marta finish in the bathroom before she ventured out to deal with her own needs. Matches followed her to the bathroom and meowed at her from the toilet while Celeste brushed her teeth and took her meds.

"Yeah, I get it, kitty," she whispered in response. "I messed up…" Matches huffed and jumped off the toilet. She pawed at the door to Marta's room, which Celeste opened a crack before she returned to the study and laid down to sleep.

10

DESTRUCTION ON THE MOUNTAINSIDE

Matches woke Celeste in the morning.

She woke in a better state of mind than she had gone to sleep. Celeste had slept deep and without dreams for the first time since she lost her job. There had been no traffic noises, no airplanes flying overhead, nothing to disturb her, and no alcohol to give her dizzying dreams. It had been three days since she'd drank even a single sip of booze.

Matches was standing on the pillow next to Celeste's head. One paw hovered in the air and Matches alternated between screaming and purring.

"Matches?" Marta whisper-yelled at the cat from the other side of the closed curtains. She was clearly trying to not disturb Celeste, but Matches had already done that.

Celeste rolled over onto her back and pushed herself up into a sitting position. Matches marched into her lap and settled down to purr. Celeste scratched between her ears.

"I'm up," she called out. "And decent." Celeste had brought full pajamas on a whim, even though she preferred to sleep in old ratty t-shirts that were three sizes too large.

Marta popped her head through the curtains. "Matches has been a *terror* this morning." She pointed at the tiny critter, now a half-asleep loaf of cat-bread in Celeste's lap.

"I closed the bathroom door so the shower wouldn't wake you, and she took mighty offense to that." She rolled her eyes.

She seems to be in a better mood this morning. But I gotta make sure I don't fuck up again.

The night of sleep had been good for Celeste and she woke with a different perspective this morning. And she was determined to make the best of the situation she found herself in.

"I'm sorry for what I said last night." She didn't want to defend herself, to justify her ignorance and poor judgment. She had spoken without thinking about anything but her gut reaction.

This is a whole new world for you, sort of. Let's try to be more open-minded and think before we speak, Celeste.

Marta smiled and nodded. "And I'm sorry that I reacted so poorly. Every year that the mountain goes unbound is harder for us than the last. And I worry about what it may do to my aunt if she cannot find a successor..." She made noises trying to coax Matches out of Celeste's lap, but the cat only made herself heavier and purred louder.

"Aunt Selena really isn't doing well. She didn't react well to chemo, so she is just letting the cancer take its course. We're managing the pain as best we can."

"I'm sorry. You two seem close." Celeste wanted to say that she understood, since her Grandma died from cancer. But Celeste hadn't been around to see her decline. *Just offer sympathy, nothing more. You know the drill by now.*

"It's fine. She's had a long life, and I've been blessed to spend many years with her." She smiled sweetly. It felt like Marta was trying to convince herself that the coming death was an acceptable end to a long life filled with purpose. But the sorrow in her eyes told another story. "But now I should relieve you of your burden." She made *tsk*-ing noises at Matches, who continued to ignore her.

"I've always wanted a cat, even though they are weird critters." Celeste slid her hands under the cat's belly and ejected her onto the mattress. Matches, offended in the way that only a cat can be, glared and cleaned one paw. Then she deigned to notice Marta and ran over, making a kind of birdlike call as she did.

Marta rolled her eyes. "You are a brat, little kitty." She picked Matches up and put her front paws on her shoulder. "I've got the waffle maker heating up and there's local bacon to go with them for breakfast."

"Oh, my favorite!" Waffles and bacon were her favorite breakfast, though she rarely got them homemade. They had been ever since she'd been a little girl and her granddaddy had made them for her and Elise every morning at the farm.

Marta and Matches disappeared behind the curtain. Marta was murmuring something to Matches about her being a *very good girl*, but she shouldn't scream at the guests so early in the morning.

Celeste grabbed her bag and headed for the bathroom.

In the mirror, pale green eyes stared back at her. Celeste looked better than a few days ago, but the effects of so much drinking were still obvious. The dark circles under her eyes were less intense. The pallor and redness were fading and her skin was returning to its usual olive tone, with the help of skincare that she'd forgotten in her alcoholic haze. Her face was still puffy, her limbs swollen and stiff, but she was recovering.

You look more like yourself now.

Celeste dressed in old hiking gear: stretchy, breathable pants and a lightweight, long sleeved shirt. She braided her long, wavy brown hair over one shoulder and secured it with a sage green ribbon that Elise had given her. She let herself look in the mirror one more time before reemerging.

Yeah, you definitely look and feel more like normal. You got this, Celeste.

Celeste slipped out the door and around the island without alerting Marta. Once she stored her bag back in the study, she was drawn to the kitchen by the sound and smell of frying bacon and toasted bread.

There were two stools on the far side of the kitchen island and Celeste took one of those. Marta slid her a plate with three slices of bacon and three thick waffles on it. Syrup, butter, and sugar were on the counter as well. Marta grabbed her own plate and took the other stool.

They ate in silence while protecting their bacon from Matches.

The waffles were light and fluffy and had a mild, slightly malted sweetness to them. The bacon was thick and crispy but not as fatty as Celeste was used to. The butter came in a fat roll wrapped in wax paper and the maple syrup was in an unlabeled jug.

Looks like these came from the local farmer's market.

Once she was done, Marta got up and put her plate in the sink. She stopped for a moment and stared at a cabinet and then started laughing. "I forgot to make coffee!"

Celeste was about to protest that she didn't need any and Marta shouldn't go out of her way to make some. But Marta opened a cabinet door and a Nespresso was sitting there, ready to go.

"A Nespresso?" Celeste asked before she could stop herself.

Marta snorted. "Yeah, I don't like putting a lot of effort into coffee at home. I usually just wait 'til I get to the shop, but I have this for emergencies. Latte or regular coffee?" Marta dug through a container of pods while she responded.

"Regular is fine." Celeste was still eating. She had always been the last to finish her meals and it had been a running gag when she was a kid. But as an adult she enjoyed savoring her food and felt like it was the one time she didn't have to rush around getting something done.

A moment later Marta had a ceramic mug of coffee for Celeste.

"Cream? I usually take some as the pods are kind of bitter and acidic to my taste."

"Yes, please."

A glass jug of half-and-half appeared on the counter next to the mugs. Also unlabeled.

"Where are we going today?" Celeste tried to keep her tone neutral, reminding herself to keep an open mind.

Marta inhaled the aroma of her coffee and took a slow mouthful and savored it. "There are a few places around the foot of Bloom Mountain, and one on the far side. It's hard to explain without context though, so forgive me if I don't tell you exactly where we are going right now."

Celeste nodded. "Fair enough."

"It'll be worth the wait, I promise."

TWO HOURS LATER THEY WERE DRIVING DOWN A weathered dirt road somewhere along the foot of Bloom Mountain. Oaks and maples stretched their branches over the road, blocking out the bright sunlight above. It was hot, even in the shade. Marta had lowered the car windows hoping to catch a breeze as they drove, but all they caught were bugs.

Celeste was quiet and contemplative. So far, they had visited two sites where Marta claimed that Bloom Mountain had wrought its wrath. And it was hard to argue that tragedies had happened, but to Celeste they all appeared natural.

The first was a farm where a boulder the size of a pickup had tumbled down the mountain and destroyed the farmhouse. No one had been injured, the family had been out at the time and the farm animals had escaped unscathed. At the time, it had been five years since Bloom Mountain was bound, and the family was already afraid of the mountain. They used the destruction of their home as an excuse to move to the other side of town, taking their animals with them. No one bothered to buy the plot and rebuild the farm.

The second site was older. And worse. A sinkhole opened up underneath a barn in the middle of the night. It took the whole structure and the animals with it. Later investigation showed that the sinkhole was caused by a cavern roof collapsing, but no one was brave enough to explore further. The farmer disappeared one night and never returned.

After they left the second site, Marta had told Celeste that the next stop was where Bloom Mountain had started lashing out at the people it was supposed to protect. The first disturbance was within weeks of the ritual wearing out, and it repeated every year without fail.

On the west side of Bloom Mountain, almost directly under the towering summit, a family of Mennonites operated the largest sheep farm in Yuback Valley. They also raised goats and chickens and kept a large garden. They were prosperous and generous, but they lived under the ever watchful eye of the mountain.

Celeste could see the slopes of Bloom Mountain towering over the large clapboard-sided house where Marta parked. From her view, Celeste thought the mountain was intimidating with its dark forests and steep rocky outcroppings. The forest at its feet grew to within a few hundred yards of the farmhouse. Ancient oaks and bristling pines and towering sycamores stood sentinel over the oldest site of Bloom Mountain's displeasure.

A woman approached them from the house as they exited the car. She was older than Marta and Celeste, probably in her early 40s. She wore a narrow skirted dress in a somber dark blue and had her hair tied under a kerchief.

There was a faint smile on her face as she walked up to Celeste. "Welcome, Outsider, to our farm. We were told to expect you this morning." She nodded to Marta and then gestured for them to follow.

She led them past two large barns and a chicken coop to a smaller, older barn. The paint had peeled off the wood and Celeste could see where warped and ruined boards had been replaced. There was a strange tension in the air that grew as they walked towards a small opening between the two doors. It made Celeste feel like someone, somewhere, was angry with her, watching her every move.

The woman stopped. "This is where we keep the *affected* ewes."

The woman did not follow as they walked towards the doors. She looked at the barn with a mixture of fear and sorrow, and perhaps the tiniest flicker of hope.

Inside were a dozen ewes and two women watching over them. The ewes huddled in the center of the barn, apparently asleep. They were as far from both doors as they could be. It was dim and smelled strongly of hay and animals and old wood, but it wasn't overwhelming.

It's been a while since I was last in a barn.... Celeste dug for the memory that was tickling the back of her mind, but it remained elusive, and she turned her attention back to the moment.

Marta sighed as she approached one woman. "So many this year?"

A soft, sad voice that was familiar answered her. "Yes, one more each year that passes without the magic being bound. We do not know what creature causes these *unnatural* pregnancies, but we are doing what we can for these poor ewes." The voice belonged to Hannah, the woman at Witch Peak the day before.

I hope her sister isn't nearby. I don't know if I can handle her prophetic shit today.

Marta moved to the side, and Hannah saw Celeste for the first time. "Ah, I see. You are showing the Outsider our woes." There was just a hint of reproach in her voice.

"What's wrong with the sheep?"

"What do you know about sheep, Outsider?"

I know a lot about trees, but I don't think this is the time for that.

Celeste shrugged. "Nothing really."

Hannah nodded. "These are ewes, female sheep. And something *unnatural* has impregnated them. The lambs they carry will not last long. They come out twisted or worse." She sighed heavily.

"We breed our sheep in October so that they give birth in early spring. The cooler weather means that the lambs are less likely to get sick. And this is the way we have always done it. We separate the ewes and the rams to ensure that the ritual is maintained."

Hannah turned to look at the ewes.

"Ritual?"

Hannah nodded, still looking away from them. "Yes, everything relies on ritual."

Before Celeste could request clarification, Hannah continued.

"We discovered the first pregnant ewe at this time the year Selena did not complete the binding. We do not blame her, of course, she was injured while trying to keep us safe. And it's not her fault that no one has completed the ritual since..." She trailed off and took a shallow breath. "It was not long after that failed attempt that we found a heavily pregnant ewe a little separated from the rest of the herd. We keep a close eye on our herd, they are our friends and our livelihood. None of us would put a lamb at risk like that."

The other woman in the barn joined them. She was older with watery blue eyes and sagging cheeks. Her voice was sharp and stern. "I told August that I saw a shadow drop down off the mountain one night, but we dismissed it until two days later when we found the first ewe. None of us want to remember that first lambing. It was traumatic and the ewe wasn't the same after, like the lamb had sucked all the life out of her. The rams wouldn't touch her either, when we put them in the pasture to breed."

Celeste shivered.

"Has any ewe been taken more than once?" Marta's voice was a sea of calm.

Hannah looked to the other woman, but she shook her head. "Some years the ewes don't survive the birth, but the ones that do never breed again. We've set aside a pasture for them and we do our best to keep them protected."

Hannah continued. "If these twelve survive then we will have nearly thirty ewes in that herd." She shivered and cast a sorrowful look at the sleeping ewes.

A bell rang in the distance, hollow and mournful. It woke two of the ewes and put the Mennonite women on edge. Celeste saw their bodies stiffen as the bell continued to ring.

11

STORMWALKER

"Have they found another...?" Hannah's voice was a terrified whisper.

"It cannot be, that *thing* has already claimed its share of our flock!" the other woman protested, voice heavy with anger. Her arms shook at her sides.

They hurried out of the barn and Marta and Celeste followed. The weather had changed while they were inside. The sky was dark, fat clouds hung low over the farm, kissing the top of the tallest barn. The wind whipped around the women as they walked, ripping their hair and clothing. A cold rain pelted them as they walked, and then ran, towards the house.

As they passed the other two barns, Celeste glanced over at them and saw the glint of sheep eyes watching the women as they passed.

Then lightning struck. So close that the bright flash blinded Celeste. The responding thunder was so loud that Celeste tripped over her own feet and fell hard onto her right hip. She was dazed but someone caught her by the shoulders and dragged her back to her feet. They led her stumbling along until her toes crashed into wood and she was pulled up a set of stairs.

Celeste's vision returned before her hearing did. She was on a covered porch behind the main house. A dozen other people including Marta were there. Marta held on to Celeste's shoulders and was paying attention to something across the porch from them. Two older men and one woman were the center of whatever conversation was happening. Then the ringing in Celeste's ears died down and she could barely hear someone as they yelled.

"Something's coming!"

One of the women pointed a long arm out towards the storm that was now raging overhead. The dark clouds swirled and the rain pelted the windows and everyone around Celeste was quiet and watchful.

It was still light out, enough to notice a towering creature of shadow as it lumbered out of the forest. It was vaguely human-shaped with gangly legs, arms that reached almost to the ground, and an excruciatingly thin torso. The wind did not touch the creature as it ambled towards the farmhouse, ignoring all else in its path. Trees and bushes were ripped up and swirled around it, a deadly vortex with a monster in the eye of the storm. Each slow, heavy step dislodged chunks of earth and stone that were sent skywards to join the rest.

It stopped when it was a hundred yards from the house. The wind battered the porch, shaking the storm door loose from its feeble lock.

Celeste stumbled away from Marta, towards the screen window that kept the debris from hitting them. The others were huddled against the house wall, but she felt compelled to get a little closer. She looked back for a second and saw a look of awe cross the face of many of the older Mennonites.

Celeste looked back as the creature raised an arm towards the house and beckoned.

Everyone else was silent and still, seeming to hope that the creature wasn't beckoning to them. But Celeste knew, in a way she couldn't explain, that the creature was there for her. She felt something in her chest, in the back of her mind, a siren's song beckoning her towards the creature.

She was terrified, paralyzed by the incredible sight before her and by the overwhelming *otherness* of the creature. All the bones in her body felt like they'd been made of jelly and she would collapse into a puddle at her feet. The desire, the need to go out and see this creature up close, overrode those feelings. In some insane way, she wanted to touch it to know if the creature felt like wind or silk or fire or an electrical shock.

Celeste watched from a distance as she moved without thinking. She was out the door and down the stairs before anyone could attempt to stop her. Her legs ate up the yards between the house and the waiting creature. The wind buffeted but did not slow her as she trudged through the tall damp grass. Debris whipped past her, smaller chunks of dirt and twigs stinging her naked skin, while the larger pieces mercifully missed. Her heart raced in her chest and she felt something electric tickle up at her spine as she approached.

The closer she came, the smaller the creature appeared. The vortex around it was dense, a shield of wind and electricity and earth and sound. It was so loud, thunder and an electric crackle and gale force winds. A thin line of light stretched to the ground as Celeste approached. It expanded into a threshold for her to step through.

Inside it was quiet.

So quiet Celeste thought she had lost the ability to hear completely. It shocked her back to herself. She couldn't hear the roaring winds outside or her own breathing or the blood in her veins. It was silent in a way that was utterly impossible, and yet here she stood, oppressed by the silence.

She stopped an arm's length away from the creature. Ribbons of shadow undulated over the edges, altering the silhouette for a brief second, giving it a changeling appearance. Flickers of light twisted through the shadow, like lightning but shrunk to size. There were deeper, darker shadows where the face should be. But there was nothing identifiable, nothing human, there. Three or maybe four pinpoints in the darkness might have been eyes or ears or mouths, but it was hard to see the details as they swirled and changed.

An outstretched arm swayed up and down, vying for Celeste's attention.

It was holding something in its flickering, long-fingered hand.

Celeste was afraid to touch the creature, but felt a compulsion to take the item. She reached out and it flipped its hand over, so that the item dangled below it. Celeste took it; an old square nail with blackened wire braided around it hung from a soft length of thin leather. A tiny yellow crystal dangled from the top, clinking against the nail head when Celeste moved it with her thumb.

Pretty…

Celeste looked up at the creature. "What are you?" she asked.

And the world exploded in response.

A pressure wave rippled out from the creature, knocking Celeste to the ground. Her vision blurred, and the last thing she saw was the creature dissipating as the sun burst through the clouds above it.

Celeste came to almost immediately. She was lying on the ground in a small crater, covered in dirt and debris. Everything smelled of burning wood and ozone and damp earth. Around the crater's lip, the trees and bushes and rubble that the vortex had torn out of the ground rested at odd angles. The sun was burning down on the world, as if the storm had never occurred.

Celeste heard voices and turned to see Marta and Hannah racing towards her, with the others not far behind.

Marta arrived first to help Celeste up from the ground. Hannah arrived a second later and took Celeste's other arm. The three of them climbed up out of the crater. The Mennonite family were excitedly talking amongst themselves, the air around them as electric as the aura around the monster.

"Are you hurt, Outsider?" asked the sharp woman from the small barn.

"I don't know…" Celeste was clutching the talisman in her hand so hard that it was going numb. While everyone was talking, she mentally checked herself over. She'd strained her ankle; she could walk, but she'd have to be careful. Everything else felt sore or on fire or numb.

"It gave me something." She dislodged herself from Hannah and held out her hand for the others to see.

"It has been a long time since we last saw a Stormwalker," one man commented, his voice low with respect.

Hannah returned to Celeste's side, her voice exultant. "Gale and Stone bless you, Celeste. You must be destined to bind the mountain and free us from the curse."

Celeste looked down at the talisman. It was cool in her hands and radiated an overwhelming sense of peace, like plunging into a calm sea on a hot day.

What are Gale and Stone?

The eldest man stepped forward. "You have the Stormwalkers' blessing and you must wear it always." He gently pried the talisman from her hand and slipped the leather thong over her head. The talisman rested on her breastbone, the thong long enough to not be irritating or make Celeste feel like she was choking. Its little crystal tinkled and scattered the sunlight into sparkles on her shirt.

The sharp woman joined the old man. "You must lunch with us, after we see to the herd."

Everyone except Marta and Hannah dispersed to attend to farm business. Two of the younger men peeled off and surveyed the crater and the debris surrounding it. There was a hum of excitement from everyone as they worked.

Celeste stood waiting for someone to tell her where to go, her mind untethered. She thought of the creature, the Stormwalker, and the talisman around her neck, and felt a knot of cold fear uncoil in her stomach. Tendrils snaked their way through her torso and up to her heart. Suddenly she was freezing despite the heat.

It's all real. This isn't a dream.

Everything that Marta and Selena had told her was true. She had irrefutable proof now. She couldn't chalk up a walking storm to a trick of the light or alcohol or an overstimulated mind.

It wasn't a dream. It wasn't a dream.

Celeste repeated those words to herself as Hannah and Marta escorted her to the house. They deposited her in a comfortable chair in a room just off the busy kitchen. Celeste could hear the clamor as food was prepared. Hannah wrapped a blanket around her shoulders and brought her a steaming mug of something strong and sweet and alcoholic.

Celeste sipped the contents and stared at the wall for many long minutes, her brain on repeat. *It's all real, it's all real, it's all real.* Her body swayed back and forth in a slow rocking motion.

She turned to Marta. "I just want to confirm that all that just happened. Right?"

Marta winced. "It was real."

Celeste nodded. She was finally starting to warm up but

her thoughts were still lost. Any strong emotions tended to get lost for an indeterminate period of time while her brain processed them. Later, though, they would all probably hit at once. The talisman was heavy against her chest, reminding her of its presence. She tucked it under her shirt and enjoyed the feeling of metal on her skin.

Hannah and Sarah brought in a tray of food and set it down on a wooden coffee table. Hannah doled out sandwiches and fruit slices and they sat in silence. Celeste ate the fruit first, letting her stomach get used to the idea of food. The bread was still warm from the oven and so soft, but it took a while for her appetite to come back.

While she waited, Celeste looked around the living room. It was large and spacious, filled with hand-made furniture covered in quilts and knitted blankets. Two doors were in the wall opposite her seat and the door to the kitchen was behind her. Sarah and Hannah and Marta were all finished with their lunch.

Sarah cleared her throat. "I apologize if I made you uncomfortable yesterday, Celeste. I cannot control the *sight*, and the days leading up to a binding are magically tumultuous at best."

And at worst? Magically tumultuous?

Celeste sighed and blinked her tired eyes. "After what just happened, I don't think you need to apologize. But…what was that creature?"

Sarah accepted that with a nod. "The Stormwalkers are benevolent spirits of Gale and Stone. They follow the summer storms to pull down dead trees and uproot rotten plants that could infect the fields. Usually they will come singly, but sometimes a group will appear if a particularly evil tree needs their attention."

Trees can be evil? Well, if storms can be monsters, then why can trees not be evil?

Hannah continued. "All farmers keep a lightning rod with offerings for the Stormwalkers. We carve wind chimes and tie lengths of wool from the first shearing of the year to ours. I know other farmers attach bells to their rods. You can hear them ringing when the wind picks up after the weather turns cold." She shivered, though Celeste couldn't tell if it was the sound of bells or the cold of winter that caused it.

"Aunt Selena leaves out jars of honey in the woods behind her house," Marta offered. "I found them while I was cleaning up litter and she told me to leave them and the glass shards out there."

"The offering varies from person to person, but anyone with land and some smarts will leave out something for the Stormwalkers." Sarah rose and collected the plates.

"What are Gale and Stone?" Celeste asked, her voice breaking slightly.

Sarah nodded to Hannah as she headed for the kitchen with the tray.

"Stone and Gale are the gods of earth and air, Ember is the god of fire and Ice the god of water. In the Liminal Worlds they hold dominion, though some are closer than comfort."

Celeste looked to Marta. As everything processed and some of her questions were answered, she felt increasingly vulnerable, uncomfortable and uncertain about the world going forward. She had irrevocable proof of magic and monsters and now she was going to have to go up a cursed mountain to deal with more of the same. Things she had only ever enjoyed in books and movies were now real, tangible. And terrifying.

And now they have a pantheon of gods too? What have I gotten myself into?

"I don't know if I can do this, Marta." Celeste pulled the blanket tighter around her, felt tears threaten to fall from her eyes. "I know I have to try, but I don't know if I can do this. I came out here cause I needed the money and then I met you and I just saw some storm monster walk out of a forest and give me a nail necklace for fuck's sake!" Celeste's voice was teetering on the edge of hysteria, her words tumbling out before she could think them through.

Another sign of an impending breakdown; at least I can recognize the signs now.

Celeste pulled the talisman out and rubbed it in her cold hands.

Marta got out of the chair and knelt before Celeste. She reached out with one hand to brush the talisman with her fingertips. "This will help, and there will be prayers…but most of this will be on you, Celeste. I'm sorry that I can't do more to help." She let her hand drop and it grazed Celeste's as it fell.

Celeste grabbed it before it was out of reach and clung to it like her life depended on it. "I'm so sorry that I mocked you and your beliefs." She squeezed Marta's hand once and then let it drop.

"You're forgiven, of course." Marta smiled and then stood up. She held out a hand to help Celeste out of the chair.

Sarah entered through one of the doors opposite the kitchen. "It's going on noon now. I imagine you two need to return to Selena."

Marta and Celeste were still holding onto each other and quickly dropped their arms to their sides. They had completely forgotten about Hannah and the rest of her family.

"We have another stop before we see her," Marta responded.

"What?" Celeste wasn't certain that she wanted to go anywhere else except home. Her hands were shaking and she felt nauseous. The fear she'd felt uncoiling had stretched its tendrils all throughout her body. There was no telling when it would finally overwhelm her.

Hannah led them through the house and to the front door. There she turned to Celeste with solemn eyes. "We will keep you in our prayers, Celeste Foster. And we will conduct the rituals, as they have been handed down to us."

After a moment she added, "May Ice, Ember, Stone, and Gale watch over you."

12

LIGHTHOUSE LAKE

Celeste was fingering the Stormwalker talisman when Marta handed her a piece of folded paper.

"What's this?" she asked, opening it to see a list of directions in spidery handwriting.

Marta looked over at Celeste. There was something soft and sad in her brown eyes. "There's no GPS signal south of Bloom Mountain, so I need you to read out directions to me. I haven't been down to Birch Branch in a while and it wouldn't be good for us to get lost."

"What's in Birch Branch?"

"Aunt Selena called me before you woke up this morning and told me to take you to a farmhouse down there. She said that it might be familiar to you and had me write down the directions."

"Did she tell you what to expect?"

Marta shook her head and put the car in reverse. "Nope, we're going in blind."

Maybe this is about my grandparents? I don't know if I want to tackle that today...

They turned left out of the driveway and drove deep into the forest. Sunlight flickered like gold under the canopy of deep green leaves. The scent of pine and falling leaves filled the car as it crept along with the windows down. The tires dampened the sounds of cicadas and bird calls and the rummaging of small creatures, rolling first over pavement and then gravel. Dust kicked up from the tires, wafting into the cab.

"Roll up your window. I'm gonna pick up the pace here in a second," Marta told her.

The trees parted and the dark waters of the Nomini River appeared on their right. The road paralleled the river for a mile or so. On the other bank, a freight train sat unmoving on the tracks.

"It's probably waiting for the Valley Express to leave Birch Branch. It sits there for half an hour every day." Marta stopped her car on a bridge that spanned a stream feeding into the Nomini. "There's only enough room for one track between Bloom Mountain and Yuback Ridge, and passenger rail is prioritized."

Celeste turned and cocked an eyebrow at Marta. "There's passenger rail through The Valley? Like, for real?"

DC can't even get the Metro expansions done and they have full rail out here?

"Yes, it's the easiest way to get around. We have the highway, but it really only goes from Springfield up north to Crestwood in the south. There are exits for the larger villages along the highway, but rail is the easiest way to get to the smaller towns and more rural areas." She pulled forward and off the bridge. "The back roads in the deeper forests are…*uncomfortable*. Especially at night."

What does that mean? But Celeste didn't ask the question out loud. She kept it to herself, wondering, hoping that she'd get the answers eventually. *It's so hard being dropped into a situation where everyone else knows more than you and they just take that for granted.* She sighed. *It's not that different from every other situation in life. Except here it's life and death, instead of social ostracization.*

They drove through dense forest for a few more minutes until they broke through into bright sunlight shining off the deep blue water of a lake. Marta turned left onto a large four lane road that circled the lake.

Celeste gasped as they rounded a bend and a lighthouse came into view. It was tall and proud, built of shining white stone that jutted up out of the middle of the lake. It was exactly as Celeste remembered it from her childhood. The brilliant white and deep blue contrasting with the distant, deep green forests and the cerulean of the sky.

Marta pulled off the road and parked next to a narrow strip of pebbled beach.

Celeste was out of the car before Marta could turn it off. She jumped a rotting fence and landed in a soft pile of pebbles, some rolling away under her feet. Celeste adjusted her stance so she wouldn't fall and stepped closer to the water, hoping to get a better view of the lighthouse. The scent of *wet* and rotting plant life wafted up from her feet.

The view was the same as from the road, but standing on the pebble beach jogged a memory from her childhood. She could see herself holding her Grandma's hand and it was night and millions of stars twinkled down on them. Elise had been there, excited, but Celeste had been scared of the dark and had stayed close to Grandma. After that there was nothing. Just an indistinct memory, tinged with fear and confusion.

Marta approached from behind, slipping on the rocks.

"This was the last place I remember going with my Grandma." Celeste was half lost in those brief glimpses of memory. "Elise was excited about something but I don't remember why.

It's hazy, but something happened that night and we never came back here."

Marta put a hand on Celeste's shoulder. It was a comforting weight, warm and soft. She didn't say anything, just stood with Celeste.

Celeste enjoyed the gentle breeze and the sunlight sparkling off the lake for a few moments and then stepped forward and plunged a hand into the water. It was cold but Celeste enjoyed the shock. She ran her hands along the rocks and scooped up one the size of her thumb. It was pale like the Lighthouse, but streaked with black and crimson and green. Her friend Mel could have told her what it was. Celeste rubbed the rock between her palms, waiting for it to dry so she could pocket it.

Another for the collection. Maybe I can find some leaves too. It's been a long time since I pressed anything.

"We should go, Celeste." Marta's voice was soft as the water sloshing against the rocks.

Celeste was starting to get lost in her memories and her hopes for the future, but she was present enough to feel the gentle pressure of Marta's hand on hers, the electric shock that passed between their fingers. She held on and let herself be led back to the car and they continued on their way to Birch Branch.

Despite her misstep last night, Celeste had grown comfortable around Marta in the short time they'd known each other. Celeste felt safe with her around.

But why does she make me feel safe? We've known each other for all of a day? Am I really falling that hard for her?

But there were mysteries that hid behind her vibrant eyes and the coy, intelligent smiles she blessed Celeste with when Marta thought that she wasn't watching. The potion-making barista who lived in a parallel world was a delicious mystery that Celeste wanted to unravel.

Those thoughts led Celeste down less innocent pathways in her mind, so she turned to stare out the window until her cheeks cooled and they approached a town.

The Free City of Birch Branch was smaller than Milton, and older by a century, so the welcome banner claimed. A small sign that declared "THE OWLBROOK MATRIARCHS WATCH OVER YOU" had been vandalized and was hanging by a single nail from its post.

"Who are the Owlbrooks?" Celeste asked Marta, pleased that her voice remained calm.

Marta glanced once at the sign before responding. "The Owlbrooks are a clan of witches who used to unofficially rule this town with the help of a goddess of autumn and decay."

"Used to?"

"Yeah, the last two Matriarchs were terrible. They ruled the town with an iron fist and misused the magics that had been gifted to them by the goddess. They horribly abused the last of their line, Josanna, because she wasn't what they wanted her to be." Marta paused a moment to negotiate a turn. "Josie's grandmother and mother were run off the road and died about four years ago. After the funeral Josie freed the goddess and ended the reign of the Matriarchs."

"You can confine a god?"

"Only if the god allows it."

They pulled off the road in front of a tall privacy fence just outside the town limits. The road was one-and-a-half lanes and lightly traveled to judge by the height of the grass, goldenrod, and honeysuckle that filled the shoulders.

The fence was familiar in a way that was haunting, but also wrong. It was taller, freshly painted, but not unlike the fence that had been there before. A door was positioned directly in the center, only a handle visible from the road. There was a part of Celeste that didn't want to open it and see the house for the first time in over 20 years. But there was another part of her, stronger and more stubborn, that wanted to know and remember everything that had been lost.

They exited the car and stood in front of the fence and door.

Celeste reached out for the handle, worried that it would be locked on the other side. But it opened smoothly and Celeste gasped. Suddenly she was a little girl again, holding Elise's hand. She could see the house as it was then, painted a bright yellow with white trim. Grandma was in the garden and Granddaddy checked the trees for fruit and signs of disease. The memories merged and she saw them sitting on the front porch, watching the chickens peck at the yard, playing with Elise and Celeste.

The grass was tall and dotted by wildflowers all in shades of blue. Phlox and Quaker ladies hugged the ground while wild cornflowers, Jacob's ladder, grape hyacinth, and blue-bells stood taller. They ranged from a pale blue-violet to bright, vibrant cobalt, all against a background of verdant grass. A light breeze carried with it a riot of smells: healthy, growing grass and the deep earthiness of the forest behind the house and the bright perfume of the flowers in the garden. Bees and butterflies flitted between flowers, the gentle buzz and flapping barely audible over the crickets and cicadas.

The two-story house was painted a dark sapphire with white trim. It leaned ever so slightly to the right where the land had sunk. Inside it was hardly noticeable unless you pulled out a level and plopped it down on the mantle.

A white picket fence contained an overflowing garden full of blue flowers: roses, violets, forget-me-nots, delphiniums, and proud orchids. To the right, hidden behind a vine-covered lattice wall, Celeste spied a garden full of corn and squash and peppers ready for harvest.

Celeste led Marta across the wild yard to the fence and reached over to let them into the garden. The grass beneath their feet was soft and springy and freshly cut. Fallen leaves dotted the yard with touches of brown and gold and russet.

"Grandma would spend hours outside with the flowers, teaching me everything she knew. Elise would sit on the covered porch, reading her books with Granddaddy when he was around."

"It sounds like you guys loved coming here."

"We did. It was always the best part of the summer." Celeste pointed to the left, through a tunnel in the trees. "Down there is the old barn and the cattle pastures." She stopped at the mention of the barn.

"What?" Marta was beside her, looking down towards the trees. "Something come to mind?"

Celeste shook her head. "Yeah, something…but I can't remember exactly what. Something to do with the barn." She could see her small self running up the tunnel, could feel a vague sense of fear and excitement. But like earlier, nothing further came back to her.

Celeste turned back to the house and climbed to the covered porch. Modern, weatherproof furniture dotted the enclosed space. "Someone clearly lives here, but I don't know who."

Marta pointed towards the door. "Knock. We're already here."

Celeste rapped on the door three times with her knuckles, but there was no response. She knocked three more times and felt frustration mounting. She had come all this way, had braved the memories locked away, and now no one was answering the door.

"Why did your aunt want me to come here?"

Marta shook her head. "I don't know for sure. Maybe she wanted you to see that you had a connection to the Valley? To make you want to help more?"

Celeste stiffened. "I've already agreed to try. I can't promise anything else."

She sighed heavily and then started looking around.

"What is it?" Marta called as Celeste walked down the porch towards a stack of terracotta flower pots.

"Grandma kept an extra key under these flowerpots, in case one of us went out playing and came back to a locked door." Celeste lifted the dusty, cob-webbed stack and laughed once. She set them down and picked up the small brass key that was underneath.

How long have you been sitting here, little key?

Celeste returned to the door, slid the key into the lock, and turned. The door unlocked with a clank and creaked open.

Marta put a hand on Celeste's arm. "Are you sure about this? We don't know if someone is home or not..." She trailed off with a look of worry in her eyes.

Celeste thought for a moment. *How much would I regret not going inside? Seeing the house is one thing, but what if Granddaddy is here?*

She looked back at Marta. "I need to see inside, Marta."

Marta nodded and followed Celeste inside.

"Hello?" Celeste called out. "Is anyone home? Granddaddy?"

There was no response. The lights were off, but the windows were open and gauzy curtains fluttered in the breeze, bringing the floral scent of the garden inside. To their right was a closed door and to the left was a large living room. "That was my grandparents bedroom," Celeste noted, more to herself than to Marta.

She turned left and entered the living room. It was done up in pale purple and pink florals and had plush, modern chairs and couch, a small TV sat on a pale wooden console table. "But this is all different. Granddaddy made or bought the old, rustic furniture that used to be in here." After a moment's observation, she added, "This looks more comfortable."

The walls had unsigned landscape and floral paintings. One of them was of Lighthouse Lake, several were views of the house and the land it sat on, the rest were views that meant nothing to Celeste. Marta lingered by one that was small and sat on a table in the corner of the room. Celeste walked up behind her to see what it was: a view of Bloom Mountain from Milton.

Celeste let out a breath, louder than she intended. "I don't remember any of these paintings. And certainly not *that one*."

Marta looked back at her. "Would you really remember these? It's been a long time…"

Celeste thought about it for a moment. "I don't remember there being any art here, but…you're right."

Back in the entry hall they had the choice of a hallway and a staircase. Celeste chose the hall which led them to the kitchen and attached dining room. The kitchen was a mix of modern appliances and antique cupboards painted a white-grey color. The bottom doors were covered in childish paintings of woods and flowers and views of the night sky.

"Oh gods, I'd forgotten about these," Celeste pointed to a doodle of two dark haired girls playing in the woods. The girls wore colorful dresses and were surrounded by a riot of blue flowers, but dark eyes watched them from among the trees.

Celeste looked up at Marta. "I always felt like there were creatures watching us from the trees, like elves or something."

Marta giggled. "There are no elves here—they all disappeared centuries ago."

"Wait, there really were elves? Like in Lord of the Rings?" Celeste had images of tall, graceful, beautiful creatures who sat around playing music and writing epic poetry.

Marta shook her head. "No, these were more like the elves of German folklore, or the fae like in *Der Erlkönig*. Not creatures that you want to idolize or cross paths with." She shivered. "But, as I said, they are long gone."

"Why would German folk tales live here?"

"Not everything that lives in The Valley originated here. Movement between Liminal Worlds is easy, if you are brave." Marta looked away, seeming to not want to continue the conversation.

Celeste moved on to one with the night sky and several constellations drawn out. "Elise drew this one. She was obsessed with the stars and space even before she decided to get her degrees in astronomy and astrophysics."

A small smile crept across Marta's face, and she relaxed her shoulders a smidgeon.

The dining room still had a large, hand-carved maple table and chairs weathered from generations of use, with a matching buffet. The table was set with battered pewter tableware of unknown origin that Celeste had always secretly coveted as a child.

That was before you knew that pewter had lead and you probably shouldn't eat from it. It still looks cool.

Beyond the dining room was a large screened-in patio with another dining area to the left and a large sitting area around an old wood stove. The gardens stretched behind the house, blue flowers gently patting the screens.

Celeste headed back through the dining room to the hall and entry and took the stairs. "Careful, they're steep," she called to Marta.

The lean in the house was more obvious up here than on

the first floor. To the left and ahead of them were open doors. Ahead was a bathroom with faded rose-colored paint and an antique claw-footed tub. To the left was a modern bedroom with a wardrobe and vanity.

"Looks like they've been selective with their renovations," Marta commented.

"Yeah, the old bathroom was rough. I used to take baths and showers in my grandparents bathroom downstairs. They also kept all the Reader's Digests in that bathroom."

Marta laughed. "A necessity before smartphones."

The door to the right was the one that Celeste had been anticipating since they had pulled up outside of the gate. Unlike the rest of the house, which had been well-maintained, the door stuck and then slowly opened, the hinges screaming.

"It hasn't changed at all." Celeste stood in the doorway staring while Marta peered over her shoulder.

Everything clean and tidy, as if waiting for Celeste and Elise to come for their yearly visits. Two twin beds flanked a large, six-drawer dresser with lamps on either side and a clock between them. One bed had cartoon forest animal sheets and a hand-sewn quilt in earthy browns, deep crimson, and golden yellow. The other bed had constellation sheets and a quilt that showed the phases of the moon. The rest of the room was decorated along the same lines as the beds. Pressed leaves and dried flowers decorated a bookcase at the foot of Celeste's bed, a black painted desk that held faded stationery butted up against Elise's. Glow-in-the-dark stars decorated the ceiling.

Celeste stepped forward to finger the quilt on her bed, soft from age but crisp with neglect. The furniture wasn't dusty and the room didn't smell of mold or mildew; it was clearly being preserved as it had been when the sisters were last there over 20 years ago.

I wonder if Grandma did this after Mom forbade us from returning...

Marta stayed by the door, watching as Celeste investigated the little things from her childhood that she'd forgotten: a box of acorns and pinecones shoved into the top drawer on her side of the dresser, pajamas with animal foot print pattern, a collection of feathers dropped in the yard, and her first book of pressed leaves.

She pulled out the book of leaves and sat on the bed. The book had come from their Granddaddy's library, a dense tome on cattle breeding that he hadn't touched since he was a young man. She opened it to the first page with a flattened, frail oak leaf, the color dulled with age to a nut brown.

"Come and look, Marta, this was my first leaf collection."

Celeste looked up at Marta. She was leaning against the door frame, a frown on her face. "We should go. We don't know who lives here now, or why *this room* is exactly the way you remember it being." Her voice rose as she spoke.

Celeste's enthusiasm ran away with her. "No one's here now. We can stay a few more minutes. Right?" She looked down at the yellowed pages of the book and could almost see her Grandma's wrinkled hands arranging a cosmos to be pressed and added to the collection. She closed the book with a muffled *thud* and looked up at Marta. "Please? Just a few more minutes?"

Celeste looked around the room and felt tears welling up. "I never got to say goodbye to my Grandma. She wanted our parents to keep her cancer a secret, so the last time I talked to her on the phone, I got off too early and she died a couple days later." She sniffed. "I have few regrets in life, but that is one of them."

I can't even remember why I didn't talk to her longer.

The look on Marta's face was halfway between agitation

and heartbreak. She shook her head, the ends of her bob brushing against her chin. "I know someone lives here, Celeste. I don't know if it's your granddaddy or someone else related to you, but they aren't here, and I don't know how I'd feel if they found us here without an invitation."

Celeste clutched the book to her chest and stood. "You're right, of course."

It felt like a fist was squeezing her heart, breaking it again. She had somehow found her way back to the home where her happiest memories were, only to break in and rifle through *someone's* belongings and stare at their empty rooms. If someone did that to her, she'd feel violated.

What have I done? What would Grandma say if she knew I just barged in here like a thief?

Celeste sobbed and held the book tighter.

Marta smiled at her. "It'll be okay, Celeste."

Celeste followed her down the hall to the stairs. She stumbled on the landing and looked up from her melancholic musings. On the wall there was a large family portrait of her parents and her mother, and a woman she didn't know. The woman looked almost exactly like her mother, with slight differences in coloring and features. She had the stronger features, a lively spark in her eyes, and healthier coloring than Celeste had ever seen in her own mother.

She stopped and reached a hand out to touch the woman's face. "Who are you?" she whispered, knowing in her heart that it must be her mother's twin. A sister and twin that she'd never heard of.

"Celeste?"

Marta was at the foot of the stairs, holding the door open.

"Hurry! I can hear someone coming up from the barn. And there's dogs."

Celeste perked up, finally feeling the urgency to leave. She hurried down the stairs and out the door, locking it with the extra key before she forgot. They ran across the yard, Celeste still clutching the book. When they reached the fence, she heard the barking of dogs and turned to see a tall woman being led by two black mastiffs. She was close enough that Celeste could make out the color of her hair and an approximate age, but far enough away that they would have no problems escaping.

They shared a look while the woman held the dogs back by their harnesses. She looked so much like her mother that it hurt.

Marta grabbed her arm and pulled her through the gate. It crashed closed as they jumped in the car. As they pulled away the gate opened and two canine heads popped through, watching them with a curious look.

13
THE NECESSITY OF RITUAL

They pulled up in front of Selena's house as the sun was starting to disappear behind the ridge to the east of Milton. It was late afternoon, almost dinnertime, and red and orange streaked the darkening sky. Celeste was on edge after everything the day had contained, and it wasn't over yet.

Why am I acting so rash? Falling for a woman I barely know, drinking myself stupid, breaking into a house? Where is the awkward, timid Celeste I know I am? Is this all just a reaction to everything that's happened since I lost my job? Is this the extremes of my autism?

The book of pressed leaves was sitting on Celeste's lap, a physical reminder of the trespassing, the talisman at her throat a reminder of the Stormwalker. Now she would learn what she had to do up on Bloom Mountain.

Marta parked and looked over at Celeste. "Are you ready for this?"

She shrugged in response. "I don't think I'll ever be ready." She rested her hands on the book for a moment before sliding it into her bag and checking her phone's battery. Celeste pulled a battery backup out of her pack and nodded to Marta.

Selena was sitting on her porch, knitting again. This time the yarn was a soft pink that reminded Celeste of cherry blossoms in April.

Celeste felt a pang of homesickness for DC that fought with the nostalgia and loss she felt from the farm visit. She was already lamenting the woman that she had been before, the one who didn't know that magic existed. The one who was confident being in the woods, the one who wasn't going to look over her shoulder at night and in the shadows. The one who had a routine and stuck to it, even when times were rough, and didn't let herself get caught up in events she couldn't understand or handle.

Celeste was a different woman now and there was no telling how much different she would be once she was done binding Bloom Mountain.

If I come down the mountain, then I can apologize to that woman… my aunt.

Selena looked up at them as they climbed the step up to the porch. She squinted at Celeste in a peculiar way that made her feel naked.

"I see you are starting to believe. That's good; that will help. But come along inside, we have much to discuss this evening."

Marta, Selena, and Celeste all filed inside and took up seats in the living room. The Persian and Siamese cats took up spots on Marta and Celeste, respectively.

Celeste pulled out her phone. "Do you mind if I record this, Selena? I sometimes have problems remembering conversations."

Selena thought for a moment. "Yes, that's a good idea. Especially for when I'm gone. But you don't need it yet. We have to talk about the necessity of ritual before we get to the Binding itself." She settled herself into her chair and took up her knitting.

"Rituals are what keep us safe, here in The Valley. They keep the crops growing, the rot away from homes, the river running in its course. They keep us healthy. Every facet of life has some ritual associated with it. You pat your pockets to make sure you have your keys and phone. You click the car lock three times, check the doors at night. *Those* are rituals that you perform to ensure that something is done. Or to ensure that you *remember* that something has been done."

She looked up to see if she had their attention, then continued. "Some rituals are important for their outcome, like leaving out a jar of honey for the Stormwalkers. They aren't necessary, so to speak, but they show the spirits that we appreciate their role. Without the rituals, they would still do what they do as it's their nature, but with the rituals they do it better and with far more enjoyment than they would otherwise.

"Then there are rituals that are important in and of themselves, like the binding of Bloom Mountain." She stopped to inspect her knitting, letting the tension build up.

"Why does the mountain need to be bound?" Celeste, briefly distracted from her personal turmoil, wanted to know as much as possible before she set foot on the slopes of Bloom Mountain.

"That is a good question, and one that is hard to answer." She took a deep breath. "The mountain was cursed because of something that the Bloom family did, either that last one I told you about, or the combined actions of the many before him.

"Over the centuries that humans have lived in The Valley, they have done different rituals to help the mountain contain that magic so that it didn't spill out into the world and affect everything around it. As time has gone by, the magic has gotten stronger, and the curse only added to that strength."

She sighed.

"In my youth, before the curse was fully settled on the

slopes, we dealt with poor harvests, or something else rather benign, in the years that the mountain went unbound. But after the curse, things got worse fast. People and animals started dying, plagues broke out among the townsfolk. One year the Nomini River turned to ash." She shook herself at the memories. "And always there was the Bloom farmstead.

"So, after the Bloom family was dead and gone, several of us got together to figure out what to do about the magic. And we came up with the ritual to bind the mountain. It would only last for a year before needing to be renewed, so they asked for younger folk to take on the task. An older friend of mine took the task first, then her sister took it when my friend married. When the sister married, I took on the task and continued with it until I broke my hip eleven years ago.

"Do you have any questions?"

Celeste thought for a moment. "Sarah and Hannah said that they would say the prayers and do the rituals while I attempt the Binding. What did they mean by that?"

And why do they need to say prayers? But she didn't ask that, afraid that she wouldn't like the answer. She'd been skirting around her own mortality all day

"There are rituals that the townsfolk have come up with that are meant to aid the binder. I don't know what they are or how well they work, to be honest. Marta?"

Oh that doesn't make me feel any better. Nope.

Marta shook her head. "I don't know what the rituals are. But I think only certain people perform them."

Selena nodded. "Could you go to my desk and get my paper and pen, dear niece? I'd like you to write down the steps for Celeste, just in case she has issues with her recording." She paused a moment. "And for posterity."

Celeste watched as Marta went to the desk in the corner of

the room and returned with a clipboard, paper, and an old fountain pen.

Of course…Selena's dying. That's why she wants it down for posterity…. Celeste felt her cheeks color. She reflected that she'd acted poorly last night and again today, like a petulant child. When Marta was facing her aunt's death and the potential destruction of her home.

Once Marta was settled, Selena continued.

"There are a few last things I want to say before we discuss the steps to the ritual." Selena leveled Celeste with a pointed, emotional look.

"I am not afraid of death, my own or anyone else's." A look she gave Marta told a different story. "I've faced many deaths and I've done the binding nearly 50 times in my long life. That is more than my predecessors, more than any single person has done. The repetition added to the power inherent in the actions. And that power will aid you while you are doing the ritual yourself.

"I don't know what will happen to Milton if you should fail and I should die without a successor. Will the curse spread and consume the town? Will we fade into myth and legend? I don't know the answer to those questions, so I will do the best I can with the time that I have left. And you are my contingency plan now."

She took a deep breath.

"You are going to have a hard time, even with that Stormwalker blessing around your neck. But I will tell you everything I know, everything that I have done that has worked, and the rest you will learn on the mountain. You will only get this one chance to bind the mountain: two days and one night. No more, and no less. The most important thing to remember is that you'll know when you're doing something right. The mountain will respond."

14
FINAL PREPARATIONS

That night Celeste and Marta ate dinner at Jed's Kitchen again. The mood was sober and contemplative. Celeste didn't feel like talking, so they shared a comfortable silence that was hard to come by. Celeste appreciated Marta more now. She was a good person, and Celeste very much wanted to help her and the other people of Milton.

Jed came by to wish her luck and to provide them with more pie than either of them could eat. Once full, Marta drove them back to her apartment. They sat in the car for several long minutes while the darkness deepened around them. Stars twinkled merrily above the shadow of Bloom Mountain.

"Is there anything else we need to get for you?" Marta's voice thundered in the silence, startling Celeste.

Celeste thought through what she had brought with her from DC. She had her clothes and hiking boots. Both were tough and comfortable. She had her hiking poles, a large water bladder, enough food to get her through the day. A small leather bag of ritual items from Selena was in her lap and the book of pressed leaves was in her bag.

"I don't think so." She turned to Marta, held up her hands, and shrugged. Celeste really couldn't think of anything else. She knew something of what was waiting for her on the slopes of Bloom Mountain, but how could mere words compare to what would actually happen? So many variables were still unknown. So many questions unanswered.

They went inside and Celeste went through the rest of the evening in a kind of fugue state, unaware of what was happening in the moment until it had already passed. She went through the motions of checking her gear and packing it away. She thought, in a disconnected way, that she would need new boots after this trip. Her boots were in rough shape; the sole was starting to break away from the rest of the shoe. The hiking pants she'd brought were thin and fraying at the pockets.

Everything is worn down, just like me. When did everything start to fall apart? Was it before or after I lost my job? Or when I started drinking so much?

"Did you say something?"

Marta was sitting with Celeste in the study.

Celeste looked up from her boots. "Did I say that out loud?"

"You've been mumbling for a while, mostly about things being worn out."

"Oh…sorry, I didn't realize I was speaking aloud." She set the clothing and boots aside for the morning then looked back up at Marta. "Do you think I'm going to die?"

She'd been skirting around that question ever since the Stormwalker appeared and her reality was shattered. What once was just a reasonable but difficult task now seemed like a death sentence towering over her. The curse was real, the monsters from her childhood stories were real, and the stakes were higher than she could have anticipated. Broken bits of the ritual steps floated through her mind, disjointed, out of order, and she felt a rush of emotions overcome her—fear and anxiety and the desire to leave now and speed back home where everything made *sense* even if she didn't fit in. But curiosity was also there too.

Marta's eyes went wide and then she sighed. "I don't know, but I hope not."

Celeste nodded, still waiting for the crash, the breakdown to fully hit her. "If I don't come back, could you do me a favor?"

Marta took a moment to answer. She seemed as unsettled by the idea as Celeste. "I'll do whatever I can." Her voice was very small.

"Could you call my sister? I'll leave you her number…she's better with our parents." Celeste fumbled for her phone, which was laying on the floor charging. It slipped out of her hands and fell under the couch. Celeste sighed, felt tears escaping her eyes, and hid her face in her hands, not wanting Marta to see her cry.

Celeste felt herself shaking. She was cold and terrified and far from home and she couldn't stop shaking. The day had taken so many turns, from monsters to memories and then the many steps to bind the mountain. It was all too much and she felt hot tears streaming down her face. She swatted at them with a clumsy hand and then rubbed her arms.

Cold, so cold…

Everything that had been building up over the last three weeks was being let out. The pain and regret, the sadness, the loneliness, the need for company, the desire to find a way out of her joblessness, the dwindling numbers in her bank account. Then there was the hope she'd felt, small and insignificant though it had been, when she'd seen the ad. And the utter confusion and fear she now felt upon answering its call.

Celeste was crying and muttering to herself and somehow there were arms around her and a cat in her lap. The sudden warmth was what stopped her tears and brought Celeste back to herself. The mental fog from the breakdown cleared slowly. The rushing thoughts became a trickle and Celeste was able to hold on to the present for a moment. At first, she wasn't certain where she was or why there was a cat or who was holding her in their arms.

Marta…

"Marta?"

Celeste stuck her head out of a cocoon of blankets and looked around for her host.

Marta was behind her, holding Celeste close. She loosened her grip when Celeste called her name. "Are you okay?" There were tight lines around her eyes and mouth.

Celeste wiped the tears from her face with one hand and emerged from the blankets. Matches, seeing that Celeste was calm again, stood up, walked to the edge of the bed, and started to clean one delicate paw. She was decidedly not paying the two women any attention.

"I think I'm okay now. How long was I…like that?"

Marta smiled. "Not long. But I was worried because you were shaking so much. I grabbed my extra blankets to warm you up."

That didn't explain why Marta had been holding her, but Celeste didn't want to push any further. The last two days had already been too much. Celeste had been fighting her attraction to Marta since they'd met. She'd felt ashamed after her miscalculated words the night before. And today she'd taken comfort in Marta's presence after the Stormwalker, and trusted her to get them away before being caught in her grandparents' home. But waking up from a breakdown in her arms was too much. Definitely too much. One more push would be enough to go down a road she wasn't certain she was prepared to walk.

Celeste wiggled to the edge of the sofa bed and stood up. Her legs were shaking and unsteady and she was lightheaded from crying.

Marta rose and helped Celeste to the kitchen to get a glass of water and a slice of pie.

Celeste ate the pie slowly, fork after fork of delicious chocolate mousse and whipped cream in a flakey, buttery pie crust. She felt a little resentful at how good the pie was, at how idyllic Milton was despite the threat looming over it, and how much she was starting to want to stay. Marta was just another knot in the thread. But everything would have to wait until after the binding. If she lived, she could consider making some changes. If she failed, nothing would matter anymore, and there was a small amount of comfort in that.

Selena had implied that Celeste *would* have to move here and continue binding the mountain, but she wasn't certain that it was required. *They can always find someone else as a long term magical binding solution, right?* Celeste wasn't certain that she wanted to live in a world defined by magic and monsters and curses.

But there was another knot.

Her family clearly had ties to The Valley, possibly to Bloom Mountain itself. There was the portrait with her mother's probably twin and unanswered questions about her Granddaddy. What had happened to him in the years since they'd last spoken? And there were the memories from Celeste's own past that were starting to trickle back after their aborted visit to the farm.

Celeste wondered if some of the magics of The Valley were already a part of her. Maybe her maternal family's proximity to Bloom Mountain was the reason why she *could* bind the mountain in the first place. It was a strange but almost comforting thought. It put everything that had happened over the last month into a different perspective. If she was *destined* to bind the mountain, then losing her job was just a product of that.

Do I really believe in fate and all that shit?

Celeste set that train of thought to the side. There was no point in thinking about fate when she still had to *survive*. If she lived, she could reassess those uncomfortable questions.

Marta took Celeste's plate and refilled her water. "Better now?"

"Yeah, but you don't have to wait on me all the time."

Marta smiled. "Well, I like you and you're going through a lot right now. I'm just helping where I can."

"I appreciate it."

Oh gods, what does she mean by "I like you"?

They stood together for a few more minutes, close enough that they could touch each other if they wanted. And Celeste was tempted to reach over and hug Marta, to thank her for taking care of Celeste while her reality fell apart around her. She wondered what Marta's lips would taste like, whether Marta felt anything like what was beating in Celeste's chest. But before Celeste could act on any of that, she started yawning.

"I guess it's time to get to bed," Marta said. "I should get you to the farm around dawn so you have enough time for the first day."

Celeste nodded, tired and frustrated and still a bit over-whelmed. "At dawn, then."

She turned to Matches, who sprawled out on the counter-top. "You'll get me up on time, won't you?"

Matches meowed in response and Celeste took that for a yes.

CELESTE STARED OUT THE CAR WINDOW, TRYING TO PICK OUT the farmhouse in the pre-dawn gloom.

True to her promise, Matches ran screaming through the apartment not an hour before, waking up Celeste and Marta at the same time. They'd gotten ready in silence, going through the motions as quick as possible to start what might be Celeste's final endeavor.

Marta surprised Celeste with a paper bag of scones and a Witch Peak branded thermos of coffee. "Courtesy of Samone, Anna, and myself. For luck."

Celeste felt her emotions roiling inside of her, but she dared not say anything. It would have been a repeat of the previous night, and she couldn't risk another breakdown. "Thanks," was all she could manage before turning to pack the bag and thermos away.

They drove in silence. The rays of early sunlight shined over the ridge to the east, piercing the dark. And it was chilly, an omen of approaching autumn. Celeste was glad she had packed a light jacket to wear.

Marta drove down a dirt road, dodging potholes until they approached an immense tree that had fallen across the road. She parked and turned the car off.

"This is as far as I can go." She sounded apologetic, almost like she would have climbed the mountain alongside Celeste if she could.

"Thanks for the ride. I hope to see you again tomorrow."

Celeste smiled at Marta, but was unprepared for the other woman to lean in and kiss her.

Her lips were soft and she tasted of vanilla lip balm. One hand reached up to lightly hold on to the back of Celeste's neck. She was there for a long moment before withdrawing, but Celeste could feel the lingering presence of the kiss. A warmth filled her chest, soothing the aches that had set in over the last month.

"Come back down that mountain, Celeste. I don't want to make that call to your sister."

"I will." And Celeste felt like she would, if only to see Marta again.

Celeste grabbed Marta's hand and squeezed it. Then she was out of the car and around the trunk before either of them could make that moment linger. Once she was on the other side, she turned around to wave to Marta, but she had already left. Celeste was alone with a gargantuan task ahead of her.

She turned back to face the distant farmhouse and started walking.

15

SHADOWS OF THE PAST

It was a quarter mile walk from the fallen tree to the farmhouse. Celeste sipped her coffee and ate one of the scones while she approached. She needed something to quell the rumbling in her stomach and the fluttering in her heart.

She passed a tall maple that had once been covered in "caution" and "no trespassing" signs, but bark had grown over the edges, consuming the signs. Only partial words were now visible. Scrubby bushes and stunted husks lined the gravel driveway beyond. No sound accompanied her trek, not the gravel beneath her feet or the wind through the trees.

Not ominous at all. Completely normal. Absolutely wonderful.

Once she was done eating, Celeste pulled her headphones out of her pocket and set them in to listen to the recording she'd made at Selena's.

"I'm gonna say it again: while you are doing the binding, Bloom Mountain will respond to you. You'll know when you're doing something right because you'll feel it immediately. And you'll know when you're doing something wrong because something unexpected will

happen. I don't know what it'll be for you, the responses were different for my predecessors than they were for me. But there will always be a response to guide you. You understand? Good.

"Now, step 1: Cross the Bloom farmstead and face the shadows of the past.

"The trail up Bloom Mountain starts on the rise behind the farm ruins. Cross the old fields and look for a large rock at the foot of the hill. The trail starts right there. You go up the rise and enter the forest between two big birch trees.

"Do your best to avoid entering the barn; things that couldn't be buried still lurk in the darkness within."

Celeste paused the recording. The sun had risen high enough to allow her to see the ground ahead of her without relying on her mini flashlight. Steam wafted up from the grass around her as the sunlight warmed it.

The tree that had killed the last two Blooms was still lying in the ruins, the bark rotting and pulling away in long ribbons from the trunk. A smaller tree had taken down a shed next to the barn and the rest of the outbuildings were covered in a tangle of kudzu and Virginia creeper. The creeper was starting to turn the vibrant red that it would wear for fall. Everything that had escaped the vines was covered in years of rain, grime, and neglect.

Nothing moved, neither wind nor creature stirred within earshot. Not even the ever-present sound of cicadas. The silence was as stifling as the heat that the day promised.

The house was decaying, rotting from the burnt core. The blue-painted exterior was peeling where the boards weren't charred. A beaten down path cut across the yard between the house and the barn, no more than 100 yards apart. Celeste approached, curiosity piqued by a scent she couldn't place: something sweet and slimy and rotten.

The grass, brown and dead, crunched under an exploratory step. The dirt beneath was pale and sandy, but striped with thick veins of what looked like mud and smelled faintly like sulfur. Celeste reached out to touch the mud with one finger and it came away with a sticky black substance that was definitely not mud, but not anything else she could identify.

"Eww," she said aloud, her voice oddly soft, like sound couldn't travel in the atmosphere that had settled onto the farm. She wiped the stuff off on the grass, but it left a sticky residue on her finger that wouldn't come off.

Celeste stood and observed the track. The stripes of not-mud appeared in two parallel tracks that ran back and forth between the barn and the farmhouse. Sometimes the track crossed over itself. It made Celeste think of a grotesque set of footprints from some unknown creature pacing between the two buildings. She approached the house first, going no further than the tumbled-down porch roof that had spilled into the front yard. She had to watch her step so she wouldn't slide on a roof tile hidden in overgrown grass.

She stood on her tiptoes to peer over the fallen tree, but there wasn't anything of interest to see in the house. The main story had held a kitchen and various living areas, but only burnt remnants of those remained. Charred bits of wooden furniture dotted the floors and scraps of faded fabric clung to frames that cradled broken window panes. The second story was completely gone.

Celeste could feel an underlying current of tension on the farm and resumed the recording.

"What happened to the man and his daughter?"

Celeste could remember Selena's reaction. She shuddered and squeezed her knitting needles in one hand.

"Well, no one ever found the bodies. They are either under the tree or burnt to ash…" She trailed off for a moment. *"Or they were taken by something."*

"Something? Like the Stormwalkers?"

Celeste heard her voice squeak in that response.

"No, child, something worse than the Stormwalkers. Not all the spirits of The Valley are kind. And not all spirits will come calling, unless everything is aligned correctly."

Celeste stopped the recording there. She wished that Selena had gone into more detail about what other spirits there were. That knowledge felt relevant to the binding, but Selena hadn't elaborated further. And Celeste could only hope that she didn't encounter any of the spirits that were *something worse* while she was on Bloom Mountain.

She decided to circle the house, starting from the front porch and going around to the left. There was an add-on with slightly newer siding around the corner. It was in better shape than the rest of the building and had escaped most of the damage caused by the tree and the resulting fire. A door around the back of the add-on led into the remains of a garden. Bricks and large rocks outlined where beds for flowers or herbs once grew, but now there were only weeds. Not even wildflowers grew there.

While Celeste was looking at the garden, she heard the soft, yet distinct, sound of something moving across old wood nearby. Whoever–or whatever–it was, was trying to be discreet. It moved slowly, trying to avoid creaking boards and sliding tiles, just as Celeste had done. But the silence that had stifled her voice earlier was now amplifying the sounds of *whatever* was creeping through the ruins of the house.

Celeste stood still, willing herself to not turn around for fear of what could be there. She closed her eyes and held them that way, directing all her attention to the sounds of wood, the creaking and clinking of disturbed remnants, the groaning of the trunk, long dormant after the sacrifice that it had made. Celeste didn't know where that impression came from, but it materialized fully formed to her senses.

Why did a tree want to sacrifice itself to kill two people?

Celeste took several shallow breaths that seemed to fill the space around her. The sounds started moving again, but this time they moved away, towards the front of the house and the path to the barn. Celeste took a deep breath and counted to 50 once the sounds disappeared into the distance. Then she counted to 50 again, just to be sure.

When she opened her eyes, the morning had grown noticeably darker. Clouds were covering the sun, still low in the sky, and it felt at any moment the heavens could open up and rain down upon her. The shadows cast by the house were deeper and darker than should be possible.

The edge of one of those shadows was close, and the thought of that deeper darkness touching her skin repulsed Celeste. She had visions of it seeping over her like oil, coating her skin, filling her lungs to drown her. Celeste sobbed once and snapped back to herself.

"Shadows can't drown you," she whispered to herself.

Celeste shook herself and continued around the back of the house, heading for the side closest to the barn. She stayed in the dim light that penetrated the cloud cover and avoided the shadows. She cleared the low garden wall and stopped at the corner of the house to peek around towards the front. There was nothing there and nothing obviously different from earlier.

She waited, listening, for several minutes. But there was

only silence and tension and the ever changing light as clouds crossed each other and the sun.

Celeste took one step forward, and another, and walked cautiously up to a spot just across from where she had stopped to investigate the not-mud trail. She knelt to get a better look.

There was a new track of fresh not-mud, dark and viscous. It stood out sleek and shiny compared to the rest. The scent was stronger now and the not-mud steamed slightly. It looked like the path someone would make if small, thin feet dragged through wet sand. There were dark spots that dotted the ground outside of the track, too. Something dripping the not-mud had walked from the house to the barn.

But it hadn't come back yet.

Had her presence on the farm disturbed whatever *it* was? Celeste felt sick in the pit of her stomach, felt anxiety fluttering in her chest.

Oh, gods, it was in the house while I was standing there.

Something creaked loudly in the barn to her left. A half-rotted door was swinging on its one remaining hinge. Celeste watched as it swayed back and forth, the metallic grating of rusted iron piercing the thick silence again and again.

Celeste felt an intense urge to stop the swaying door, to return the farm to its previous silent watchfulness.

But she couldn't move.

She was pinned to the spot, kneeling beside the brown grass and the trail of viscous, sulfuric not-mud, staring at the barn and the door.

Something was watching her. Celeste was aware of a presence, the intense attention of *something* in the barn. It felt like something that had once been human, but was no longer. It was considering her and what it should do about the intruder in its domain. Celeste couldn't see anything in the darkness.

Whatever it was, it was just out of the light. A shadow moving within the shadows.

Celeste waited and watched and was rewarded with a memory that came unbidden from her childhood, knocked loose by the visit to the farm the day before and the barn before her.

Once, when she was six or seven, Celeste had been playing by herself down at the old barn on her grandparents' farm. It was the oldest building on the property but it hadn't been used in decades and the doors were always open to allow access to the fields beyond. There were some large rocks along one of the front walls that Celeste liked to climb on and pretend she was hiking in the backwoods.

This particular time, she heard the sound of soft padded paws on dirt and the occasional clack of claws on stone. She stopped her playing and crept to the open doors and peeked through. A large leonine face was doing the same from the other side, staring at Celeste while she stared at it. They stood there considering each other for long minutes before Celeste ran back to the house to tell her grandparents. Her Grand-daddy had laughed and told her that she'd made a friend, but her grandmother said that she must have been mistaken. That there were no mountain lions in the mountains.

But Celeste could see the entire scene again and was certain that she'd seen a mountain lion. Bobcats and coyotes don't have that large head, the thick rounded ears, or the wide smooth nose of a mountain lion. Celeste was even more sure of herself now than she had been back then, having 20 more years of experience than her child self.

Celeste pulled herself back to the present, noting that something had changed outside of the memory.

The creaking door had stopped swinging and was silent again. The air was thick with tension and Celeste was still rooted to the spot. She couldn't tear her eyes away as something dark that flickered like fire crawled out of the front door. The sickness in her stomach churned and bile spattered the top of her throat.

It was something humanoid.

Something small and childlike.

It was bent over with its hips squatting over its feet and arms splayed out ahead. The skin was charred and dripping ichor. It lifted its blank, burnt face towards Celeste. It took everything in her power not to cry out as the creature settled its unseeing gaze upon her. She felt terror like she'd never felt before.

It reached out one arm, dug its fingers into the crusty earth, and *pulled* itself forward, sliding on its feet like skis. The skin on its arm cracked and ichor dripped out, lubricating the track for its feet to slide unhindered. Celeste watched as it pulled itself forward, one slow arm length at a time. Details materialized out of the darkness as it dragged itself closer. There was nothing left except white bone peeking through the cheeks and voids where nose and mouth and eyes once were. The skin was charred and stretched tight over the skeletal frame. Scraps of pale hair clung to the scalp.

The closer it got, the more terrified and disgusted Celeste grew. She couldn't move, couldn't scream, couldn't even close her eyes. The creature demanded every ounce of her attention. Celeste was certain that it would reach her and she would never see the light of day or hear her sister's voice or see Marta's beautiful eyes again. And somehow, that last loss hit harder than the rest.

It's over…before it's even begun.

Celeste's eyes glazed over, not wanting to see the creature any clearer before it reached her. She was still aware of it, of her impending doom, but she had detached herself from her vision and was floating there, waiting for the end.

But just then, when she had given up all hope, warmth sprang to life from the pendant at her neck and a great *crack* reverberated across the farm.

Celeste returned to herself and saw that the creature was stopped. One arm held out and its head cocked to the left, searching for the source of the noise. It turned away from Celeste and focused on the barn. Once it turned away, the intense weight of fear lessened by a degree.

Another crack followed the first.

Then another.

The creature dragged itself around to face the barn. A little shiver ran through its body as it did. It started pulling itself back towards the creaking door. It moved faster now than before. Its skeletal arms reaching forward. Hands digging into the earth. Ichor dripping faster and thicker to speed it on its way.

A large sycamore tree was swaying behind the barn. It rocked from side to side. It hit another nearby tree and ribbons of thin bark ripped away from the trunk. One final *crack* sounded. The tree shuddered and broke free.

It started to fall.

The creature was almost at the door, unaware of the immense tree trunk that was on a collision course with the barn. It turned back to look at Celeste and she felt a rush of anger and accusation and something terrifyingly close to hunger assault her. She had a brief glimpse of another tree falling, felt fear as fire spread, and charred her flesh, choking her. And then Celeste was free again, back in her own body.

Celeste watched the tree land on the barn roof and meet no resistance. It burst through, sending shingles and boards flying in every direction, and landed where the open door had been, where Celeste had last seen the creature huddled. Wood splintered and scattered across the grass, the door slid out towards Celeste, and with a final rush of air and the delicate tinkle of branches and leaves, the tree came to rest.

Another tree sacrificing itself to seal away the dark legacy of the Bloom family.

The tension on the farm dissipated and Celeste fell backwards onto soft, living grass, gasping for air. The clouds broke as she watched and sunlight blazed across the farmstead, too bright to see anything clearly. Warmth followed the sunlight and when her vision cleared, Celeste found a small bird sitting on the toe of her boot watching her with benign interest. A shower of green leaves were falling around her and one larger than her hand landed in her lap. It was a bright, almost violent, yellow green with thin, spidery veins of brown. She ran her fingers over it and felt that she should take it with her, to add it to her collection.

Celeste heard Selena's voice in her head:

"The mountain will respond."

She looked up at the fallen tree and felt sorrow and gratitude for its sacrifice. She had been doomed, but something else had decided that now was not the time of her death and sent the tree as her savior.

"Thank you," she whispered to the tree, but her voice was lost in bird song and insect calls as life swarmed back to the old Bloom farm.

16

THE OLD OAK TREE

Celeste found the trail up the rise and sat down on the rock that marked it. She pulled out the thermos of still hot coffee and watched as animal life appeared from the woods to investigate the farm. A pair of mourning doves landed nearby to peck at the ground, a fat groundhog stood to survey the fields before disappearing into the tall grasses. Two does and their fawns sprinted out of the trees and stopped near the old vegetable garden to crop at the plants.

Celeste stored the sycamore leaf in the book of pressed leaves from her childhood. She spared a few moments thought for the day before, for the house and the memories that it had unlocked. For the woman whose house they had broken into because Celeste had needed answers.

Did I even get any answers? Or just more questions?

Celeste set aside thoughts of the farm and put in her headphones to continue Selena's recording.

"Once you've crossed the farm, you'll find yourself in the old fields

where they grew wheat and corn and other crops. They've been fallow longer than I've been binding the mountain.

"Follow the trail across to the foot of the mountain where there's a large rock. That marks the start of the trail proper. You'll go up and skirt around the trees until you find two large birch trees with branches over the path. You'll have a bit of a hike until you reach your next objective: The Old Oak Tree."

Celeste stopped the recording again.

Celeste pulled her hiking poles out of the pack and returned the thermos, now half empty. It'd been a while since she'd actually used the poles, but she had brought them along to help with any aggressive downhill hiking she might have to endure. Something about the way an old knee injury healed made it harder for her to go downhill than up. She tied the poles to the outside of the bag and stood.

The trail was beaten earth and easy to follow, but steep in some places. It was about a foot wide in most places, but there were spots where grass or moss had grown over the dirt or where it diverted around a large rock.

The two birch trees were set slightly down the trail from the bulk of the forest, sentinels set to watch over a tomb. Or perhaps they were like the Gates of the Argonath from The Lord of the Rings, welcoming her at the old border of Gondor. Their leaves were already changing from green to bright yellow in anticipation of autumn.

Celeste stepped under the branches and into the forest. Her eyes needed a moment to adjust to the dim light and the cacophony of sound. She was surrounded by healthy, green growing things that hadn't been affected by the hand of man. The undergrowth was dense with needles, bark, and leaves on either side of the path. The depth suggested that there had been no forest fires or prescribed burns in a long time. The scent of rotting leaves and pine needles was pervasive, earthy, and comforting.

Celeste could feel the life that thrived in the forest: the trees, moss, ferns, animals creeping through the underbrush, the birds flitting from branch to branch. She stood still with her eyes closed and let the life of the forest rush over her and wash away the fear that had consumed her on the farmstead, the uncertainty of her journey, the heartache that had consumed her life. The sounds of the wind and the feeling of damp air on her skin were a balm for her trembling soul.

When she opened her eyes again, every color was bright and vibrant. The forest was older, larger, and more alive than anything she had experienced in years. She had felt nothing similar since she was doing fieldwork out west, so long ago.

Celeste followed the path through the forest for 15 or 20 minutes, climbing gentle switchbacks and steadily gaining elevation until she broke out of the tree cover onto a narrow rocky ledge that overlooked the farm. She stopped and watched the animals below for several minutes until she heard the faint sounds of footsteps and a cheerful whistle from the trees on the other side of the ledge. There was the occasional clatter of small rocks as they were kicked out of the way.

A man appeared on the other side of the ledge. He was tall, lanky teetering on the side of gaunt, with tanned skin and straight brown hair that reached his shoulders. He had a kind of eternal quality to his features that made it hard to guess his age. He could have been a rugged 40 or well-aged 70 for all that Celeste could guess. His clothing was casual, dark pants with signs of wear and a green button-up shirt. He carried a walking stick in one hand and wore a floppy leather hat. Small rocks were strung from the walking stick on leather thongs. They made a soft clanking sound as he walked.

"Aha!" he exclaimed when he saw her. His voice was deep and rich and carried well.

Celeste felt herself tense up. The experience at the barn had been tempered by the raw beauty of the forest, but she was more on guard now than when Marta had dropped her off.

Anything or anyone could turn out to be a spirit or a monster.

It was also strange to see someone else on the mountain that was shunned and revered and cursed. She'd gotten the impression that few people were brave enough to willingly breach the bounds of the mountain, especially when it had gone unbound for so long. Celeste stepped near the edge of the trail to let him pass, hoping that his exclamation didn't mean that he wanted to stop and chat. She was on a hard deadline after all.

"I been watchin' for you, miss."

Celeste swallowed hard to try and control her voice. "I didn't know I was expected."

Selena said that I wouldn't meet anyone on the mountain until later.

He stopped a yard or so from Celeste and looked out over the farm. The tension in her rose with proximity and being able to better see the man. There was a strange aura that surrounded him, like that of a hidden predator, dangerous and cunning. He stood slightly higher in elevation than her, which exaggerated his height and made her feel very small in comparison. A wooden pipe materialized in his hand out of a hidden pocket and was lit it in one smooth, practiced motion. Once lit, he turned his attention to Celeste. His bright brown eyes barely contained something deep and dark and powerful.

"'Tis a pity about the family an' farm," he said, gesturing with his pipe at the ruins below them. "The Blooms were good stewards of the land 'til that one was corrupted by the big war

Outside. They had their secrets, sure, but they did no harm to the land or animals."

"I don't know much about it." Celeste felt compelled to respond, just like she had been compelled to stare at her approaching doom back at the barn. "It looks so peaceful from up here."

And it did. From the ledge the damage to both house and barn appeared different. Like the family had moved away and then the Earth had started to take back the land without killing anyone.

But even with the return of animal life, the Bloom farmland was still blighted. Celeste could feel that in some unknown, unnamed part of her soul. And she knew that the blight was centered on the barn, where that creature had lurked and hunted. Celeste didn't know for certain that it had been destroyed by the falling sycamore tree, but she hoped that it was gone for good. That shadow of the past now destroyed.

"Peaceful sure, but there be a curse upon th' land. A fool went Outside t' fight in a war that didn't concern The Valley or the mountain. An' when he came back, he were damaged."

Curse or blight, they seem the same to me.

He stopped puffing on his pipe and stared at Celeste. He leaned into the stare, putting all his weight in his walking stick and the toes of his shoes. The intense attention made her skin crawl and her throat constrict.

"We haven't met before, have we?" His tone was curious, almost playful. Like he knew the answer was yes, but couldn't pinpoint the memory. But Celeste knew she had never met him before.

Or maybe I did. When I was a kid visiting Grandma and Granddaddy.

Celeste searched for a polite way to escape the conversation. But the man cleared his throat and Celeste reflexively looked at him.

"You are not much of a talker, are you?"

His voice was different now. He talked slowly, enunciated every word perfectly, with no trace of the accent that he'd had before. Celeste had only ever met a handful of people who talked that way, and she'd been disturbed by them all.

Keep calm.

"With the right people, I am." She felt a thread of defiance creeping into her voice. There was something incredibly wrong with the man, but instead of scaring her, she was annoyed. She knew that the fear would come later, knew that her emotions were buffering behind the veneer of calm that she had practiced over her lifetime.

He laughed and a sparkle glinted in his alien eyes.

Celeste felt herself flush and dropped her gaze to the ground between their feet. Moss was growing between them as she watched. It unfurled and crept out away from his boots, reaching for Celeste in a way that plants never should.

What the fuck.

She stepped back from the man and his creeping moss and looked up into his face, searched for whatever it was that set her on edge.

But everything was slightly *off*: his face slightly too long and his nose too short, the skin stretched too tight over his cheeks, with a sickly moss-colored undertone. Subtle changes happened in the time it took Celeste to blink. His eyes were first too small and then too large. His cheekbones sharp and then rounded. Over time they coalesced into a slow, churning mass of motion that was only perceptible when she stared. If she looked away and back it was as if it never happened.

It was strange and sickening, and Celeste suddenly understood what other people meant by the uncanny valley. The creature or spirit before her appeared human on the surface, but it couldn't contain itself in a perfect replica of humanity. Something was lost in translation, something in the eyes, in the stance, in the liquid way he moved. There was a fluidity to his inhumanity, something else was different every time Celeste searched for one comforting bit of human reality.

The longer Celeste looked, the more she felt like she would never find it. And she felt fear start to creep up her spine.

He had turned back to the farm, puffing mechanically on his pipe without seeming to savor it. One heavy breath in and an immediate exhale. He watched the farm and the ruins with an intense detachment. Everything he was and did appeared right on the surface but was deeply, terribly wrong.

"You're trying too hard to be human." Celeste's voice was a whisper. The words unplanned and unchosen, they slipped from her lips like petals falling from a flower or autumn leaves from a tree. The fear reached her heart, chilling Celeste to the core.

He turned his attention back to her. A change came over his face and he appeared sly and foxlike for just an instant before a shadow seeped into his eyes and then he was back to seemingly normal. "I do not know what you mean by that, Miss…?"

"Celeste," she responded without hesitation. And there was a moment where she was on the brink of telling him her full name but stopped. The fantasy stories of her youth had taught her that names held power and if you ever encountered a fae creature you should not, under any circumstance, give them the power of your name. If there truly were fae creatures like in her books, the man before her was one of them.

He cocked his head to the side, almost as if he was listening to her thoughts. "They call me Abram Waite."

"Is that your real name?" The fear had won over her other

emotions, but curiosity was Celeste's greatest vice and sin. It would always find a way to inconvenience her, would always show up at the worst times. Like now.

"My original name is lost to the ages, just like those who named me." His voice was wistful as he spoke. "And, as you have just put it, names have power."

Great, he can read minds too. Lovely. I'd like to leave now.

Celeste nodded, accepting that Abram Waite could read her thoughts just as she accepted that a tree had sacrificed itself to save her and a creature made of storm clouds had given her its blessing. She wasn't comfortable with the thoughts, but she accepted them.

"I have to go now," she told him. "Lots to do."

Celeste stepped back onto the path and started up the trail behind Abram. She almost made it to the far side of the overlook before his voice whispered over one shoulder.

"Keep an eye on the sky, and an ear to the ground, and you'll be fine, Celeste."

Celeste turned her head and saw him standing in the same spot he had been in, watching her intently. The pipe hung from his mouth and a curl of smoke drifted around him. She nodded once to Abram, then turned around and marched up the trail, putting as much distance between them as quickly as she could without running. Fear kept her from turning around, lest she discover he was following her up the trail.

Once she had gone a quarter of a mile further up the trail, she came to stop and rested for a few minutes.

"What the hell was his deal?" she asked the wind and the glittering sunlight as it filtered through the tree cover.

She listened to the chattering bird song and the lilting insect calls as she drank the rest of her coffee and picked at another scone. This one was spicy with cinnamon and cloves, and covered in a sweet glaze. It would have been better warmed up, but it was still tasty.

She fingered the Stormwalker medallion on its leather thong and wondered what kind of protection it would grant her on this ritual hike. It had seemed to react to the creature at the barn, but had done nothing to Abram Waite.

Only time will tell if it is really useful.

Celeste was also certain that the meeting with Abram had been contrived, that he'd been lurking in this stretch of woods, waiting for her. It was still early, just gone 8 AM, and she had the whole day and half of another to survive. And she was afraid that it wouldn't be the last time that she saw him, whatever he was.

"What have I gotten myself into?"

She finished the scone without answering the question.

It was darker and more damp here than it had been lower on the slopes. The trail was smaller, the grasses growing in abundance across the dirt track, and she crossed a dozen trickling streams on her ascent. She followed it, carefully setting each foot so she wouldn't slip on wet moss or loose stones. The path meandered up the slope, sometimes deep in the woods, other times skirting the rocky ledge, where only a couple of feet were between Celeste and plummeting to death.

Celeste hummed a song from the '80s. "Death is everywhere…" She sang off-key under her breath, not remembering the rest of the lyrics. She was cheerful despite the feeling that the lyrics were appropriate. She continued on, humming snippets of songs as they came to her, singing the lyrics she remembered in a whisper.

The woods abruptly ended around a sharp corner, where there was an uninterrupted view of one of the largest trees she'd ever seen. Celeste stopped to stare.

"The Old Oak Tree," she whispered, her voice filled with awe. She slid her headphones back in to listen to Selena.

"Step two: Climb up to the Old Oak Tree and soothe the Hangman's soul.

"You'll know the Old Oak Tree when you see it, there isn't another like it this side of the Mississippi. The corruption of the Hangman's soul makes the leaves turn crimson early. I've taken to calling it the Herald of Autumn."

Celeste stopped the recording.

There was no question that the tree in front of her was her next goal. It sat higher up on the slope and was cloaked in autumnal leaves of fiery orange-red, standing out against the pale brown-grey stone behind it and the deep green of the woods she had just escaped. Its branches reached for the heavens and its roots burst from the earth. It was a giant and a god among trees.

She started forward, up the rough stone steps that led to the tree. A chill wind rose off the side of the mountain and blew through the branches, dislodging leaves to fall like crimson rain around Celeste.

The tree unveiled its true form.

The world expanded in a rush. Her eyes widened. Breath was struck from her lungs. All Celeste could do was stand and watch.

The trunk swelled. Branches stretched higher into the sky. Reaching for the moon. Thick, knotted roots delved deeper into black earth. When it was finished, it could easily be compared to the great Redwoods she'd visited when she was young.

The power of the tree followed. On the breeze an inhuman voice groaned. Howled at Celeste. She was buffeted by its malevolent fury. Hatred for all things living and breathing and growing. But also pain. Love. Resignation. A sense that the Old Oak Tree and the Hangman were crying out for relief. They begged. Begged Celeste to perform the ritual that would calm their conjoined soul.

The wind and the howling grew. A gale pushed against Celeste as she stood. Hate and pain and longing and deep sorrow overcame her. She lost her footing. Stumbled away. Tripped over roots and rocks that had emerged during the unveiling.

Celeste backed away until the howling was barely a whisper and the wind was a gentle caress on the tears streaming down her face. She could finally breathe again.

Once outside the immediate range of the Old Oak Tree, Celeste felt a strange throbbing in the earth below her feet. There was an unseen current of *something* under the surface, hidden in the air. It was rushing towards and swirling around the Old Oak Tree, but a shield kept the current at bay.

What is that?

She focused on that feeling and sucked in a breath as her vision expanded. The world appeared in sharp contrast for a moment before settling. A halo surrounded everything, a haziness that she could ignore when she wasn't focusing on it. A few minutes passed as she observed, watching the halos and feeling the currents running beneath her. The new sensations settled into her mind, barely perceptible unless she actually looked for them. A headache started in the middle of her forehead, but she tried to ignore it.

Celeste sucked on her water bladder and continued Selena's recording.

"Who was the Hangman?"

"He was a murderer." There had been a gleeful tone to Sele-

na's voice when she responded. Like a storyteller retelling their favorite part of a gruesome tale. *"Lots of people used to say that the Hangman was from one of the offshoots of the Bloom family. There were many branches that moved throughout The Valley, with only the eldest male branch staying in Milton. People also liked to say that the Hangman was the reason that the Bloom family was cursed, but I ain't so sure of that. I think they brought the curse with them from Outside."*

"What about the one who came back from the war? Didn't you say the curse was laid down then?" Celeste didn't remember what Selena had said exactly, but she had gotten that impression.

"No, that's just when the curse settled on the mountain and killed the main branch of the family off. The Hangman lived in the middle of the 18th century, and was hung for his crimes. The records conveniently don't mention who his victims were.

"Anyways, the Hangman was taken up to the Old Oak Tree and hung from its branches. Once dead, they buried him at its base, and eventually the tree and the Hangman became one and the same being. The Old Oak Tree is the Hangman's reluctant jailer, or so that's the impression I get. There are dark nights when you can hear screams and laughter on the mountain and see jack-ma-lanterns around the Old Oak Tree."

"What's a jack-ma-lantern?"

Celeste had never heard of that bit of folklore before. Selena had paused a moment to consider.

"They're little floating balls of light that you can see on certain nights."

"Like a will-o'-wisp?"

Celeste remembered those specifically from The Lord of the Rings, when Sam, Frodo, and Gollum were in the Dead

Marshes, but she knew they popped up in literature all over the place.

"Sure, if that's what they remind you of, think of them like that.

"Now, once you've gotten to the tree, you'll see a deep indent in the wood. You'll place the first two fingers of your left hand in the divot and walk anti-clockwise while chanting. You can get two lines of the chant done each rotation. You must remain in contact with the bark as you chant, otherwise you'll have to start again. The binding might not take right, and who knows what would happen to Milton after..."

Celeste remembered Selena sighing with her whole body, seeming to collapse in on itself. Marta had started getting up from her chair when Selena rallied with the next breath.

She turned her bright, defiant eyes back to Celeste.

"Remember, you'll know when you're doing it right—"

"The mountain will respond," Celeste finished for her. She skipped ahead, past Marta asking Selena if she was alright, and Celeste needing to take a bathroom break. She started it back up with the chant.

Celeste could see Selena as the old woman's eyes glossed over and she held out her left hand, the fore and middle fingers extended, while she chanted.

"Hangman, Hangman, knife in hand,
Caught in act of murder planned.
Hangman, Hangman, on the limb,
Stoney face, gaunt and grim.
Hangman, Hangman, under tree,
Where'd you hide the bodies three?
Hangman, Hangman, in the ground,

To these roots your soul is bound."

Celeste steadied herself and took another drink of water. The headache was less intense now and she was feeling more clear-headed. She could feel the currents swirling, lapping, playing around the tree, testing the barrier that hung there.

The sun was bright in the sky above her, high over Bloom Mountain. Now that she was out of the cover of the trees, it was hot and humid. A haze had settled on the farm and town below her. In the distance she could see the bell towers that framed the downtown neighborhood, and the apartment buildings on the outskirts near the Nomini river. She saw the sparkle of sunlight on the Nomini and all of the mountains that surrounded Yuback Valley to the east and west and far to the north. It looked so quaint and peaceful from up on the mountain, and Celeste was determined to do whatever it took to keep it that way.

They deserve it. And I deserve this too, whatever the outcome of these two days.

Celeste stretched her shoulders and settled her pack, then started back into the gale towards the Old Oak Tree's base. But it was easier now, like the tree and the Hangman had given their best before and were now resigned to whatever fate had in store for them. There was barely a whisper of wind and a moaning from the tree.

The closer she got, the larger the tree appeared. Its trunk was wide enough that the Camry could have been on the other side and Celeste wouldn't be able to see it. The branches were so tall that they could have caressed the moon had it been out at the time. Other branches reached out towards the edge, towards Milton, and others rested on the ground, bound by roots and rocks and the remnants of vines.

Celeste was comforted by the wholesome earthy smell of

the bark and the soil. She watched ants and beetles march up and down the tree, ignorant of the soul of the Hangman and Celeste. Sunlight streamed through the swaying leaves, tinting everything the color of autumn and blood. She saw the deep divot in the grey-brown bark and reached out to place her fingers in it. It was about chest height and completely smooth inside.

Ahhh…

Something passed between Celeste and the Old Oak Tree and the soul of the Hangman in that first gentle touch. She could feel both creatures, bound as they were deep in the roots of the mountain. There was a deep well of anger and evil there, memories of crimes long since lost to history, but also a passion for growth and sunlight, and the tickling sensation of wind in the leaves and the knowledge that the tree was home and haven to many creatures. The tree's good nature dwarfed the evil of the Hangman's soul and caressed it, soothing the soul with gentle sensations, but allowed it to express itself when overwhelmed by its own memories.

Celeste got the impression that soothing the Hangman's soul, as Selena directed her, was also soothing the Old Oak Tree's soul. And that both were excellent ideas.

"You are a noble soul," Celeste told the Old Oak Tree.

She circled the tree, stepping carefully over the thick, gnarled roots and loose rocks, repeating the first part of the chant in her head. It took three circuits to get the timing down right, to find the right footing so she wouldn't trip and break her connection to the Old Oak Tree. Celeste stepped back and took several deep breaths. A breeze that had played with her hair and the small branches on the tree died down with a watchfulness. The birds and insects stalled their calls and Celeste felt the mountain take a breath and hold it. Even the strange pulse and current in the land slowed to a trickle.

Everything was waiting for her to begin.

Celeste shivered and stepped forward in one smooth motion, laying her fingers in the divot. She took a shallow breath and started.

> *"Hangman, Hangman, knife in hand,*
> *Caught in act of murder planned."*

Her voice broke on the first verse, but she completed the first circuit without breaking contact.

> *"Hangman, Hangman, on the limb,*
> *Stoney face, gaunt and grim."*

Celeste heard a whisper echoing her words. Something was urging her on, giving her strength, adding power to the ritual she was performing.

> *"Hangman, Hangman, under tree,*
> *Where'd you hide the bodies three?"*

The echoes were louder now, her voice and the whispers resonating, bouncing off the stone wall, ricocheting through the heavy branches. She felt the tree start to sway and shiver beneath her fingers. The roots moved beneath her feet, settling and sinking back into the earth. Her steps were easier, more sure, as the roots wormed their way back underground and the rocks freed from captivity tumbled towards the edge. Branches that had rested on the ground lifted themselves up to join their brethren.

She felt a strange thrill as she rounded the tree one last time.

"Hangman, Hangman, in the ground,
To these roots your soul is bound."

On the final syllable Celeste returned to her starting position. Her fingers were still on the trunk, but it had shrunk and bark had grown to fill the divot that had been her guide. There was a slight indent now, but nothing more.

Celeste took her hand off the tree and felt a shiver in the earth below her feet and an electric feeling in the air around her. The currents that had lapped around the tree like waves were now rushing into the space that had been denied to them, swirling and soothing and calming the souls of the Old Oak Tree and the Hangman.

Celeste felt the magic swirl around her too, poking and prodding at her form, at something inside of her, some well that she hadn't known existed. And there was a response, small and slow, but a trickle soon turns into a torrent when it rains.

A great gust of wind blew down the mountain, rattling the branches of the tree, dislodging the great crimson leaves. They fluttered out over the mountainside, riding on the wind towards Milton. When she looked back at the tree itself the branches were bare, and Celeste felt that the tree and the soul it contained were both resting after a long, waking nightmare. The power and anger that had battered her were slumbering once more.

The magic that had stretched the world making the tree gargantuan and oppressive dissipated and Celeste felt a sense of vertigo as she reconciled her impressions of the tree before with the tree now. A flock of birds launched themselves into the air and Celeste heard the sounds of insects again.

Celeste took a deep breath.

"The mountain will respond."

She didn't think she would need the reminder again.

17
THE STAIRWELL

The path away from the Old Oak Tree curved around the western side of the mountain, skirting a sheer stone wall, and plunged back into dense forest. Pine, maple, and oak towered above Celeste as she walked. Wonder and sorrow competed for prevalence in her heart; wonder at the beauty of nature and the strange magics of this new world, and sorrow for the years she had missed with her grandparents. Sorrow for the life she might have had if she had been allowed to learn about the Valley as she grew up.

It was cooler on the south side of the mountain. Trees blocked the sunshine, but humidity clung to the forest, drenching Celeste in sweat. She didn't mind it too much, her mind focused on observing the currents of magic around her.

The currents were stronger now, easier to follow. She could feel the magic in the ground as they swirled around her footsteps, the ones in the air as they caressed the changing leaves above her, the ones deep in stone thrumming with the heartbeat of the mountain. They flowed along the trail, leading her on, guiding her on the path up the mountain. She felt a little lightheaded while concentrating on *seeing* and *hearing* the currents, but it got easier every time. When she didn't concentrate, they dissipated into the air or the ground or the bark of the trees as she passed. Some newly awakened sense told her that they were still there, in the corner of her vision, just under the background hum of the forest.

She enjoyed the new feelings as she continued through the trees until she reached a sheer stone wall and The Stairwell.

She put her headphones back in.

"You're going to think you are off to a good start after the Old Oak Tree. It'll hem and haw and do its little dance and wiggle its branches and you'll sing it and the Hangman back to sleep. But this is where the real test is going to begin.

"The Stairwell. Gods of the Valley, I hate that thing. Last time I attempted the Binding it was after a pretty nasty spell of rain and I slipped and fell and that's how I broke my hip."

"Aunt Selena, you shouldn't have been binding the mountain in your 60s."

Marta's voice was soft, gently chiding her great aunt. Celeste felt herself melt a little and hoped one day Marta would use that voice with her. Maybe when there were too many books of pressed leaves and did Celeste really need another one from the same tree?

"Marta here loves to remind me that I am
getting old."

There was a moment where Celeste had wanted to laugh at Selena and Marta, who were glaring at each other, but she'd smothered it, fearing that they would start glaring at her.

"Anyways, the Stairwell. There are 500 steps carved into the rock of the mountain. Most of them taller than you'll be expecting, so be sure to stretch before attempting the climb."

Celeste looked up at the Stairwell and thought Selena's description a bit understated. The steps were about two feet wide and one foot deep and carved deeply into the stone of the mountain. The outside wall was about waist height on Celeste and the inside was the cliff face. It climbed at a steep incline and switched back on itself until it was high out of sight.

Celeste considered stretching before tackling the Stairwell, but she had hiked uphill all morning and felt very loose. The magical currents in the stone were cheerfully flinging themselves from step to step, inviting Celeste to join them. She felt ready for the stairs.

As she set her foot on the bottom most step, Celeste heard the distant sound of a whistle and the clack of a walking stick on stone. She couldn't pinpoint the direction it came from, but she thought it was above her, at the top of the Stairwell. She turned to face the forest and cocked her head to the side to listen, but she didn't hear the whistling again.

Celeste turned back and started up the stairs.

She started to regret not stretching after the first 50 steps.

The stairs were roughly carved, each step was a potential twisted ankle from the uneven surface. Celeste had to pay attention to every step she took, ensuring that she wasn't going to be stuck on the mountainside without any way down. Or worse, fall down the stairs like Selena had done. There was pain in every muscle from her ankles to her hips.

Out of shape and cocky. You got yourself into this mess by not taking Selena's advice. How 'bout we not do that again?

Celeste rested every 40 to 50 steps on the small platform at the switchbacks, where she had more room. She sat with her back pressed against the outer wall and focused on the steps leading up while she drank water and tried to control her ragged breathing. She wasn't afraid of heights *per se,* but she was wary of them and occasionally suffered from vertigo. It was much more comfortable being on wide open ground, preferably with a sturdy railing between her and any nearby edges.

Though she listened for them during her breaks, Celeste didn't hear the whistle or the clack of the walking stick again.

Once she reached the halfway point, Celeste had to keep her breaks short. Her knees wobbled from sheer exertion and old injury. Ragged breaths tore at her throat and lungs. She frequently stopped, slumped over, as dizzy spells came and went. There was a spot on her left side that was in pain, but she kept climbing.

Celeste all but crawled up the last 20 steps, pulling herself up with sore hands as much as she pushed with her aching feet. But then she was out on open ground with only the sky above her and she collapsed on a stretch of soft grass. She lay for a long time with her eyes closed, her breath easing slowly, the pain in her side dulling to an ache. When the dizziness passed and the pain was just a twinge, Celeste pushed herself into a sitting position and looked around.

Around her, the trees were younger and further spread out, allowing a larger variety of shrubs, grasses, and flowers to thrive below their branches. She could see further into the depths, spy little creatures as they minded their own business. The air was heavy with the scent of late-blooming honeysuckle. But the real view was over the edge of the cliff.

Her first thought was to look for Milton on the landscape below, but when she couldn't find it, she remembered the trail had taken her around to the far side of Bloom Mountain before reaching the Stairwell. Celeste was now facing south, towards

Birch Branch and the farm. The ledge overlooked a dark forest that stretched to Lighthouse Lake. The lighthouse appeared tiny, its lamp still shining despite the daylight. Celeste heard the distinct sounds of a train horn somewhere below. In the distance, the dark form of Blue Mountain loomed over the deep waters of Lighthouse Lake.

"How close I was, and how far I ran from here." The thought was strange and depressing. She still couldn't remember what had driven a wedge into her family, whether it was her or Elise or something else. She just knew that the trip to the lake was the catalyst. Something that day, or night, had changed her childhood forever, had changed her family irreparably.

Or was our family broken before that? Mom never talked about Grandma or Granddaddy and never drove out to drop us off or pick us up. No, we were broken before that night. Mom was always walking around like something was following her or she was taking out her anxiety on us. That just was when the Band-Aid was ripped off, no matter how much it hurt Elise and I. I wish I knew what happened.

She shuffled those thoughts to the side and pulled herself to her feet, happy that she didn't experience a wave of dizziness and that her knee was steady. There was a lot more to do here on Bloom Mountain before she could consider visiting the farm again, before she could meet her aunt. She looked out across The Valley, at the distant form of Blue Mountain.

"Why did they give the mountains similar names? That's kind of ridiculous, isn't it?" She hadn't thought about the names before, but they were close enough to have caused someone trouble in the past.

No doubt it will cause me some trouble in the future. Whether that future is just my memories of this trip or a future where I live here in the Valley. Maybe with Marta…

Celeste turned away from the edge and started down the

wide trail. It was drier up here and her boots kicked up dirt in a small cloud behind her. Because the trees were spread out, it was also hotter and Celeste soon was sweating. To distract herself she listened to the next step in Selena's directions while drinking from her water bladder, now more than half empty.

"Step 3: Light a candle at Coal Mine Number 3 and wait till it burns out.

"When you get to Coal Mine Number 3 you are going to light your candle stub in remembrance of those who died in the collapse."

Celeste pulled the leather bag off the side of her pack where she'd attached it last night. The leather was soft and supple with age and wear, tied with a leather thong. Inside was a variety of seemingly random objects that Celeste would use during the next 24 hours: a very short beeswax candle, a straw effigy, a small bottle of local brandy, a metal cup, matches, and the instructions, handwritten by Marta.

"What was the collapse?"

"You don't know much, do you?" Selena answered with a hint of scorn. *"Mines collapse sometimes, especially in backwater areas where the companies think they can cut corners to maximize profit. That happened here, in about 1861, when a company from Outside came in and tried to profit off our labor."*

"How many people died?"

"Fifty-seven souls died that day. Forty-nine men, six women, one teenaged boy, and a dog all died when Coal Mine Number 3 collapsed." She trailed off for a moment. *"Their bodies rest in the darkness of the mine. Or they disappeared, like many bodies do. No one is quite certain.*

"You'll want to find a spot for your candle, light it, and wait for it to burn out. It shouldn't be longer than five or ten minutes. The size of

the candle doesn't really matter, for future reference, but I don't want to waste the beeswax."

The trail turned and headed into denser forest and followed alongside a rocky slope. The first candle sat on a dislodged boulder. It had melted into a wide puddle of wax that clung to the curves of the rock with only a finger width's wick sticking out. The second candle was a little further down the trail, stuck in the dirt, surrounded by a circle of small, polished stones. More and more candles appeared as she walked, until she rounded a large tree and saw the mine entrance.

The forest around the mine entrance had been cleared and saplings cut back over the years. Stumps too large to dig up dotted the clearing. The mine doors, which Celeste could see from within the trees, were fully 10 feet tall and made of thick wooden beams and dark iron fittings. There were chains looped through the door handles and locked with two rusty padlocks.

And then there were the candles.

Candle stubs of all shapes and sizes covered every surface surrounding the mine doors. There was a pool of wax three feet wide around the base of the doors. Candle stubs and wicks dotted the wide expanse, with more hanging off of the handles, the chains, and the top of the door frame. Wax had cooled in rivulets that ran down the wood.

Celeste worked her way forward around tree stumps covered in stubs and stopped just outside the wax pool, looking for a spot for her candle. Here she could better see the varying shapes and sizes of candle. Some were as thick as her wrist and three inches tall; others were like a pencil, tall and skinny with only the thinnest layer of wax over the wick. Some candles were spindly cones, others had ornate spirals up to impossibly thin points.

Celeste dug through the leather bag for her own. It was a stub, barely an inch tall and only as thick as her thumb. She stared at the candle for a moment and then looked around the door for a place to set it.

It's just a little guy, could fit anywhere. But what about up there?

It was small enough that she could wedge it onto one of the exposed door hinges. She had to stand on her toes and stretch to reach the hinge without disturbing the existing wax and candle remnants. She didn't think anything would happen if she did, but it felt sacrilegious in a way that she couldn't explain.

Lighting the candle was harder: she had to light the match on the box and quickly stretch to light the wick. The first few matches blew out before she could reach over to the wick. The fourth attempt was successful, and Celeste stepped back to wait.

Next time I'm going to bring one of those grill lighters. That'll work a lot better. Just one click and WHOOSH!

The flame burned hot and bright, melting the wax to run down the candle and the rusted hinge. The sun was beating down on the door, where Celeste stood away from the shadow of the trees. She was sweating heavily by the time the candle burnt down and the flame started to flicker out. A whiff of burning wax and cotton filled the air for a brief second.

But before the flame burnt out, another candle ignited. Then another, and another, each flame popping into existence with a hiss. Dozens of candles ignited every second, burning hot, blue-white flames and forcing Celeste away from the door. She backed away until she hit a stump, felt the edge dig into her calves. Chunks of wax broke off the stump and fell to the ground, hitting her skin on the way.

The whiff she'd smelled earlier grew more intense as more and more candles lit. Suddenly the whole area burst into a supernova of light and heat, blinding her eyes and searing her skin for just a second. And just as suddenly it dissipated. Stars peppered Celeste's vision for a moment, but they cleared before her little candle sputtered out in a puff of grey smoke.

The heat from the candles and the sun had remelted the wax at the foot of the door. Celeste felt the urge to run forward and dip her fingers in the pool of hot wax. The burning, tingling sensation was one she had grown to love as a child, coincidentally at her grandparents' house. They had enjoyed the ambience of candles at night. But they never allowed Celeste or Elise a candle of their own and they had to make do with electric light in their room when they read themselves to sleep.

Such a strange, yet beautiful way to memorialize the dead. May their souls be at peace.

Celeste waited a few more moments as the pool of wax cooled and solidified. She felt more sure of herself, of the ritual, now that she'd completed some of the steps without issue. She knew, vaguely, what was ahead of her. Selena had shared the broad strokes of the ritual, but kept all the details to herself. Celeste didn't know if that was because she *must* or because she wanted to. And now it didn't matter.

Celeste turned her attention back to Coal Mine Number 3. The wood and hinges and wax shined bright under the light of the day, and now there was nothing left to do but leave.

18

PRINTS IN THE DIRT

Celeste was tired and hungry after climbing the Stairwell and visiting Coal Mine Number 3. Her legs ached and her bad knee trembled occasionally. Her water bladder was almost empty and she wondered if she'd have to resort to using the purifier straw. She didn't want to—it was nearing the end of its life and she really didn't want to get sick. There was one last scone. Celeste was kind of sick of scones by now, but the bacon and cheese smelled good so she started munching on it.

The trail away from the mine led into denser forest where the undergrowth was thick with brambles and bushes, making it hard to see any distance to either side. Celeste walked on, not really paying any attention to the trail, thinking that it would just lead her on to whatever the next objective was. She didn't remember what it was, and didn't bother listening to the recording while she was eating. She could do that later. Food was more important right now.

Celeste was so preoccupied with her snack that she missed the first fork in the trail, and the second, and didn't realize that she was walking in a long loop in the same stretch of forest until she'd walked past a clump of phlox that she had noticed more than once.

Huh?

She stopped and looked to either side, and then behind her. In the far distance she could see the doors to Coal Mine Number 3.

"The fuck?"

To her left was a small, flowering bush with an intensely sweet smell. A variety of golden yellow flowers had bloomed on the bush: three golden asters in different stages of blooming, four black-eyed Susans, a cone of goldenrod, a dozen tiny buttercups, and several yellow poppies that shouldn't have been growing in September. A large patch of yellowing honeysuckle that covered a nearby evergreen bush was the source of the intense smell.

Celeste knelt beside the bush and gently touched one of the poppies. "You are out of season, little flower. And your bedmates are a curious bunch." The flower bounced on its stem, seeming to laugh at or with Celeste, knowing that it shouldn't exist in that time or place were it not for the magic of Bloom Mountain.

"I'll leave you to your mischief." She stood back up.

Celeste looked back at the mine doors and then down the trail. It led through densely grown pine and birch trees, but at the furthest extent of her vision, she saw what she thought was a fork in the trail. That reminded her of Selena's recording, something in there about taking a specific fork.

"Step 4: Take the left fork at the crossroads, and continue taking the left forks until you come to the Giant's Grave.

"Step 5: Share a drink with—"

Celeste shut the recording off and checked her phone's battery. It was nearing 40% so she plugged in the battery back-up and stuffed them both into her pack's side pocket.

Don't forget or ignore the instructions. Got it.

Celeste started down the trail, watching the first fork far ahead of her. As she approached, she saw a moss-covered boulder sitting nicely between the two.

Celeste took the left fork, and the ones after that, until she came to a five-way crossroad with two forks that led distinctly *left*. She sighed and tried to look down both paths, but they quickly turned out of view.

Celeste stood, tapping her foot on a small rock, while she considered which to try first. She took the first fork that veered left from the center, not the left-most fork. The forest grew taller and loomed over Celeste, the quiet watchfulness intensifying until she felt a rush of panic and paranoia and stopped. She felt her heart racing in her chest and took several shallow breaths to steady it.

"Okay…that was the wrong fork. I get it."

The panic eased and Celeste took a deep breath.

Celeste turned around and returned to the juncture, glad that she didn't have to go back to the beginning. As she did, she saw shallow footprints in the trail's dirt. She crouched next to the clearest print: it was the size of Celeste's palm, with four pointed oval prints over a large central portion. Celeste knew that print like she knew her own boot prints.

"Mountain lion," she whispered.

The tracks were recent, and they led down the right-most fork in the trail. It could have passed through the crossroads while Celeste was wandering along, thoughtlessly ignoring the directions that Selena had given her. Celeste turned and stared into the darkness down the fork, but neither saw nor heard anything to indicate that the lion was still around.

Celeste stood and felt the currents of magic in the stone below her feet again. The feeling came unbidden; she had nearly forgotten about them after the exertion of climbing the Stairwell and the brilliance of the candles outside Coal Mine Number 3. The majority of the currents flowed down the left-most path, the one she hadn't taken yet. But a trickle of magic followed the mountain lion's prints.

There was a faint difference to the way the magic felt on the path up the mountain and the path that the lion took. The path up the mountain felt like a summer day and the mountain lion's path felt darker, damp, like an overgrown forest on a misty morning. She could breathe in and taste the forest, pine needles and moldering undergrowth and the sweet scent of hidden flowers.

Celeste wondered if she would feel that difference in the magic if the lion started to follow her. She wanted it to happen, to test out this new ability. But she also hoped that the mountain lion wasn't one of the spirits that was *something worse* than the Stormwalker.

Celeste followed the currents down the left-most path. They led her through five more junctions and out into a wide grassy meadow dotted with white and yellow and orange wildflowers. The pine trees formed a dark border along the edge of the meadow, the path a thin line of brown amongst the tall green grasses. The middle of the meadow was dominated by a large mound of stones.

Celeste waited for her eyes to adjust to the sunlight and then approached the mound. It was about 15 feet long, 10 feet wide, and almost 6 feet tall. The largest stones at the bottom were covered in a thin layer of moss. Smaller stones were stacked on top and an immense flat stone capped the pile.

"Step 5: Share a drink with the spirit of Giant's Grave.

"Once you've passed through the crossroads, you will come to a large meadow surrounding the Giant's Grave. At the head of the grave, you'll find a large stone carved into the shape of a cup. Fill that up with the brandy in your bag, saving only a little for yourself.

"You'll want to eat something before you drink the brandy, it's powerful stuff. Try not to cough it all up."

The last comment made Celeste laugh. Maybe when Selena was young people didn't drink much, but there were some nights from undergrad and grad school that Celeste couldn't remember. And brandy had been one of her spirits of choice in the long weeks since she'd lost her job.

Celeste circled the grave and found the stone cup. She tossed her bag to the ground, sat, and pulled out the little bottle of brandy and the small metal cup. The brandy was a deep amber in color and when she uncorked the bottle she got a whiff of strong alcohol that stung her nose.

Celeste poured two fingers into the metal cup and set it on the ground next to the grave. The rest she poured into the stone cup on the grave.

"Cheers!" she said before she took her first sip.

The brandy burned as it went down and Celeste had to take a long drink of water to keep the coughing at bay. The second sip burned less and she was starting to enjoy the brandy's subtle sweetness. There was a part of her that worried that she would relapse, go back to drowning her sorrows with booze. But things had changed over the last week in ways that were hard to explain.

She sat with her back to the grave, the bumpy stones cool despite the heat of the day. A gentle breeze rocked the wildflowers and tall grasses, bees buzzed over the flowers and birds flitted from tree to tree singing their summer songs. Somewhere nearby more honeysuckle was blooming, adding its fragrance to the grass. The small amount of brandy made Celeste sleepy. She leaned against the grave and emptied her head of thoughts.

When she was on her final sip, the sound of a rock rolling across the ground brought her out of subtle, sun-drenched daydreams in which Marta played a leading role. Celeste sat forward and craned her neck to look out over the grass. There was nothing in front of her, towards where the path exited the meadow. She had to get up on her knees and look around the grave towards the entrance. A flash of sunlight rippled on an arched back of tawny fur. A large leonine head poked up over the top of the grass, the dark eyes of a predator locked with Celeste's own.

It was a mountain lion, probably the same one who had made the prints she'd crossed earlier.

Celeste sucked in a breath, too loud, too fast, and saw the lion flinch.

Celeste set the metal cup of brandy down and stood, careful to make her movements slow and steady. She kept her eyes locked on the mountain lion. It remained in place, watching Celeste.

Okay, nice and easy. Try to seem bigger than you actually are and scare the lion off.

Once she was fully upright, Celeste raised her arms and spoke. "Are you following me?" Her voice carried well across the meadow.

In response, the mountain lion relaxed its stance and sat down on its hind legs. It divided its attention between Celeste and something stuck on one of its claws. One moment passed, and then another.

She thought back to the mountain lion from her childhood, and how after that trip she'd been obsessed with them. She'd pestered the librarian at school and the public library to show her all the books they had that contained information on mountain lions. It was almost as if she'd tried to convince herself that the lion had been real, despite her grandma and several others telling her that it couldn't have been there.

Celeste waited and watched, her heart pounding in her throat, while the mountain lion stood back up, stretched, and gave her one last long look before turning and disappearing under the trees. Celeste lowered her arms and shook the tension out of her limbs. She turned to her bag and saw the stone cup, forgotten when the mountain lion made its appearance.

It was empty.

Celeste chuckled. It was a forced laugh, reluctant in a way she couldn't explain. "I should've known that would happen."

She picked up her metal cup and tipped it to the grave. She hoped that the last of the brandy would give her a measure of courage instead of making her drowsier.

"Cheers," she said one last time.

OVER THE NEXT 20 MINUTES, CELESTE SWORE THAT SHE heard the soft padding of paws on dirt behind her. She stopped the first few times but saw nothing hiding in the underbrush or skirting through the shadows.

It didn't hurt me before, but maybe it was just checking to see if the prey was worth the hunt.

She shivered and fingered the Stormwalker talisman against her chest. So far it had only shown a form of warning, spiritual but not physical protection. Spiritual protection wouldn't stop a stalking predator. Or maybe it would, maybe she would get a warning before the lion attacked. The Valley clearly didn't run on all of the same natural laws that she was used to. Maybe spiritual protection was enough.

I'm probably not worth the effort, unless the lion likes pickles. Celeste snorted at her own joke.

Those thoughts soothed the rising paranoia and stopped Celeste from looking over her shoulder every 30 seconds for something that was not there.

It was well past noon when she came to her next goal: The Ledge. The path ran close to a steep slope covered in dirt and gravel, dotted with stunted trees and squat bushes. Then it all but disappeared and only a thin section of rock stood between the rocky edge of the slope and the edge of the walkway.

"Step 6: Cross the Ledge without looking up.

"This part is really quite simple, but still dangerous. There's a narrow ledge that you are going to have to sidle across for about, say, 50 feet. It used to just be a narrow path along the back side of Bloom Mountain, but one day the path just wasn't there anymore. Something knocked most of it off the mountain. Now it's about two feet wide.

"A couple years after it happened we were able to save up and pay some people to install a rope along the whole Ledge. That's made it much easier for me."

"Why shouldn't I look up?"

It was the most bizarre step in the directions so far.

Selena had cleared her throat and looked down at her knitting for a moment.

"There are some things you will just need to trust throughout this process, and this is one of them. Do not look up. For any reason. You can look down all you like. There is a drop of 20 feet or so onto the parts of the path that fell. Don't think you can get back up unless you can crawl up stone."

Celeste sighed. "If I could crawl up stone, I'd have reached the peak of the mountain by now. But I guess that wouldn't really help with the ritual, would it?"

Then Celeste wondered if there might be a creature in the mountains that *could* crawl up stone. She imagined something perched on the side of the mountain, waiting for unsuspecting passersby to pass below it.

I'm gonna have to pass on meeting any creature like that.

Celeste's phone was fully charged now, so she disconnected the battery back-up and secured it in her pack before walking forward to inspect the Ledge. Saplings and wildflowers dotted the far side of the Ledge, and it seemed *so close*. Close enough that it shouldn't take over ten or fifteen minutes to safely cross the distance, even at a glacial speed.

The path, however, was more worse for wear than Selena had described. Its edge was crumbling and weatherworn in several spots and large chunks had fallen to join the rubble below. The rope was fraying too. There was enough room for her to face the slope and slide along to the other side. But it was going to be a nerve-wracking experience.

Celeste had little experience with rock climbing. She tried to keep both feet flat on the ground as much as possible. She wasn't thrilled with how small that stretch of ground was for the next *however* long it took to cross the Ledge.

She slid a foot forward onto the Ledge and tested it with her weight. It held without crumbling or complaint.

Celeste stepped back and took a deep breath. She had to do this. There was no other way forward. And going back was not an option now. Going down the Stairwell would be much worse than it had been coming up.

And, you know, the whole "doom us all" thing that Marta said.

"If I have to do this again, I am having a bridge built over this."

Celeste pulled a pair of gloves out of her pack and pulled them on. They were newer than anything else, hardly worn in the last five years. They were still stiff and crunchy. Celeste flexed her hands to warm the gloves and loosen the fabric.

The rope was an inch thick and fit comfortably in her hands. She gripped it and pulled, watching as it grew taut. Twice she yanked on it, hard, and it didn't come loose. It still held strong despite age and fraying. She faced the rocky slope and took her first step.

Celeste slid along the first ten feet without issue. She shifted her weight to her right foot, slid the left over to join them, repositioned her hands, and then slid the right out again. Over and over like clockwork.

Then the whispers started.

At first Celeste thought it was just the wind blowing, but then she started to make out words and voices. The first she recognized was a voice of the dead.

"Celeste, dear, would you kindly look at me when I am talking to you?"

Her Grandma's voice slipped down the slope to envelop Celeste. She stared straight ahead at a pile of shining cream colored stones sitting precariously on the slope.

What. The. Fuck.

Aloud she said, "No."

The voice dissipated. Celeste got the sense that it was searching for some other way to taunt her.

"One foot at a time. One hand at a time. Slow. Steady. Keep your breathing calm. Keep your heart rate normal." Celeste focused even harder on moving her body along the Ledge, trying to keep that voice out of her head.

The whispers started again, low and hidden in the folds of wind that swirled around Celeste, playing in her hair, tugging at the elastic keeping it contained. Celeste ignored it, not wanting to pull even one hand from the rope. She made it another five feet before the whisper changed.

"Celly? Celly, is that you?"

Her granddaddy called to her with the nickname only he had used. It was a whisper above her, playing on the slope, sliding through the trees, crunching over gravel that tumbled to pelt her feet. It felt surer of itself, happier in its choice of torment.

"Celly, I'm here, come to Granddaddy."

Celeste stopped and started to raise her head, but a sound on the rocks below her drew her attention away from the ghost. She looped her right hand in the rope and turned to look behind and down.

The mountain lion from the Giant's Grave stood on the largest of the fallen rocks, staring at her. It was closer now than it had been before and she could clearly see swathes of reddish fur across its head and back and darker brown fur on its legs. Its body was muscular. Celeste recalled from the depths of her memory that mountain lions could sometimes jump close to 20 feet in the air. She couldn't tell for sure, but Selena had guessed the drop to be just about that.

"Hello, there," Celeste called out.

The mountain lion closed its eyes and Celeste heard what she thought was the deep rumble of purring.

"Celeste! I'm talking to you!"

The voice was sharp and stern, her mother's voice when the sisters vexed her.

Celeste yelped and snapped her head back to face towards the slope, causing pain on the right side of her neck. She rubbed the sore spot and then grabbed on to the rope again. She took several deep breaths, to calm the fluttering in her chest.

Stop blindly reacting to the voices. They cannot possibly be on the side of this godforsaken mountain.

The lion made a sound, a kind of growl and meow at the same time. Celeste turned just her head to look at it.

"I'm sorry, big kitty, but I have to go now. Please don't eat me later!"

Celeste closed her eyes and slid her right foot out and shifted her weight.

"Celeste Lucia Foster, I am speaking to you, you better look at me!"

"She's not there, she's not mad at you, Celeste. Keep going," she muttered over and over. The left foot came to join the right and the process began again.

The whispers shifted from her mother to her sister and back to her mother. Each voice demanding or accusing. But Celeste kept her eyes firmly shut and focused on moving one foot and then the other, keeping close to the rope and far from the edge.

Selena whispered to her next, then Jed, then Sarah and Hannah together speaking grave prophecies. These were all low and almost inaudible, she could only catch the gist of what they were saying. The whisperer was cycling through all the voices that Celeste had heard over the last several days. The mountain lion made an occasional comment, usually when something really terrible was whispered to her. The leonine sounds broke through the fear, reminded Celeste that she wasn't alone, that the mountain lion was there, watching over her. She still didn't dare open her eyes and be tempted to look up, where all the voices originated. She didn't dare face whatever was there, whatever it was that she was not supposed to see.

Celeste's right foot came down on a loose bit of ledge that crumbled under her weight. Her leg banged on the edge as she slipped and she grabbed onto the rope with every ounce of her strength. She made a curious sound halfway between a scream and a gasp and her eyes were fully open looking down at the rocks below.

Celeste was crouched down, with all her weight on her left foot and in her hands grasping the rope. Her right leg dangled over the edge. She felt the trickle of blood dripping down her leg inside her pants.

The mountain lion was still there, monitoring her progress. It watched Celeste with concern as she hung from the ledge.

Celeste watched it watching her while she gathered the strength to pull herself back up. She was able to and then shifted all her weight onto her left leg. Her right ankle burned from twisting on the crumbled stone.

Once upright, Celeste looked to her right and saw that she was only a couple of yards from the end. She scuttled to the edge of the new crevice and moved over it. Her leg was sore and bleeding, but she could make it. She had an old athletic bandage in her pack that she could put on when she reached the other side.

So close. You got this. Just a few more feet.

She shut her eyes again and prepared for the onslaught, but the only sound was her feet dragging across stone. The whisperer's absence was deafening.

Good. I'm sick of its shit.

Celeste hurried to reach the other side, taking her steps too quick to accommodate her aching leg. She rolled her ankle again and cried out. Tears burned in her eyes as she limped along, her focus on the other side. So close, and yet so far away.

"Celeste? Are you there?"

Marta's voice broke through the silence, soft and cold and small.

"I'm so alone. Won't you comfort me?"

"Fuck off with that noise!" Celeste was sick of being toyed with, sick of being taunted and teased. "I'm making it to the other side."

Her lungs heaved with effort and barely contained emotion. Celeste moved fast, ignoring her hurting leg. Once she stepped off the ledge, she turned around to glare up the slope at whoever or whatever the Whisperer was. She didn't stop to consider if the instructions meant she was *never* allowed to look up the slope.

"And when I come back, I'm building a fucking bridge!"

There was nothing crouching on the slope, nothing hiding in the bushes or behind the trees. The slope was clear of anything unnatural.

Nothing spoke on the wind. It was as if the whispers had never taunted, teased, or threatened her. As if the Whisperer had never existed at all.

Celeste waved a hand at The Ledge and the mysterious Whisperer and limped over to a fallen tree. It was an old loblolly pine, rotten at the core, but sturdy enough to hold Celeste's weight.

Celeste whimpered as she slid her boot off her swollen ankle. She let it sit in the open air for a few minutes while she finished her water and removed her still crunchy gloves. When she tentatively poked her leg where she'd felt blood, she found a small section of her pants damp. She would've had to pull them off to clean and inspect the wound, so she let it be.

What's the chance of infection? Low? Yes, definitely low.

Celeste pulled out her bandage and started wrapping the ankle. The first try was too tight, but the second was comfortable. She flexed her ankle and gingerly stood up to test her weight on it. The wrap provided enough support and range of motion for her to walk. She pulled on her boot and was finishing lacing it up when she heard a loud, curious sort of meow from below the Ledge. It was not unlike the sound Matches made before jumping onto Marta's kitchen counter.

The mountain lion's paws appeared a split second before the rest of the animal scaled the rocks. It stood and shook itself and approached, nostrils flaring.

Oh fuck.

Celeste stood still as she watched the lion approach. It didn't matter that it had distracted her from the worst of the whispers, it could kill her if it wanted to. And there wouldn't be much that Celeste could do about that.

The lion's head came up to about hip height on Celeste, with powerfully built legs and large dark paws. It sauntered right up to her and prodded her right knee with its broad nose. Then it turned its attention to her hand and rubbed it with the side of its snout.

Celeste opened the hand and let the mountain lion sniff it, the large nose tickling the fine hairs on the back of her hand. Once content, it shoved its hand under her palm and made a small noise. Celeste scratched between its ears. It closed its dark yellow eyes and rumbled.

"You scared me earlier, big kitty, when I was back by the grave." She scratched with both hands behind both ears, enjoying feeling the fur. "I think that you're trying to help me. Aren't you? You and your little round ears!" That last exclamation was in a cooing sort of voice Celeste had adopted when talking to domestic animals, no matter the species or size.

The lion pulled out of her hands and jumped to put its paws on her shoulders. Its weight startled her, almost toppled Celeste over, but she was able to steady herself. It stared into her eyes for a long moment and then pushed its forehead against Celeste's. Images washed through her mind.

A woman, tall and proud, standing with her back to a bonfire where it rested its tired bones. She looked back with dark eyes and dark hair falling almost to the ground. Her face was indistinct, not feline and therefore the details were distorted. Hair and eyes and scent it could understand. But human faces, even beloved ones, were hard for her.

The same woman, this time a bandage in her hands, slowly being wrapped around the lion's chest. She whispered strange words and cooed at her, like a mother to her kittens.

The lion in a field of flowers, the woman ahead, glowing under the full moon. She floated a foot off the ground. The scent of honey and nectar and burning wood filled its senses.

The images repeated, till Celeste had seen each three times. All throughout were impressions of *pack* and *love* and *caring*.

The lion licked Celeste once, the rough tongue abrasive against her cheek. Then it hopped down and hurried up the trail. It stopped once to look back, and Celeste raised an arm in response. Then it disappeared into the trees.

19
MOTHER BIRCH

Celeste passed the spot where the mountain lion had disappeared into the forest and continued up the slope. It was steeper on this side of the ledge, so she stopped to pull out her trekking poles to assist.

The trail was smaller too, barely wide enough for her feet, and she had to watch for rocks hidden in the grasses that could re-twist her ankle. She used the trekking pole to help judge how solid individual rocks were.

The currents of magic were stronger, flowing in and out of the plants, dusting the dirt trail, floating in the air like pollen in springtime. Before she left, Celeste had looked back at the ledge and focused on the currents of magic. The magic flowed down The Ledge like a river, bubbling and churning to rest in a lake with the rocks. But there had been one area that was devoid of magic, one stunted tree growing out of the slope that repelled the magic currents, causing eddies in the flow. Whatever lurked there was surely the cause of the auditory hallucinations that Celeste had experienced. Maybe next time she'd uproot that tree too, though that might harm the effectiveness of the binding ceremony.

Fuck that bush and whatever happened to it.

Celeste thought that she was beginning to understand the ritual. She had a feeling that each step was meant to have meaning for the mountain and for the binder. The meaning for the mountain was clear: each step happened in a location that was an obstacle on the path. Meaning for the binder would be personal, hard to guess or interpret. The ritual was a test of will, the magics of the mountain and the curse against the will of the binder.

But what is the meaning for me? Is it just a test of will? Of endurance? Or is there something deeper that I will glean in the months and years to come? Will each binding bring that meaning into sharper detail? Or further obfuscate it?

Celeste let the questions rumble quietly in her head as she walked. Around her the forest felt cooler and calmer compared to the other side of the Ledge. The trees loomed taller, older, wiser; watchful in a different way. A weightier, more powerful way. Celeste felt like she was transgressing on some sacred space.

The trail led deeper and deeper into the forest where densely grown pines dominated above and stretched far into the distance. The scent of their needles was thick. They blanketed the trail where the stunted grasses and creeping vines hadn't covered it. The sun's rays rarely graced the trunks of the trees around her, so dense were their branches.

Celeste walked along, listening to the hum of the pines and the wind as it attempted to penetrate the outer shell of the tunnel. She started to hear the gentle sounds of a creek: shallow water rippling over rocks, small splashing noises, and bird song. She rounded a corner and saw where the creek wound through the forest ahead.

The trees broke off five feet from the creek. Soft grass studded by rocks crept from beneath the pines to the rock-lined creek bed. The rocks were smooth and shiny, polished by running water and the passing of time. Some were a shimmering pink while others had a subdued reddish-brown tint. The water was shallow and clear, foaming over and around larger rocks in its path.

Overhead, a little diluted sunlight shined down on Celeste.

This is lovely. I wish I had time to stop and relax. I bet that water would feel wonderful on my ankle...

To her left, the creek veered right and started downhill, creating tiny waterfalls. It was reasonably flat to her right. Three large, flat rocks allowed Celeste to cross the creek. The water splashed her boots as she stepped from one to the next.

"Hold a minute!" a voice boomed from her right, nearly causing Celeste to fall over into the creek. It was familiar, but changed in timbre.

Oh no.

Celeste hopped to the far side and looked up for the voice: Abram Waite was walking towards her down the grass on the left side of the creek.

His long legs ate up the space between them, approaching like he was on a mission. He sported a long auburn beard, hip length hair of the same color, a floppy straw hat, and a different pipe was stuck between his teeth. She shouldn't have recognized him, but there were the same brown eyes full of power and darkness and the same changeling aura to him.

"Abram," she greeted him. She kept control of her voice, made it sound normal despite her fear and irritation at seeing him again. Something about him was different this time, other than the clothes he was wearing and the style of his hair. Something deeper.

"Celeste," he replied, drawing it out with a serpentine hiss.

Celeste felt her heart stutter and race. Felt fear rising up her throat like sap to coat her tongue in ash.

No, no, no. This is wrong. This is very wrong.

He stopped an arm's length away again and *loomed*. There was a menace to his stance and the timbre of his voice that had not been there that morning. His eyes were blanketed in shadow and his features gaunt. There was nothing of the kindly man she had first encountered that morning, only the spirit that had peeked through the human veil.

And seeing that malignant spirit peeking through made Celeste's fear turn to anger.

They faced each other for long moments while Celeste worked her throat, tried to get control of her voice, of her fear and anger. She mustered up the anger she still felt for the Whisperer, the annoyance of having her Grandmother and Marta used against her.

"Fancy seeing you all the way up here. I could've sworn I left you behind at the farm overlook." Celeste's voice dripped with sarcasm and bravado that she didn't quite feel. But anger was always easier than fear. "And yet, here you are, ahead of me. Now, if you will excuse me, I have a schedule to keep."

Oh yeah, that was the wrong thing to say. Time to go.

She stepped to the side to scan the forest's edge for the path. It was up the creek on the other side of Abram. A clear dirt track led up ten yards and then turned left and passed through the trees. She started to walk around him.

"Did I give you leave to go?"

Celeste stopped, unable to go any further, wishing she had been faster. But most of all, she wished Abram hadn't spoken again. There was something dark, akin to hatred, that resonated in his voice.

"Do not make the same mistake others have, Celeste." He drew out the 'c' into another hiss, heavy and ominous.

"Others have ignored me and my warnings, ignored my generous advice. And they failed, Celeste. Whatever their goals were, if they set themselves against me, they failed."

He paused a moment, quirking his mouth into a semblance of a smile. "On this mountain I am God and I rule alone." The façade dropped, all humanity gone from his voice. An echoing dissonance that grated on her mind replaced the previous richness in his voice. It felt like he was speaking to her through a long, echoing tunnel.

Celeste was suddenly aware of how close they stood to each other. He walked around to face her and reached out one long arm, the hand tipped with sharp, dark nails. He touched her forehead with the tip of his forefinger and trailed it down the bridge of her nose to her chin. His head cocked to the side, eyes widening, pupils dilating until only the thinnest rim of brown remained. Something happened at the edge of his body, some trick of the light that cast undulating shadows that *leapt* off of him and back.

"You are walking a dangerous path," he continued, "with many opportunities to fail."

His finger trailed down her neck, the nail slicing into the flesh under Celeste's chin. She whimpered, still unable to move, as blood trickled down her neck. Abram's nail trailed further down, crossing her jugular, with menace lurking in the pits of his eyes. Down, down, down it went, so slow and torturous that Celeste felt like she would faint. She could feel a welt rising on her face and neck, the wound under her chin pulsating with the beat of her racing heart.

"And if you fail, you will die." His voice was distant thunder on a summer day.

His finger reached the bottom of her neck. It hooked onto the leather thong and scooped the Stormwalker talisman out from under her shirt.

"Ahhhh…" he hissed and pulled his hand back in obvious surprise.

Celeste was aware of a faint glowing light between them. It was a pale yellow, like the stone that hung from the nail head. The glow reflected off the blacks of his eyes and the red of his current hair, but did nothing to the shadows that flickered at the edges of his form.

"So, the spirits of Gale have given you their blessing."

The tension eased a little and Celeste could think beyond the feel of the welt and blood on her skin, the beat of her heart, the constant litany of "No" and "This is wrong" that shuffled through her head. She felt the warmth of the talisman against her chest, felt it vibrating with some hidden power.

"Ah, but that blessing is worth nothing here," Abram said, drawing her attention.

He reached out his hand for the talisman and wrapped his fingers around the nail, preparing to pull it from her neck. "You won't be needi–" he cut himself off and howled in pain.

The scent of burning flesh assaulted Celeste and she was suddenly free, able to move and think again.

Abram's hand was still wrapped around the nail but a pressure wave and a brilliant yellow light burst forth from between his fingers, pushing the two of them apart, pushing the talisman out of his hand.

Celeste had enough time to catch her breath and see that Abram was stunned before she turned and bolted up the trail towards the trees. Panic replaced fear and annoyance.

Gotta get away. Far away.

"Run!" He shrieked from behind her. "Run as fast as you can. When I catch you, I'll rip that nail from your neck and punch it through your eyes!"

Celeste made the mistake of looking back at Abram, shocked by his threat.

He was a shifting mass of shadow, human, and animal parts. His legs were the hind legs of a deer, then a bear, then a human again. His torso changed just as swiftly, his hair and beard and clothing following suit, but his face and those dark eyes full of uncertain violent emotion remained. The shifting slowed, dragged out in a nauseating display of twisted limbs and muscle growth.

It was too much for Celeste. Her mind couldn't comprehend the horror displayed for her. Her head snapped forward and she took off at a run. She was up the creek side in an instant, following the dirt trail that would lead her back into the safety of the woods. She glanced to the side once more before entering cover again.

Where Abram had stood was a twisted creature. Human and animal parts merged into a deranged, nightmare-inducing concoction that should never exist, even in the darkest dreams. It crawled on a dozen oversized possum legs, carrying a bloated bear-like body, the long neck of a deer, and Abram's human-seeming face pasted onto the deer head like a mask. It was covered in red fox fur with black raccoon stripes and all around it was a maelstrom of shadow and flickering light, an aura radiating malice.

And worst of all, it was following Celeste, laughing with every step.

She regained her footing and ran into the trees. The pines seemed to stretch out their branches towards her, blocking the path, trying to trip her, allowing that-which-once-was-Abram to catch up. Celeste's arms and legs were cut by the stinging branches as she protected her face and continued to run. When she slowed, she heard padded feet on the grass behind her and the breaking of branches that blocked Abram on the path.

When the trail narrowed further, Celeste pushed her way through the tree branches. It was slow, painful work. She constantly looked over her shoulder expecting Abram to be there in some horrible form. She pushed her way into a small clearing and stopped for a moment to catch her breath. There were no sounds behind or around her and she hoped that Abram had been too large to follow her into the trees.

Through a gap in the trees on the far side of the clearing Celeste could see a wider path. Slowly, her breathing started to return to normal, but the stitch in her side from the Stairwell had returned with a vengeance. She clutched it, hoping that pressure would help, but it didn't. In the far distance Celeste heard something move through the trees and decided it was time to leave. She didn't want to be caught by Abram.

"Fuck that guy," Celeste wheezed as she started across the clearing. "I don't have time for his shit."

"What was that?"

That horrible, dissonant, otherworldly voice was right beside her. Celeste looked down to see Abram's face staring up from another hideous concoction. This time his face was grafted on the back of a raccoon's body with eight hobbling rabbit legs. It was the worst type of spider ever imagined.

Without thinking, Celeste stomped on Abram's face. She did it again and felt something crack and give under her heel. A howl ripped through the clearing as Celeste took off through the trees, heading for the wide path she'd seen. She could hear Abram shifting again, the swirling of wind and the pop and crack of joints and tendons and bones as they reconfigured into something new and even more horrible.

A shadow flew between the trees above her and she heard the pained and angry cawing of a crow. "Eyes to the sky," it yelled over and over from some hidden branch.

It flitted from tree to tree, keeping up with Celeste, cawing and screaming its refrain. "Eyes to the sky," it would scream, then occasionally another voice would respond, "Ears to the ground." It was the same thing that Abram had told her that morning after he revealed his true self to Celeste.

The pine trees gave way to a wide stretch of thick grass dotted by large white rocks with an opalescent sheen and stubby bushes with dark leaves. On the other side tall white birches grew in regimented lines on a shallow incline. Small purple flowers grew in the grass on the approach.

The light was beginning to fade, and the sky darkened from cerulean to a deep, muted sapphire. Celeste picked up the pace without running. "I'm running out of time," she muttered over and over as she crossed towards the birch forest. The heat of the day was dissipating and a cool breeze blew across the meadow, rustling the bushes as she passed.

Celeste turned back when she reached the first sentinel birch. She heard the continual calls of "Eyes to the sky" and "Ears to the ground," but they were far away at the edge of the pine forest. She could only just see light reflecting off two sets of eyes close to each other deep in the branches of a particularly tall Norwegian Pine.

Celeste breathed a sigh of relief. It appeared that Abram would not be following her any further. She passed beneath the birches and stopped to rest on a boulder. The encounter with Abram and the chase had taken a lot out of her. Her side was burning and she felt drained of all the emotions that she'd been struggling with earlier. And still she worried that she wasn't quite done with Abram Waite yet.

There's a lot of time left until noon tomorrow. But I'm so tired now.

The atmosphere under the birch trees was a distinct change from the pines across the meadow. It was cool and clear and the air was pure, untainted by the heat and humidity of the day. Celeste was surrounded by that intense smell of green growing things but without the edge of rot that spoke of autumn's touch and the looming presence of winter. There was a light perfume from the purple flowers that dotted the moss and grass growing beside the trail.

She stood up after a few minutes, not exactly refreshed, but feeling less overwhelmed than before. And there was still so much to do.

The birch trees grew on a grid, row after row of almost identical trees, with their peeling bark and yellowing leaves. The trail wound up the hill, meandering from one column of trees to the next, taking whichever path was easiest. Celeste made good time climbing the hill and her heart finally felt lighter for having escaped Abram Waite at last. She breathed a sigh of relief so deep that it shook her shoulders and almost caused a coughing fit.

A low mist gathered at Celeste's feet. It swirled around her and flowed through the trees in currents that didn't correspond to the wind or the magic or the undulations in the earth below. With each step she took, her feet disturbed the mist like a rock skipping on water, ripples radiating out until they met another or the trunk of a tree.

Celeste stopped to feel the rough, textured bark on the tree, brown and black breaking through the soft white. It was a very old *betula lenta*, the black birch, common in Appalachia and the northeast. Celeste had birch beer, made from the sap of the black birch, once when she was camping in Pennsylvania. It had a really *distinct* flavor, bitter and herbaceous, that she hadn't enjoyed and a friend had finished the bottle for her.

While she was feeling the bark, a trio of deer stepped into sight, picking at the grasses that grew below the birches. Two does followed a stag with long antlers that glowed golden in the twilight. The light from its antlers shimmered on the short fur of its companions. They stopped and stared up at Celeste, their dark eyes reflecting the gold.

One of the does stepped around the stag and approached

Celeste, its little tail swishing behind it. Celeste stayed still while the doe inspected her. It sniffed her hands and the spot on her pants that was now crunchy with dried blood and the pine needles that clung to her boots.

"You're beautiful," Celeste whispered, trying not to scare the doe.

Once it was done with the inspection, it looked up at Celeste. They stared at one another for a long moment and then the doe trotted back to her companions and the three of them disappeared into the darkness of the forest.

Celeste waited until they were gone and continued up the hill.

She enjoyed the strange sight of so many birch trees that had grown according to some higher plan, some grand design. Trees in nature did not grow in the way this birch forest had grown. Only man demanded orderly rows and columns from nature. And though that disturbed Celeste, she found she couldn't be afraid of the trees. Even after the Old Oak Tree. They were still trees, organic living things that didn't judge or gossip. Celeste found more comfort in their aged presence than with most people.

There are always exceptions, like Marta.

A smile played at Celeste's mouth as she thought about Marta. She wondered if Marta was at Selena's, both of them waiting for a sign of success or failure from the mountain. Or was she with Matches in her apartment, unable to focus on a distraction? She had been worried that morning when she dropped off Celeste.

Why does it feel like that was days ago? It's been barely 12 hours.

Celeste left the mist below as she climbed a steep slope between large boulders. She crested the hill and saw that there was a large glade with an immense birch tree in the center. It had three wide trunks, each reaching over 100 feet into the air, with thousands of branches and a crown of leaves that almost blocked out the sky. There was a shimmering quality to the air under the leaves, as if stars fell from the gently swaying branches.

The tree called to Celeste. It sang a song of comfort and fulfillment; it sang of its long life and the many children that took root from its seeds. How it had done it, Celeste didn't know, but she was certain that this one birch was the source for the entire forest below it. Every single black birch had sprouted from the seeds of this one tree, this Mother Birch.

"Oh, shit! I forgot again!"

Celeste realized she hadn't listened to Selena's recording in more than an hour. The last thing she remembered was the warning about the Ledge.

Celeste dug in her pocket for her phone and headphones, hoping beyond hope she hadn't fucked anything up by completely forgetting about the recording. She headed for the Mother Birch, trusting the feeling of the forest and the smell of good earth below her feet to protect her. There was a large root that had twisted out of the ground and was at just the right height to be a bench. Celeste flopped down on it and shoved her headphones into her ears.

"Step 7: Cross Battle Creek.

"This one is going to sound pretty straightforward, but it really isn't. Once you've reached this point in the journey, you are more than halfway up the mountain and you've almost reached your bed for the evening.

"But time is also running out.

"You'll climb up through an old forest and eventually come to Battle Creek. It's a stream that runs from a spring up in the mountain. It eventually meanders through Yuback Valley to join the Nomini. There are flat rocks that will allow you to cross the stream,

*but here is where one of the Mountain Folk will probably come to say
hello."*

"The Mountain Folk?"

Celeste felt her stomach drop while listening to this again.
She had completely forgotten that Celeste had forewarned her
about Abram. Or at least alluded to Abram's presence on the
mountain.

*"Yes, the Mountain Folk. They are spirits of Stone, and Ember, and
Gale, that make their home on the mountain.*

*"If you are lucky, it will only be a little winged sprite come to tease
you a little, to play with your hair, and to lead you on to Mother Birch.
If you are less lucky, it might be a troll or another spirit of Stone. They
might ask you for something in return for their help, and I don't
suggest turning them down. They know the mountain better than
anything else and they can shorten or lengthen your trip depending on
how you respond."* Selena took a deep breath that Celeste could
hear on the recording.

*"If you are unlucky, you will meet the…ruler of the mountain.
You'll know it's him because he will appear as a man, at least at
first."*

There was a long, silent pause here. Celeste knew that it
would be hard to describe Abram to anyone else. She could
sympathize with Selena, who had probably interacted with
Abram many times during her long tenure as the binder of the
mountain.

*"I cannot say more than that; he is mercurial, and I've never been able
to predict when he would or wouldn't show up. Some years he has practically joined me on the hike, other years he came and went as he had
time, and sometimes I went years without seeing hide or hair of him.*

Who knows what duties he has? What he does to keep the mountain in check himself?"

Selena had asked those questions to herself.

"After you have met whatever or whoever is waiting for you at Battle Creek, you will continue through the pine forest until you come to an open meadow and see a hill covered in birch trees. Climb up to the top of the hill and you'll find Mother Birch.
"Step 8: Say a prayer before Mother Birch."
"A prayer?"

Celeste was still suspicious of this part. Despite everything that had happened today and the previous day, despite the repeated *responses* from the mountain, she still was suspicious about saying a prayer. It would take more than a few days for her to overcome a lifetime of doubt.

"Yes, a prayer. Don't you have religion Outside?"

Celeste had shaken her head at that. No one in her family was religious, none had even spoken of going to church or to a temple for any reason at all.

"No, we're not religious."
"You don't believe in anything? Nothing higher than you or beyond death? Even after today?"

Celeste still didn't know how to respond to that, but she stood by her previous reply.

"When I die, my tissues will feed a forest, and my bones will house a family of field mice; I'll go back to the earth that birthed me."

"That's very poetic, dear. Say a prayer to your forest if you want, but you must say a prayer to something. And it must be at the base of Mother Birch."

Selena's voice had taken on the tone adults use when they aren't impressed by something that a child did or said.

Celeste looked up at Mother Birch. The white bark shone where it wasn't scaled and broken and black. Twilight glittered in her shimmering leaves, reflecting the sky painted peach and pink.

Celeste stood and walked around Mother Birch's trunks and headed for the far side of her clearing. The path continued, down into the darkening woods and out of sight. She considered heading down without saying a prayer, it felt foolish to even try to pray for the first time in her life on a cursed mountain. What god would hear her?

Yes, but you can feel foolish instead of being stupid.

Movement in the trees drew her attention. Shadows slinked. Lights flickered.

They lit like matches, first white and then blue, brightening to glowing orbs that flitted between the trees. Shadows stirred below them, wrapping the mist about their forms, with bright eyes that peered up at Celeste. One shadow shuffled slowly out onto the path. It was tall and humanoid, bloated around the abdomen, with shapeless arms and legs. The head was long and narrow and it raised an arm towards Celeste, beckoning her closer, a mockery of the Stormwalker that had blessed Celeste.

Celeste looked back to Mother Birch, shining in the twilight. There was no doubt in her mind that the shadows were waiting for her to continue without praying, to break the steps of the ritual on purpose. Some parts of the ritual were as natural as following the path. She hadn't missed a step *yet*. But she'd come close in the last encounter with Abram. She *had* met him at Battle Creek and they *had* talked. But it had not gone well.

He's right about one thing: I am walking a fine line between success and failure. He's just on one side, pulling me into the abyss. And how do you fight that?

Celeste needed to be careful, more mindful as she went forward into the twilight. She needed to not trust anger and stubbornness to get her through the day.

She looked back. The shadows were still lingering, just under the white branches of the birch forest below her.

Celeste sighed and turned back around. "Fine, I'll pray at the damned tree."

She left her pack a few feet from the tree and dropped down on her knees before the middle trunk. She looked around, as if someone might see her there and then she would have to be even more embarrassed than she already was.

Her mind went blank when she tried to think of a prayer. Who would she pray to? She had never called upon any god, never given them more than a passing thought. What words should she say? She didn't even know what prayers were said in Christian churches, which this surely was not. She looked up at Mother Birch for guidance, but found none.

Selena's voice, talking about Ice, Ember, Stone, and Gale came to mind. Celeste wondered which one was "closer than comfort allowed," but ultimately brushed the topic aside.

That is not a now problem. That is a later problem. Focus.

Finally, she decided to pray to the mountain itself. She didn't put it into words, just intention focused at whatever was the heart of Bloom Mountain. Intention to finish the ritual, to find a place for herself in the days and weeks and years to come, to see her mother and her father and her sister again, to see Marta and Matches again. Celeste had lost her job, her dream job, but she was beginning to think that maybe it was for the best. That maybe there was something out here for her that was not just a burn schedule or seeds and saplings. Something more than she'd had before.

Celeste put all that and more that she didn't have the words for into her prayer to the heart of Bloom Mountain. And when she was done, she felt lighter, braver.

She stood and stretched, hoping that she was almost done for the day. She was hopeful that Old Ellie would have a bathroom and a hot meal waiting for her, maybe even a bath.

Maybe I can see some more of those golden deer. They were pretty.

When approached the far edge of Mother Birch's clearing, she saw no shadows in the forest below, nor any lights flitting in the trees. Celeste sighed with relief, glad that she had gone back and prayed despite how silly it had made her feel. She swung her pack onto her shoulder and started down the hill.

Once she crossed the rest of the birch forest, she would arrive at her destination for the night. She could do it, it wasn't that far.

Just walk down the hill and through the forest. You'll come to a wide clearing and Old Ellie's cabin. Nothing could be easier than that.

Right?

20

NIGHT ON BLOOM MOUNTAIN

Shadows surrounded Celeste as soon as she stepped into the forest, and all of her hope dissolved back into fear.

Tall and skinny, short and round, the shadows came in every shape and size, some shifting like Abram as she watched. They lined the path, a multitude of grotesqueries that reached towards her with their long, snaking fingers. They stayed off the trail itself, but Celeste had to duck to avoid them as she made progress deeper into the forest.

In the settling gloom, the birch trees looked more like bone than bark.

Yes, that is an absolutely useful thought.

Wisps, or jack-ma-lanterns as Selena called them, floated above the trail, casting it in a cold, flickering light. The lighting and the shadows and the tall, skeletal trees made Celeste feel like she was in a horror game. And if she was, she already knew who the final boss would be.

She walked on, dodging reaching hands and spectral tentacles, until the trail circled around the right side of a clearing and ended. Celeste stood on the last dredges of trail and despaired. There was no way forward and no way back; shades that crouched over the thin line of dirt that had been her lifeline and blocked the path behind her. The shadows clung to the tree trunks, some clawing at the bark, others climbing to perch on low branches, letting their long limbs dangle like jellyfish tentacles. Their piercing eyes faced the center of the clearing where a blackened tree trunk rested.

With nothing else to do, Celeste paced back and forth around the clearing, never leaving the dirt trail. High above her, the wisps hung on the branches of the birch trees, the colors changing from ice blue to periwinkle to sapphire to amethyst and back. It was a sparkling display that Celeste would have loved to watch in other circumstances. The changing colors cast strange light on the multitude of undulating shades that watched Celeste.

It was still warm despite the deepening darkness of twilight. Night would fall soon and bring with it horrors unknown. Celeste couldn't remember if Selena had any warnings for after nightfall. Would terrors emerge from the dark recesses of the mountain's interior to hunt her?

The currents of magic disappeared with the trail, though whether that was because of the presence of the shades or some other magic, she didn't know.

The tension in the clearing grew in leaps and bounds. Celeste wasn't certain what would happen, but she knew she was being forced to wait in this clearing until *something* happened. And surely that *something* would involve the so-called god of the mountain, Abram Waite. She regretted the earlier reflex to stomp on his horrid, spidery form.

Well, not regret, so to speak. He deserved that. I just wish I'd have run instead.

Celeste stopped pacing and sat on the trail and watched as the last vestige of twilight darkened to night. The sky deepened to a dark, velvety blue-black studded with crystal stars.

Focus on the sky. On the stars. Just like Elise told you.

The night sky was beautiful out here, so far from DC and the airports and the light pollution and smog. The stars shined bright and clear, their muted colors visible against the vast void. She picked out the familiar constellations that she knew from her childhood: the tail of the big dipper peeked over the tree line, Polaris shined bright and true, but nearby Cassiopeia was almost completely blocked by trees. A fresh wave of home-sickness washed over Celeste. She curled her knees up and wrapped her arms around her legs, thinking about her sister and wishing that Elise was here to watch over her.

Surely I wouldn't have gotten into this mess if she had picked up the phone. She'd have told me to come visit her and we'd work through it together.

No, you probably would have still come out here, 'cause that's how you are. You gotta try your way first, then ask for help after you've fucked up again.

The mounting terrors and stresses of the trip had grown too large for her to continue shoving to the side. She would have to confront them soon, if she survived whatever would be happening next.

"I don't think $20,000 will be enough to cover the therapy I'll need after this," she told herself, then half-laughed, half-sobbed into her knees.

I'm still hoping that this is all a bad dream. She thought of Marta and silly little Matches. *Not all bad. But I might give them up to go back to my normal, boring, overwhelming life.*

Despite the tension and anxiety, it was calm and warm in the clearing. Celeste could have fallen asleep, if it weren't for the presence of the shades, the curling mist, and the feeling that *something* was going to happen. And that it would happen soon.

Celeste watched her captors in return and saw when they stopped their incessant shifting and twitching and grew still. Their glowing eyes stared unblinking at the tree trunk, where the mist grew thick and started to creep up the bark. It wound up the gnarled trunk in a slow, slug-like motion to float in one spot. It grew, first in slow inches over long minutes, then in lurches, and finally in a cascade. The wisps lowered themselves closer to the clearing, the coalescing mist casting roiling shadows infused with their multi-colored lights.

Celeste climbed to her feet and steadied her shaking limbs. She clenched and unclenched her hands as a chill wind blew down from above and swirled through the glade and pushed the mist into shape. Limbs sprouted and lengthened, the frame was tall and perilously thin; a head appeared in a poof of smoke and the rest of Abram Waite followed.

He sat on the trunk, appearing exactly as he had been that morning, with a pipe in one hand and a floppy hat on his head. He smiled at her in that sly, serpentine way that Celeste associated with his hidden, *true* self, whatever that may be. The self that he had shown by Battle Creek, the shifting, twisting horror that hid beneath his imperfect human disguise. She preferred how he had first appeared: a helpful, ageless man. But that was not who sat before her.

"Fancy seeing you here, Celeste," he greeted her. His tone and words carefully chosen to mimic her from their earlier meeting at Battle Creek. "We could have had this conversation earlier, but you were being quite disagreeable, were you not? So I had to ask a few of my…friends to corral you here while I attended to other business." He waved a hand at the shadows that reached for him like adoring subjects.

Celeste clenched her fist again, allowing the nails to sink deep into the flesh. The pain helped clear the fog of anxiety that had started to cloud her mind. She took a deep breath, enjoying the cool mist in her lungs.

"I was expecting you sooner, Abram," she managed to say through clenched teeth. "It's rude to keep your guest waiting." Again she was being audacious in the face of inevitable danger.

At least you are consistent. Not much else can be said for you, but you are consistently a dumbass in the face of horror.

He laughed and slapped his knee with his free hand. "You do have spirit, I will give you that. But your manners are sorely lacking in the presence of a god. I can see into your head, read your darkest secrets. And I can smell your fear." He sniffed for dramatic effect. "And you reek of it!"

"I see no gods here, only an old man and his sneaking shadows." Celeste had no idea why she was saying everything possible that would rile Abram up.

Abram was unfazed by her blasphemous words. "It appears we will have to wait to have this conversation. I feel the need to reinforce that I *am* god here." He stood and walked over to Celeste, the ground quivering with every step. He circled her once, his face mere inches from her, making her body hair stand on end. He returned to his trunk, but he did not sit back down. The lingering scent from his pipe made Celeste's stomach queasy.

"I see you have walking poles attached to your pack. I am told that hiking with those is incredibly healthy exercise. But I was thinking of something else to entertain us this evening. Another form of exercise." His eyes narrowed. "Would you like to know what I have in mind?"

Celeste shook her head in response. There was no way that anything he could suggest would be pleasant for her.

"Ah, that is too bad. Because your participation is required." He pocketed his pipe and stretched his long arms up above his head. He pointed one arm towards the trees to

Celeste's right. She glanced over to see that the specters had shifted to allow a gap in the circle. Celeste looked back at Abram, fear bubbling over in her gut.

He smiled one last smile, showing rows of sharp, shining teeth.

"Run."

THE STITCH IN CELESTE'S SIDE FORCED HER TO WALK. SHE didn't know how long she'd run before it started again, if it had ever subsided. It was a miracle that she hadn't tripped and fallen, but she would only get clumsier the longer she ran.

There was little light to see by. Wisps hung high on the tree branches. But she rarely saw more than one at a time. Their cold, diffused light didn't carry far in the darkness. She stopped to catch her breath when she came across one. But only if it wasn't surrounded by twinkling shade eyes. She didn't dare test the safety of the light against Abram's...*friends*.

Celeste had no guide in the forest save for the wisps, her own instincts, and the magical currents that she had trusted so far. And she couldn't be sure that either were leading her on to safety. She knew that her next goal was a cabin in a large clearing. But how would she get there? Nothing manmade appeared in her limited night-sight. The magical currents were confused, crossing themselves and looping in long, winding curves. She had a small flashlight in her pack, but she was reluctant to pull it out. *Things* shifted and followed and called out to her from behind ghostly trees. She didn't want to give those a definite form.

Fuck, fuck, fuck, fuck. This is not good. Fucking Abram. And my fucking stubborn ass.

Something large moved on her left, hidden by the trees, but

still rustling the thick underbrush. Celeste groaned. She'd hoped that she'd earned a short reprieve from the constant running, the shadowed hands reaching out of the darkness, the piercing eyes that watched her every move. They were a warning, the dead end sign on the road that was the unending forest. Celeste continued taking cues from the shades on both sides.

Until she stepped off the path and fell into deep water.

She gasped as the chill seeped into her bones. Soaked her hair and clothing. Her limbs grew heavy and cold. She started to sink. There hadn't been enough time for her mind to catch up and she was already far below the rippling, star-studded surface. Celeste tried to kick her legs. But something held on to her ankles. Drawing her deeper into the depths and further from the stars. She looked down and saw only darkness engulfing her legs. Pulling her down into black oblivion.

The last breath she'd taken ran out.

The hands disappeared from Celeste's ankles. She struggled, trying to reach the surface. But it was too far away. There was no more air to fuel her frenzied attempts at self-preservation. She reached one last time. Her legs kicked lamely below her. And then she gave up. Celeste floated in the deep. Waited as each excruciating second passed, hoping she would die soon rather than linger. She closed her eyes one last time.

And when she opened them again, she was standing below a wisp, its cold purple light surrounding her. She gasped, drawing in all the air she'd lost, but there was no void to fill. She was fine, her brain was clear again and her clothes were dry and warm.

Behind her was nothing but trees and night. There was no pond or lake or river, not even a puddle. She hadn't drowned, she hadn't even been wet.

It was all in my head? But I could feel the water and the hands around my legs. I could see the stars above me. It felt so real...

Celeste shivered and continued, still looking for the elusive clearing where Old Ellie lived. Another wisp blossomed into sight to her left, so Celeste turned and approached. It was a light turquoise and brighter than the rest, its little light illuminating a wide circle below it.

To Celeste's right something large stirred in the trees. A heavy footstep crunched leaves and fallen branches, another cracked a rotting truck. One after another, they continued, ponderously following Celeste further into the night. A hiss twisted through the trees above her, like the labored breathing of some massive serpent.

Once she reached the perceived safety of the wisp's light, Celeste turned to face whatever it was that had followed her. It stayed in the shadows, but she could see the blue-green light flicker over a massive, bloated body covered irregularly in reflective, pearlescent scales. It didn't have that unsettling, shifting quality of the shades and specters, or the gloating face of Abram stitched across its form. It was something new, and Celeste didn't want anything to do with it.

She turned and continued, and the wisp followed, floating a few feet above and behind her head. When she came to a stop the wisp moved to float a few feet above her head. She looked up at it and marveled at the little creature. There was something small at the center, some tiny flying creature that was engulfed in a flaming aura that gave it its light and color. She could just see a tiny face looking down at her, human and yet not.

"Looks like we're in this together, little wisp," Celeste said up to the creature. "I feel better with you by my, uh, side."

The wisp floated up and down and flickered in response.

Celeste reached down to adjust the bandage around her ankle. It was itching and constricted after all the running.

"Alright, let's go," she whispered to the wisp and the snake creature following her.

For the first time since sunset, Celeste could see where she was placing her feet. The forest floor was suspiciously free of clutter here. Only a thin layer of leaves and small twigs covered the dirt and moss and rocks under her boots. There was no obvious path, only the hint that other people had passed this way before. But the currents of magic were less confused now. She could still see ghostly paths twisting and turning through the trees, but she found one that was stronger, clearer, and followed it.

Well, at least that has settled itself. Now just ignore the big guy behind you. He's probably okay, right? Totally not going to swallow you whole and then sleep for a century.

The hissing creature continued at a distance, never coming close enough for Celeste to see the details. Once, when Celeste stopped for a rest, a large shadow stepped into the light to her right, threatening her and the wisp with its writhing limbs. Celeste was frozen, watching the creature when a fallen tree trunk hurtled out of the night into the creature, dissolving it. It hit another tree and splintered into a thousand slivers of wood, but none of them penetrated the wisp's light.

Celeste looked back at the hissing creature and felt a sense of satisfaction. She re-categorized the hissing creature from *possible foe* to *friend*.

As they progressed along the hidden path, shadows no longer reached out from the darkness. Celeste could only see their distant, unblinking eyes. Their strange trio made fast progress through the woods.

They reached the edge of the birch wood. Beyond its bounds a wide meadow was lit by starlight, bright after the dark forest. The lumbering creature held back behind the safety of several old trees while the wisp stopped just at the edge of the wood.

Celeste looked back at them and nodded, sensing that they could not leave the bounds of the wood.

"Thank you for lighting my way," she said to the wisp. It floated and flickered a response before rising to be lost in the foliage above.

To the large creature, she nodded, thankful for its protection, but uncertain what to say.

It's hard to tell who is friendly and who is not. This creature that, from all appearances, should be dangerous and predatory, protected me. While Abram, who appears human, is the worst of the lot.

She turned her back on the birches and entered the meadow. It stretched on into the distance where the dark silhouette of another forested section of Bloom Mountain loomed.

"You are not running, Celeste!" Abram's voice boomed, each word punctuated with hate.

"Fuck you, Abram!" Celeste responded. She turned and walked parallel to the trees, wanting to stay in the meadow where visibility would be marginally better. She didn't run, she didn't want to give Abram what he wanted. But she wished the wisp had stayed to light her way.

A shadow slunk from the forest to her left and hurried toward Celeste. She tensed up and watched it until it was close and she recognized the feline silhouette. She felt a surge of relief: the mountain lion had returned.

I won't say no to another protector. Though I wonder who sent the wisp and the big, hissing guy.

Celeste stopped in the starlit field and waited as it sniffed her and then peered around into the gloom. Content with whatever it found, the mountain lion head butted her leg and trotted down the meadow towards some unseen goal.

A few moments of relative silence passed. Celeste could just hear the padded feet ahead of her and her own boots on the thick grass. But then the mountain lion came to a halt and started to growl. It was a low, terrifying sound and Celeste was glad it wasn't directed at her.

Abram appeared out of the mist, still in his human form. "I thought that I told you to run!"

He circled Celeste and the mountain lion, his bright eyes two glowing pinpricks that she could follow in the mists that swirled around him. When he was behind her, he called out again.

"Since you will not run of your own accord, I will have to chase you!"

Claws raked across Celeste's shoulder. Ripped a scream out of her. Pain trickled down her back like blood from a wound. But blood was there too. The mountain lion screeched and launched itself at Abram.

"Down, filthy beast. Go back to your mother!"

The lion backed off and butted Celeste again. Then it turned and started running.

Just like he wanted. But at least I'm not alone.

Celeste was only a few seconds behind it. She found a reserve of energy she didn't know she could tap. She held her arm close to her side to prevent jostling as much as possible. Celeste barely felt anything. Not the pounding of her boots over rock and grass and hard packed earth. Not her lungs and heart as they pumped wildly in her chest. The adrenaline pumping through her veins was swifter than caffeine and sweeter than morphine.

A dark form in the mist to her left betrayed Abram before he lunged. Black arms with shadowed claws tried to catch

Celeste. But she was more agile than him. She ducked and spun away. The mountain lion put itself between her and Abram. They kept running.

Didn't know I could move like that.

Abram growled as they left him behind.

The mountain lion caught Abram by surprise the next time he appeared. It slunk around in the dark to attack him from behind. Formidable teeth sunk into his shadowed leg. Abram howled in pain, curses dripping from his mouth like blood from a wound.

Celeste and the lion kept running. Kept encountering different forms of Abram. She wasn't sure what the endgame was for him. Why was he chasing her? Was it really to teach her a lesson? To show off his powers? Or was there some other hidden goal in his mind? Did he not want the mountain's magic to be bound? Would that then bind him as well?

A bear charged them from the woods on their right. But disappeared into mist before it could reach them. Shadow-drenched hawks and eagles dived from above. Their grasping claws sliced through Celeste's arms as she protected herself. More subtle and terrifying creatures harassed them. But on they ran. Down the middle of that meadow. Searching for sanctuary.

Then, in the distance, a light appeared out of the darkness. It was the warm orange and red of a large bonfire and the tall, dark shape of a building behind it.

Celeste coaxed a little more out of her ragged limbs, starting to feel the edge of pain returning as the adrenaline drained from her. She ran faster than she had ever run before.

As they approached, Celeste could see that the light glinted off thousands of flowers that grew around the bonfire and building. The silhouette of a woman stood among the flowers, wild hair flowing behind her, a crown of twinkling stars floating above her head. The fire was behind her, so the details were in shadow, but Celeste could make out the gun in her hands.

Celeste waved her arms, trying to signal the woman. Hoping that she would not be on the receiving end of whatever was loaded into the barrel of the gun.

The forest fell away to either side and Celeste and the mountain lion were in the final stretch when the woman shouted at them.

"Hit the ground!"

21

THE STONES

THE SOUND FROM THE SHOTGUN BLAST REVERBERATED through Celeste's skull. She pressed her palms to her ears and willed it to stop with every fiber of her being. There was only the ringing; it blocked out sight and smell and pain. It rang and rang until it was suddenly gone.

As her senses returned, Celeste was overwhelmed by the smell of grass and rich earth and a multitude of flowers. Crickets chirruped nearby. The mountain lion approached; its wet nose touched Celeste's forehead. It huffed at her, turned around, and disappeared into the flowers. She continued to lie in the grass.

Celeste had enough sense to understand that the mountain lion wanted her to follow it again. It took a moment for her to regain control of her limbs, and another to realize that they were shaking from exertion. She slid her uninjured arm under her chest and used it to push herself up off the ground and back on to her knees.

She was on the edge of a field of mixed wildflowers, though it was hard to tell exactly what they were in the low light.

Behind her mist shrouded the empty meadow and ahead warm, flickering light from the bonfire drenched the house.

Celeste stood slowly and searched for the mountain lion or the woman, but saw neither. Her shoulder was throbbing and there were sticky spots on her shirt where blood had soaked through and started to dry. She could feel it, dull though her brain was. The fabric stuck to her skin and the wet feeling of it releasing. It was nauseating.

She stumbled through the flowers, heading for the bonfire, hoping it would warm the chill that had crept into her sluggish limbs. And that she'd be able to pull the over shirt off to relieve one of many irritating sensations.

A circle of flat stones shoved into the ground circled the bonfire. Large stones and wooden benches framed one half of the bonfire. Celeste dropped her pack and collapsed on the ground next to the nearest seat, and hoped the woman would be back soon. She tore off her over-shirt, hating the feeling as the fabric detached from her skin and the blood dripped, sap-like, down her back. In the warm firelight, she could see three long cuts in the fabric, dark with her blood.

I wonder how much blood I've lost. I feel woozy, but it's been a day.

The fire's warmth mingled with her exhaustion, making Celeste drowsy. But the warmth couldn't touch the cold that had settled into her bones. It was more spiritual than physical. As she drifted off to sleep, Celeste wondered if that cold would linger for the rest of her life.

When she woke up, Celeste found herself curled up against a warm body. This one was solid and covered in short, tawny fur. It rumbled like an earthquake and smelled of large animal, an earthy, sweaty scent that Celeste knew from the National Zoo.

A paw pushed against her leg and Celeste moved away from the mountain lion.

"Finally awake?"

Celeste turned too fast for her fuzzy vision and exhausted brain. The world turned sideways for a moment before it stabilized and she could focus again.

A tall woman with deep bronze skin sat on the next closest rock, the barrel of the shotgun resting against her thigh. Her hair was dark brown with a soft wave to it and her eyes were pools of deepest black reflecting the red and orange of the fire.

"You're Ellie, right?" Something about the woman tickled her memory. "You were at the courthouse, weren't you?"

She smiled at Celeste, warmth softening her features and aging her. "You're right, I am Ellie and I was there. I sensed that someone was coming to attempt the binding and I wanted to see who it was."

Celeste pushed herself up into a sitting position, feeling the bandages on her shoulder as she did.

"Lorna was keeping you warm when I came back from setting my wards. Your shoulder was pretty messed up, so I took care of that while you slept."

Celeste looked at the mountain lion, who had gotten up and stretched before sitting next to Ellie to receive scratches. "Lorna is the lion?"

Ellie nodded. "She's my friend and one of my familiars. I sent her down to keep an eye on you. Abram has gotten dangerous these last few years and I was afraid he was going to do something…unhinged."

"I don't have anything to compare him to, but he definitely wasn't welcoming." Celeste ran a hand over her shoulder where medical gauze was tightly taped and wrapped with a bandage.

"How long will this take to heal?"

Ellie shrugged. "If you're lucky, you'll heal by the end of the week. If not, you never will. It's hard to tell with wounds from that bastard." She sighed. "I had hoped that you would've arrived earlier, sunset at the latest, before his powers grew to their fullest on this auspicious, moonless night."

Celeste took a deep breath, feeling how damaged her shoulder was from the movement. It twinged and there was something viscous on it, keeping the pain at bay. "I would have made it here earlier, but Abram interfered."

Ellie nodded. "Do you feel well enough to go in? I have Berry minding the stew on the stove, and I think you could do with something to eat."

Ellie offered a hand and Celeste took it. She was unsteady for the first few steps, but regained her balance before reaching the porch around Ellie's cabin. It was hard to see in the light, but the cabin and the porch appeared to be made from the same aged wood. Celeste wondered how long the cabin had been here, near the top of Bloom Mountain.

Ellie held the door open and Lorna paced in, heavy on her paws. The day had been long for her too. Celeste followed, noting that Ellie had her bag over one shoulder and the shotgun slung over the other.

The interior of the cabin was lit by bright, warm firelight. Across from the door, a large stone fireplace dominated the main room, a wood-burning stove set to one side. A square table and two large armchairs occupied the middle of the room. The furniture was handmade wooden pieces with colorful quilts and cushions stacked nearby. The table had a basket and a stack of cards on it. Two closed doors were in the right hand wall, a row of cabinets and shelves filled the wall to the left, with the only free spot being taken up by a large curtained window.

The shelves were full of books, opaque glass jars, bottles, stones, sticks, and other miscellany. The cabinet top had bowls, plates, knives, a pestle and mortar, and a fiddle and bow resting among papers. Herbs, flowers, and vegetables hung from the rafters, giving the room a wholesome, earthy smell. Small lanterns with candles hung from the ceiling too, boosting the light.

Cozy. But crowded.

A large metal pot simmered away on the stove and Ellie moved across the room to ladle stew into wooden bowls. "Take the left seat, and mind Berry on your way around. Her eyesight isn't good and she can't move fast anymore."

Celeste didn't know who Berry was. Lorna had taken up a spot next to the fireplace, sleeping on a dark purple cushion.

Celeste stepped around the back of the furniture and slid herself into the chair. She spotted a very large rat on a cushion half under the table between the chairs. The rat opened one black eye and considered Celeste for a moment, its whiskers twitching, before settling back down. It was as large as Matches, with brown fur going white.

"Is this Berry?" Celeste asked, pointing down at the rat.

Ellie turned back and her face went soft. "Yeah, that's my old girl. We've been together almost since the beginning of all this." She reached for some spoons and handed Celeste a bowl of savory stew with large chunks of meat and vegetables. Ellie sat in the other seat and offered Berry a sniff of the stew. "She was with me before Lorna, and age wears heavier on her little form." Berry took a stewed carrot in her little hands and ate it slowly.

Celeste watched Berry eat for a while before turning to the bowl in her lap. The stew was beef or venison with carrots, onions, and new potatoes. The thick broth was rich with wine and herbs. Celeste was very hungry, but she savored the stew, eating one slow spoonful after another. A little of the chill inside her dissipated while she ate, but it and the pain in her shoulder remained.

This is the first hot food I've had since yesterday. Strange. I almost miss the scones.

Celeste snorted into her bowl and ignored the look that Ellie shot her.

When they were done, Ellie collected their bowls and spoons and set them in a wash basin on the countertop. Then she pulled out a bottle of clear, yellow-ish liquid and poured it out in two, small antique wine glasses. They were made from faceted glass in a shade of amber that merged with the fire.

"We have some time now before you should rest. I imagine that you have more than a few questions that need answering." She took a sip from one glass and handed the other to Celeste. The liquid had a sweet, floral scent. "Elderflower cordial," Ellie commented. "I keep bushes behind the house for the deer and the birds."

"The deer with the golden antlers?"

Ellie's eyebrows raised a fraction. "You saw one?"

Celeste nodded. "I saw three by Mother Birch, and a lot of other strange creatures too: wisps, a big thing hiding behind the trees, shadows."

"A big thing hiding in the trees? A troll, maybe?"

Celeste shrugged. "It was big and had iridescent scales and threw a tree at one of Abram's shadows." She thought for a moment between bursts of brain fuzziness. "And it hissed, or wheezed. Like it had asthma and didn't know where its inhaler was."

"That's…interesting." She took a sip of the cordial. "I don't know the names of every creature on the mountain. Many keep to themselves and only interact with Abram. He is their lord."

"Their lord?"

"Yes, he is the god of shadows and the creatures of the mountain. Even then, most of the creatures don't show themselves when a binding is taking place. It can be dangerous, especially now that Abram is in a more savage state." She sighed and took a long sip of the cordial. "It's been centuries since the mountain went unbound for so long. Even Abram doesn't know what will happen, and his connection to the mountain is *different* from mine."

"You sound like you pity him." Celeste had a hard time keeping the fear from her voice.

"I do pity him. He and I are connected, and I can feel the anger and power flowing through him." Ellie set the glass down and turned in her chair to face Celeste, her long hair flowing over one shoulder. "I suppose Selena didn't tell you about the beginning, because she doesn't know that story. But I will tell you some of it now, if you are interested."

Celeste thought about it for several moments before responding. It was tempting to learn something that even Selena didn't know.

How much will that help you? How much will you even retain tonight? With your brain fuzzy and your nerves shot and being on the edge of your third breakdown in almost as many days?

The information could be useful in the future, but for now, she was focused on surviving and completing the ritual.

"No…not right now."

Ellie's dark eyes went wide in surprise. "I—that was not the answer I expected."

Celeste stared into the fire. "Right now, I just want to live. I'm tired and in pain and so overwhelmed. I don't know that I'd even remember what you tell me in the morning."

"That's pragmatic of you, considering the situation. I would think a scientist would want as much information as possible."

Celeste finally tasted the cordial. It was thick, sweet, and floral, just like its scent, and strong. She rolled it around her mouth, savoring the burn and the sweetness.

Hmm, I could get used to this. Never had a cordial before. It never seemed right to drink one. Like I was drinking wrong.

"I have so much to process right now and I really don't need to add anything else to the queue. I've seen things that shouldn't exist and learned that my family has been hiding secrets and met someone…Nothing makes sense, but…" Celeste paused for a moment. "Well, I don't really care if it doesn't make sense right now. It feels right, and that's why I'm here. I'm exhausted, and my only goal is to finish the ritual and live."

Ellie's eyes narrowed. "And go back to Selena's niece, right?"

Of course she would know about that.

It was Celeste's turn to narrow her eyes. She was exhausted and annoyed by all the questions and the insistence that Ellie knew her better than she did. She let a hint of rising anger seep into her response. "Yes, I'm going back to Marta, too."

Ellie smiled, wry and knowing. "Calm down, I'm not threatening you or her. Marta is a sweet girl and she makes a very good latte. How about this…If you survive, bring Marta up and we can all have a nice chat together. I know she wants the information as much as you do, despite your protestations."

Celeste sighed. "Fine."

Ellie took their empty goblets to the sink. "I think it's time we get to bed. You need your rest and I need to keep an eye out for Abram tonight."

The remaining anger cooled to fear in Celeste's stomach,

mixing with the cordial into a potent cocktail. "What will he do?"

Ellie grinned, showing her teeth. "He can't do much now, not with two shells of sacred salt in him. But he can still command shadows and many of the other spirits on the mountain. Lorna will keep an eye on you, and Berry will keep the hearth safe. There will be patrols until dawn, when Abram's power will wane." She stood and walked to the door where her shotgun was waiting. "The left door is the bathroom and the right door is the bedroom. Sleep well, Celeste."

Ellie was out of the door before Celeste could reply. She heard a lock turn with a metallic clank.

That was abrupt.

Berry got out of her bed and walked over to the fire pit with slow, methodical steps. Once there, she settled down on the flagstones and started to *glow*. The glow spread to the hearth and the fire banked itself.

As if that was her signal, Lorna rose from her spot and stretched a full-body stretch. It was dizzying how large she was. Or maybe that was the fire, or the collected energy she'd spent that day, or something that Ellie had put in her food.

Or I'm just in a perpetual state of being on the edge of a breakdown. Maybe I'm the problem here.

Celeste got up and stumbled to the bathroom to wash her face and teeth and reapply deodorant. She had sweated profusely today and hoped that tomorrow's trek would be easier.

I want a shower so bad.

The bedroom was small and simple. A hand-carved bed, wardrobe, and table took up the bulk of the room. More quilts covered the bed and thick woven rugs covered the floor. Two tiny windows hung high on the walls, too narrow to squeeze through and too high to see out. Celeste wondered if their placement was a safety precaution. The other window in the cabin had curtains drawn over it.

Lorna stretched out at the foot of the bed. Celeste climbed in and curled up, hoping that sleep would replace the dizziness. Somewhere far away a train horn broke the silence of the night. From the bed, Celeste could see the gentle glow from Berry on the hearth. Lorna purred from her spot and the gentle sounds and warm glow led Celeste into a deep and dreamless sleep.

SCRATCH, SCRATCH, SCRATCH, SCRATCH.

Fingernails scratching at wood and glass woke Celeste with a start.

Scratch, scratch, clink.

Scratch.

Scratch.

Riiiip!

A sliver of wood fell from above and bounced on the mattress next to her head. It was as long as her hand and sharp. She was lucky that it hadn't impaled her. She couldn't have done anything if it had: she was paralyzed in the bed.

Lorna was sitting upright, her glowing eyes staring at the windows high on the walls. A deep rumble filled the room.

The scratching stopped and a darkness trickled in through some tiny crack in the wall or from around the window frame.

Celeste watched as it seeped in, coalescing into an opaque cloud. Something moved within the cloud. It sprouted limbs and quivering tentacles that felt for the wall. And when it found it, it started pulling itself down towards Celeste.

She wanted to scream. To launch herself from the bed and cower in the bathroom where there were no windows. But the screams were trapped in her throat and she was still paralyzed beneath the blankets.

Something *vibrated* the house. Pots and pans in the main room clattered and items fell from shelves. The glow from the hearth intensified until Celeste could make out every detail in the room and the cloud that hovered above her.

The cloud was churning and swirling like a storm cloud. Its limbs pulling it down the wall at a slow, steady pace. It had no eyes, but she felt its attention on her. Its intention to slip down the walls and suffocate her while she slept, to seal the fate of Bloom Mountains and Milton.

Time stretched out, seconds lasting hours, as the cloud descended. Once it was only a foot or so from Celeste's face, it stopped and hovered.

Lorna tensed up by her feet.

Somehow Celeste knew that the cloud was not aware of the lion. She felt the lion raise one paw and adjust its weight.

Celeste watched as Lorna pounced on the cloud. The lion slammed into it and the cloud hit the headboard, rattling the bed.

Lorna was standing over Celeste, growling deep in her chest. She raised one paw and hit the headboard where the cloud had landed. She hit it again and again, until there was an audible *pop!* and Celeste was able to move again.

Outside something screamed and Ellie's shotgun roared. Lorna leapt off the bed and bounded out of the room.

Celeste sat up. She could hear footsteps outside and someone speaking low in a language she couldn't understand. Then everything went soft and hazy and she was so tired that she laid down and went right back to sleep.

WHEN CELESTE WOKE THE NEXT MORNING, A COOL LIGHT was sneaking through the window. The only sign that anything had happened in the night was the splinter of wood laying benignly next to the pillow. Lorna was no longer at the foot of the bed and the doors to the bedroom and outside were flung wide open.

Celeste pushed the quilts aside, got up, and stretched. Her phone said it was just about 6:30 in the morning, but it felt like she'd slept for an entire day. She took her bag into the bathroom, scrubbed her face and torso, brushed her teeth again, and dressed in fresher clothing. As she pulled the shirt out, something dropped to the floor: a worn and unraveling mouse toy, the same one that Matches liked to play with. Celeste smiled and tucked the toy into her pocket. It would be another good luck charm for the final phases of the ritual.

While she got ready, Celeste put on the recording from Selena, completely forgotten in the wake of last night's events.

"Step 9: Spend the night at Old Ellie's cabin.

"Ellie is a dear friend of mine and another caretaker of the mountain. She will help tend to your wounds and feed you. She might offer some advice, but it is your decision whether to take it.

"After you have slept and eaten, you'll head west up the slope, through the boulder field, towards the summit. There's one last stand of trees between you and the peak, some of the oldest and tallest trees on the mountain. They are safe."

Celeste snorted at that.

I haven't felt safe in the forest since before I came out here. These woods are alive and filled with hidden creatures. And Abram and his ever-watchful eyes. Celeste looked at herself in the mirror, her eyes wide. *Where did that come from? What ever-watchful eyes am I thinking of?*

After you've spent the night with Ellie, there ain't much left to the ritual. I'll sum it up quickly:

   Step 10: Climb to Bloom Mountain's peak

   Step 11: Burn the effigy at noon and wait for the storm to pass

   Step 12: Return down the mountain by the coal road and don't look back

Celeste listened to the final steps twice to internalize those simple directions. The recording finished playing before Celeste finished in the bathroom.

No one was in the main room when Celeste emerged. Neither Lorna nor Berry were near the hearth, and the only sign that Ellie was around was her shotgun propped against the doorjamb. Celeste slipped on her boots and headed for the door.

The morning was cold and crisp, the dawn a pink tint in the east. Clouds crouched low on the mountain, so close that Celeste might have reached up and pulled a handful down. The bonfire still burned. Berry rested on one seat, enjoying the heat. She made little squeaking noises when she saw Celeste and reached out her front hands, beckoning Celeste to join her.

Celeste did as the rat requested and sat on the stone. Berry snuggled up against her thigh and squeaked appreciatively when Celeste scratched the back of her neck.

Celeste looked around while she ministered to Berry's itchy skin.

The flower gardens extended for 50 yards or so in every direction. Some beds were a single variety of flower while others were a mix of flowers and flowering shrubs. All the flowers were at peak bloom, despite the majority being out of season. The bed closest to Celeste had a type of white and pale yellow daffodil that she didn't recognize. Next to it was a bed of blue poppies, tall purple orchids, fist-sized orange tulips, and pink hydrangea bushes.

Footsteps behind Celeste signaled that Ellie had joined them.

"She's more energetic in the mornings," Ellie said from behind Celeste.

"She started squeaking when I came out the door." Celeste had moved on to a particularly good spot on Berry's back and the rat was in a fit of ecstasy, squeaking in delight.

Ellie entered the cabin and returned a moment later with freshly baked bread and reheated stew. Celeste gratefully took the food and offered a carrot to Berry.

Ellie was wearing dark red pants tucked into high brown boots and a flowing blue shirt with embroidery at the cuffs and collar. Her long hair was in a thick braid down her back.

"Do you have anything you want to ask?"

Celeste sighed. *This again?*

Aloud she said, "Why do you keep asking that? Is this some riddle I am supposed to know the answer to?"

Ellie shook her head. "Just genuine concern on my part. I know we didn't exactly have the best first impressions."

Celeste shrugged and swallowed some stew before responding. "I'm not sure that's true. You did shoot the crazy guy who'd been chasing me for a couple hours. That's a pretty good first impression in my book."

Ellie blinked a couple of times before responding. "I guess that's true. But then I left you to bleed out in the garden while I chased him off."

"Were the cuts that bad?"

Ellie smiled. "Not even close. You were more at risk for infection than bleeding out. But Lorna helped with that before I could properly clean and bandage you. How is it today?"

Celeste rotated her shoulder. She had been going very easy

with it while she got ready. "Stiff and sore. But better than last night."

"Good. Do as little with that as you can for another day and then take off the dressing. It won't be pretty, but it needs to breathe."

"I'll do that. Thank you." Celeste finished the stew and set the bowl down for Berry to investigate. Celeste started on the bread, which was coated with butter and some sort of berry jam. The bread was soft and the jam was sweet, perfect after the savory stew. Berry sat looking at Celeste the same way that her family's dog did when he wanted a portion of whatever someone was eating. She saved the last bit and handed it over to Berry.

"I guess I do have one question," Celeste said, thinking about the night.

"What happened last night?"

Celeste nodded.

Ellie sighed and stared off towards the trees. "Something came out of hiding when Abram was hunting you. I don't know if he woke it or if his shadows did or if it woke when it heard the call."

That's not very specific.

"What was it?"

"Something akin to his shadows, but worse. They don't really act without orders, they don't have the capacity to think for themselves. This, though—it has killed in the past. Back before the ritual first bound the Mountain and made it content..." Ellie trailed off and continued to stare into the distance. Something crossed her eyes and a sad smile tugged at her mouth.

But what about Berry? And the glow? The vibration? Celeste sighed. It didn't seem like she would get full answers now, despite finally having a question to ask. She waited until whatever reverie Ellie was lost to ended. Berry grabbed at her hand, demanding a continuation of the scratches she had gotten before.

After a few minutes, Ellie shook her head softly and looked back at Celeste. She had a soft cloth bag in her hands. "If you don't have any other questions, can I cast the runes for you?"

Celeste furrowed her brow in confusion. "Cast the runes? What does that mean?"

Ellie sat on the adjacent stone and faced towards Celeste. She opened the cloth bag and let a set of pale stones tumble into her hands. They were smooth and shiny with use and sparkled green in the light. She chose a few and held them out to Celeste. "My runes," she said.

The ones she held out were the size of Celeste's thumb with curling symbols carved into one of the two flat sides. No two symbols were the same: antlers, the moon, a cloud, a spiraling flower, a maple leaf. Celeste handed them back to Ellie.

"Is this like a tarot reading?"

Ellie nodded. "They are alike, certainly. But the runes can tell you more than the cards, depending on the situation. They can warn of more specific danger, or give guidance on a path, or tell you what the weather is going to be like. It depends on who the casting is for and what path they are on in life. These are keyed to the mountain."

"What do I do?"

Ellie shook her head. "Nothing hard." She took the small handful of runes in both hands and held them out to Celeste. "Hold them in your hands for a moment and then drop them on the ground when I tell you to."

Celeste took the stones. They were cold and smooth, almost soft against her skin.

Ellie was muttering something under her breath, with one hand hovering above and one hand below Celeste's. The air between the two women grew warm, centered on their hands, but the stones remained like ice. Pressure grew in the air. Behind her, Berry was huddled against Celeste's back, squeaking in rhythm with Ellie's muttering.

The pressure built until Celeste had to pop her ears. In the distance she could hear an echo of Ellie's words.

Then Ellie spoke aloud.

"Now."

Celeste opened her hands, and the rocks dropped to the dirt below.

"Huh," Ellie said, no inflection in her voice.

Celeste looked down and saw that all the runes had fallen with the symbol side up.

"What does that mean?"

Ellie looked up into her eyes. "That hasn't happened before. In all the years I have been casting the runes." She thought for a moment. "But it seems like they are telling you that anything can still happen."

"And Abram?"

Ellie looked back down at the runes and plucked out one with an open, pupil-less eye and held it up for Celeste to see.

"Abram is always watching."

22

THE MEMORIES OF ANCIENT TREES

Celeste and Ellie cleaned up the breakfast and put the cabin to rights. Most of what had rattled free during the night were small bits of crockery, herbs drying on shelves, and an unfortunate glass bowl that had shattered. Amber colored glass shards reflected the morning light, but Celeste still sliced her finger open while collecting the pieces.

It didn't take long for Celeste to gather up her stuff. She fretted over what the runes had told her while she made sure that everything was in her pack.

He has been a constant presence since you started this journey. And he is always watching. He could be in the trees now, waiting for a chance to get his hands around your neck.

She shivered. She had to continue, and Ellie was going to accompany her. At least to the edge of Boulder Hill.

Ellie had cleaned up and changed and now wore a long tunic belted over thick leggings tucked into her high boots. She was dressed in shades of green: pale sage and striking emerald, with touches of subdued brown. She carried her shotgun slung over one shoulder and a walking stick.

They left Berry comfortable in her basket, drowsing after expending her energy overnight. Lorna waited at the western edge of the flower field, keeping a watchful eye on everything.

"Are you ready? There isn't much left." Ellie's words were calm, but there was an undercurrent to them that Celeste couldn't decipher. She sounded worried, for Celeste and for something else, something less tangible than human life.

"If I delay any longer, I don't know if I'll be able to finish the ritual." It was the truth. Tension had continued to build just as the clouds above them came to rest on the mountain top. The atmosphere made it harder to breathe and Celeste took shallow, deliberate breaths with more attention than was normally necessary. She felt more like fleeing now, when she was so close to the end, than she had at any point yesterday. Even when she was being pursued by Abram and his shadows, she had always run forward, looking for the next goal, looking for Ellie's cabin. But now she wanted to turn back.

Why do I want to leave now? Because I'm uncertain what finishing the ritual will actually mean?

But her courage had finally run out. She wanted to go home, wherever that was going to be, and just rest. There was a bone-deep weariness that had settled on her that no amount of caffeine was going to fix.

"Let's go," Celeste said.

She followed Ellie across the colorful garden, wishing she could stop and wander among the beds identifying the flowers she knew and learning the ones she didn't. A brief image of a similar garden came to mind. Her grandmother's blue flower garden, still surviving at the farm. Celeste wanted to visit it again.

But still that thread of anxiety had ahold of her and she kept looking over her shoulders at the far tree line, worried that Abram was watching. He was probably still terrifying, even injured and in daylight. Just the threat of Abram was enough to make her want to flee.

Celeste sighed heavily as they passed Lorna at the edge of the garden, who stood, stretched, and followed.

They crossed a field of long grasses, interspersed with goldenrod. Saplings grew at random among the grass, nothing old enough or interesting enough to really draw attention. They approached a thick stand of sycamore. The tops of their trunks were white from the grey-brown bark peeling away, and the usual detritus of small branches, strips of bark and leaves littered the field as they approached.

"This is an ancient stand of sycamores," Ellie told her. Celeste had no reason to question it—they were immense, towering over everything else she had seen. The leaves she saw on the ground ranged in size from her fist to almost a foot across. "They were here before Abram and I came out of the mist of time. They have seen most of the life of the Valley and they will share it with you, I think."

What does that mean?

Ellie stopped at the first one and pressed her open palm against the trunk. Her shoulders sank and she exhaled sharply. She turned to Celeste. "Come and feel it for yourself."

Celeste approached the twin trunk and placed her hand on the bark. She felt the great age of the tree. It was kith and kin to the sycamore who had sacrificed itself to save her from the creature on the Bloom farmstead. Perhaps the seeds had carried from this ancient tree and planted themselves on the farm so far below. All the sycamore in Yuback Valley could have come from this ancient stand.

But there was something else there too. She felt the shadow of all the ages that the tree had experienced rise and fall. She felt a sharp pain and then long, slow growth. She felt the wisdom in its roots and branches, felt it flow in the sap in its veins.

"Ahhhh," Celeste exhaled aloud.

Then her eyes went wide as flashes of the tree's memories came to her all at once.

A tall sapling stood lonely on the top of a weathered mountain.

Time passed. It felt the tiny roots of its siblings reaching through the earth, the steady trickle of water up its veins. Celeste felt herself stretching upwards towards heat, felt the strange sensation of limbs growing from nothing, the tickle of seeds and leaves sprouting, falling. The cycle repeating.

Then a vibration in the tiny rocks embedded by their roots alerted them to another presence. Something moved among the sapling grove, touching trunks and caressing leaves. Power surged from the figure into the trees, connecting their roots together, merging their collective senses into one consciousness. The presence passed beyond the grove and everything fell silent.

Time passed. The cycle of heat and cold, seeds and leaves continued. Then another presence appeared. Similar to the first, but darker, earthier, more like the creatures that scurried around their bases, little pinpoints of pressure as they climbed their bark and skittered along branches. This presence stopped and shared power too, but nothing perceptible changed for the trees.

Time passed. A third presence appeared, and reappeared through the cycle of seeds and leaves and soft snow and gentle, cool rain.

Time passed. The third presence did not appear in the cycle. Darkness seeped into the water that fed the deepest roots of the grove. Strange sensations foreign to the trees seeped into their hearts and festered like rot. The trees went dormant, one after the other, until the grove stood silent and still.

Time passed. The leaves were falling, the cycle continued while they slumbered. A trickle of power seeped up through the roots, waking the trees. Something, a presence that was familiar in a way, had arrived. Sap and water both moved faster through the trees' veins, through the connected roots. A sensation passed through the collected consciousness.

And then nothing.

Celeste pulled away, freed from the intensity of the memories. She held her hand away from her body, relishing the remnants of the tree against her palm and the tingling memories mingling with her own.

She closed her eyes for a moment, trying to absorb everything she had seen. Everything she had felt. Those few moments were the closest she'd ever had to a religious experience. And there was something else, something that lingered.

"They knew, didn't they?"

"Knew what?" Ellie's voice was perfectly neutral, like she already knew the answer and wanted Celeste to come to it herself.

"The trees knew I was coming. They felt me below the mountain."

Ellie laid a hand on Celeste's shoulder.

"More than that, Celeste. They were calling you home."

THE TRIP THROUGH THE SYCAMORE TREES WAS QUICK AND silent. They stood guard over Ellie, Celeste, and Lorna as the trio passed under their leafy boughs.

Celeste was still dazed by the memories. Of all the things that she had seen and experienced since she entered The

Valley, that communion was the most poignant, the most magical. She had felt and seen and lived as ancient trees did, even if only for a moment, and long years would have to pass before she could forget that gift.

But there was something about it that confused her.

I don't think I ever came to Bloom Mountain as a child, did I? Would I remember when I have forgotten so much? How would the trees know to call for me? And how would that reach me Outside?

Ellie led them on and Lorna kept Celeste from stopping or wandering off to commune with the other trees.

It was a tempting thought, but Celeste hoped that there would be other opportunities in the future. Perhaps she could bring Marta up, by some easier route if possible, and show her the memories. She had the magic of The Valley within her, so maybe she could see them too.

Would she appreciate the experience? Celeste considered that for a few minutes and concluded that Marta probably would. *But you are jumping ahead of yourself…you don't know what the future will hold, or if Marta will even be a part of it.*

They reached the other side of the sycamores too soon for Celeste's liking. She rubbed a hand over the bark of one of the outermost trees, feeling sparks in its core, but she pulled away before it drew her into its thoughts.

Ellie and Lorna were waiting for her on a large, flat rock that stuck a few inches out of the ground. Pale green moss grew up the sides and stretched over the top. Celeste joined them and looked at what lay ahead: the final stretch to the peak of Bloom Mountain.

The path led up a steep hill towards the summit. The clouds were higher now, fluffy and fat, and sunlight peeked through the spaces between. Pale white stones jutted out of tall grass dotted with goldenrod. Tall creatures moved among the grass, carrying boulders and bundles. Celeste wasn't close enough to them to make out what was in the bundles.

"Here we part," Ellie told her. "I cannot step into the field or the trolls will take offense, but they will let you pass."

Trolls? Is that what those creatures are?

Celeste looked over at the woman. She had hoped that maybe Ellie would accompany Celeste to the summit to see that the ritual was properly completed. But another part of her mind told her it was something she had to do alone, that no one but the Binder was allowed at the summit.

"Thank you for the food and shelter and first aid."

Ellie smiled. "You do not have to fear anything now. Just up that slope is the summit, and noon is approaching." Her smile faltered as something behind Celeste caught her eyes. She pointed to their right, to a shadow hidden in the trees not 100 yards away.

"Abram…" Celeste hissed.

A chill rushed down Celeste's spine as his shape appeared out of the shadows. He was as he appeared to her early yesterday morning: an old but ageless man of the mountains, a pipe in his mouth and a walking stick in his hand. Around him darkness roiled, obscuring his form, clinging to the ancient sycamore trees like children on a summer's day.

"Will he follow me?"

Ellie looked down at Celeste. "I don't know. If he were in his right mind, I would say no, he wouldn't break that covenant. But he hasn't been himself for many, many years now. I don't know what the unbound magics would push him to do."

They both looked at Abram. He stood still, surrounded by his writhing shadows, and stared at Celeste. Even from this distance she could feel the dark emotions that engulfed him, the madness that had taken over him. It was unnerving to be the center of such intense attention.

Celeste looked away and took a few timid steps forward, trying to keep herself from staring at Abram as she did so. Lorna followed her, keeping near her right side. Her attention switched from Celeste to Abram and back.

Celeste looked back at Ellie, a question unasked on her lips.

"Lorna is not subject to the same laws as me. She is an animal and she goes where she will, when she will."

Celeste held out a hand to Lorna, who nuzzled it briefly. "I'm glad I won't be alone."

Hopefully she will keep Abram at bay…

"Thank you again, Ellie."

Ellie smiled in return. "Good luck."

Celeste turned and started walking along the path, careful to not step on any loose rocks. Lorna followed, sticking to the softer grass. The first 100 yards were grass and saplings and goldenrod, but then the path turned left and started up the incline.

The first of the trolls waited there, sitting on a rock and basking in the sun. It looked down at Celeste and cocked its head to the side. Deep green eyes like an emerald peered down at her and Lorna, unblinking and unreadable.

"Hello," she said.

I don't think it would fit under a bridge.

Its skin was pale and sparkling like the stone it sat upon, with green and grey and brown marbling. Its torso was as tall or taller than Celeste and was heavily muscled. It was naked, save for a skirt of woven fabric around its waist and a large goat's horn hanging on a leather strip over its shoulder.

Celeste waited several minutes while the troll leaned over and stared at her, its face close enough that she could see the pores in its skin. It had a pleasant earthy smell, like rocks after a rainstorm and fresh spring plants growing in a garden. It breathed shallowly and then started to sniff the air above Celeste.

Finally it relaxed and leaned back on one arm while the other wrestled the horn off its shoulder. It popped something out of the end and brought it to its mouth. Thick lips pressed against the end and Celeste had only a moment to cover her ears.

A long, low call that Celeste could feel in her bones cried out over the mountaintop. It shook the birds out of the trees and rumbled through the stones beneath her feet. After what felt like an eternity, the troll stopped, took another deep breath, and blew the horn again.

Seven times in total the troll blew the horn. After the final blow it set the horn down at its side and listened to the wind. Celeste pulled her hands down, uncertain if they had done much to protect her hearing. Lorna was fidgeting at her own, more sensitive ears, wiping them with a paw. Then she settled down and the three of them waited.

A crow circled overhead and cawed twice before flying off. Far in the distance, almost too low to hear, another horn returned the call seven times. The troll looked down at Celeste with its carved crystal eyes and pointed up the slope.

Did I pass some final test? Approved by possessed trees, a haunted mine, and now trolls. Signed, sealed, delivered: one fool in search of money wins a cursed mountain and a lifetime of nightmares.

Celeste nodded to the troll and wondered if she should leave anything for it. She rummaged in her bag and found a forgotten scone, much battered over her long trek. She unwrapped it and held it up to the creature, hoping it would understand what she was doing.

It cocked its large head to the side again and reached out to delicately take it between two large fingertips. It sniffed the scone, tiny compared to its face, and then popped it into its mouth. Celeste got a glimpse of large pearly teeth. It savored the scone for a moment and then swallowed without chewing. Its crystalline eyes were closed in pleasure.

It reached out one large finger and patted Celeste on her head and then sat back on its elbows and stared up at the sky.

Celeste looked down at Lorna, who was staring back at her with a quizzical expression.

"Let's go, Lorna."

Together Celeste and Lorna walked up the slope, pausing to watch each troll they passed. She gaped at the first standing troll–fully three times her height, with most of that in its long, powerful legs. Another squatted down in front of her and used its fingers to gently twirl Celeste around in a circle. Lorna sat by with a patient, amused look on her feline face.

Some trolls were busy using massive scythes to cut the grass and goldenrod, while others dug small boulders out of the ground and hauled them out of sight. Two that they passed were carrying massive armloads of dried grasses and conversing in low, melodic voices. They were the only ones she passed that spoke, and Celeste yearned to be able to converse with them.

You aren't even good with English, you'll never be able to talk to the trolls.

But, oh, I can dream.

They passed twenty trolls on their way up the slope, which would have taken a fraction of the time, but Celeste kept stopping.

The way they walked and moved was so measured and deliberate and delicate in its own way, despite their size. Their language was strange and beautiful. There were variations in their skin tones that a geologist would have loved to study. Celeste wondered if there were trolls in other parts of The

Valley, or in the other Liminal Worlds. Were there trolls with skin like bark, or sand, or moss, or wheat?

The part of her that was already in love with The Valley overrode the last of her uncertainties. She would stay and visit these trolls and learn the stories of the sycamores and soothe the soul of the hangman. She would learn the name of every tree and bush and flower on the mountain and introduce herself to all who called it home.

You go from wanting to flee to planning to stay in less than an hour. Very in character. Was it the sycamore that convinced you? Or the trolls?

Celeste turned back to watch a troll haul a boulder the size of a car down the slope, heading for wherever they stored them. She drank in the scene with the green grass blowing in the breeze and the pale sparkling rocks and the bright blue sky. Her watch buzzed. It was 11:30 and the summit was just ahead.

Celeste and Lorna left the trolls behind. They clambered over rocks and passed by young trees, and finally came to the peak of Bloom Mountain.

Celeste took a deep breath of chilly mountain air and reached for the leather bag attached to her pack. She didn't need the instructions anymore. There were only four steps left to the ritual: place the effigy on the altar and burn it at noon, wait for the storm to pass, bury the offering at the summit, and then descend the mountain.

But Abram waited down the slopes she would have to tread. And would binding the magic do anything for his madness?

23
PENUMBRA

THE SUMMIT OF BLOOM MOUNTAIN WAS SMALL AND teardrop shaped. There was a flat grassy area where Celeste and Lorna stood that tapered to a point where a large grey stone jutted out over the mountainside. There were only 20 feet or so from end to end.

Celeste and Lorna walked the perimeter.

She looked over the edge and saw the steep sides of the mountain, covered in gravel and dotted with stunted trees growing at improbable angles. It was a long way down. Celeste stayed a few steps in from the edge and actively tried to avoid looking over it again.

The stone on the far side of the peak was on a slight incline, making the unsupported tip the highest elevation on Bloom Mountain. It was smooth except for a small indent blackened by fire. The currents of magic pulled everything towards the stone. They swirled around the stone, lapping at the sides like waves, only to leap up and swirl in a vortex that drained down to that small, blackened spot.

This was the altar.

Celeste had the bag of ritual items in her hand. It was almost empty. The brandy bottle sat at the bottom of her pack, along with the little metal cup and Marta's handwritten directions. The candle stub was resting at Coal Mine Number 3 with its fellows. All that remained were the effigy and the book of matches.

There is no turning back now. You've made it to the summit and you're still intact. Your conflicting emotions about staying are moot now because you are going to bind this mountain today, and probably many more times in the future.

Celeste took a deep breath and pulled the effigy out.

It was a small doll of dried straw bound and dressed in yarn. It had tiny feet and hands, braided hair, and an elaborate outfit of colorful yarn. Celeste caressed it, sorry that such a small thing must burn. She wondered who made the doll and who had spun and dyed the yarn to make the outfit. Was it Sarah and Hannah? Or another of their family? So much care and skill went into such a small thing, and it was going to be destroyed.

Celeste sighed. It was for their benefit, their protection. They all knew that the mountain was their savior or their destroyer. It all depended on uncertainties like the breakability of hips and the naivety of Outsiders lured in by hope and desperation. She smiled and snorted a laugh. The people of Milton were hardy and strong and continued on in the face of near certain death. Of course they would put everything into a ritual item to keep themselves safe and the mountain sated.

Celeste's watch started vibrating. 11:50. Ten minutes until noon.

Where did the morning go?

She set the straw doll down on the altar and placed the matchbook in her pocket. She continued her circuit and then investigated the center of the rounded portion of the summit. There were a series of three concentric circles made of stones, the largest in the center and smaller ones in the two outside circles. Whatever was left on the altar after the storm passed would need to be buried in the center of the stone ring.

Lorna had settled herself near the altar and watched Celeste as she paced around, looking at the tiny buttercups and daisies that grew among the low grass around the stones. She wondered if the trolls tended this place as well as their slope, something to add to her growing list of questions. Some would be answered soon.

What is the storm? What will be left over after the storm?

Will Abram attack on our way down the mountain? Or will the binding cure his madness?

Will Marta be there to pick me up? Does she feel something—anything—for me?

What will binding the mountain mean for me? For the future?

Celeste let those questions swirl around in her head and went to stand next to Lorna and look out over The Valley.

The summit faced due west. To her left, south of Bloom Mountain, was Lighthouse Lake and distant Blue Mountain. Below her the river wound through the forest, accompanied by the Valley Express train tracks, to eventually empty into the lake. It was easier to see the winding path the Nomini took from above.

To her right, far to the north of Milton and Bloom Mountain, Celeste could see the low haze of a metropolis blotting the skyline. It wasn't as pronounced as the smog that covered the DC Metro area, but she thought that people here would be more environmentally minded. If they didn't, Celeste had no doubt that the environment would fight back with a ruthlessness that would shock anyone from Outside, herself included.

If just one mountain can cause so much damage, what would happen if the whole Valley were to fight back?

Ahead of her, so close she could almost reach out and touch them, was a ridge of mountains a little shorter than Bloom Mountain. There was a fire watch tower, so tiny to her eyes, that perched halfway down the ridge. Beyond those was a wide stretch of sunlit farmland and rolling hills dotted with towns and forests. The highway she'd seen several days before was large and stretched from north to south outside of her range of vision. Beyond the edge of the Valley stretched dark blue-brown mountains far into the distance.

The Valley, in all of its strange and glorious beauty, stretched out before her from horizon to horizon.

Celeste noticed the world was darkening. The shadows of the mountain ridge lengthened over the forest and Lighthouse Lake.

What's the odds that this is a coincidence?

Above her a shadow was crossing the sun. She watched the shadow stretch over the land as the moon began to eclipse the sun. A part of her mind, disconnected from everything else, wondered whether Elise was watching the sky in Charlottesville. She was an astronomer doing research and teaching at the University of Virginia and they had watched many together over the years. Always with protection for their eyes.

I hope that you see this too, big sister.

Her watch buzzed again.

11:59. Only one minute until noon.

Celeste stepped forward and pulled the matchbook from her pocket. She watched as the seconds ticked away and crouched over the altar stone, a match tucked between the two folds of the matchbook.

Time slowed as the final ten seconds passed, until at last, there was only one left and Celeste pulled the match, lighting the head. She dropped the match on the little straw doll, which lit as though it was soaked in oil. A whoosh of air and the stench of burning straw caused Celeste to scramble back next to Lorna. She watched as flames licked across the doll, burning straw and yarn alike.

Step 11: Burn the effigy at noon and wait for the storm to pass

The doll burnt to ash just as the shadow of the moon fully eclipsed the sun.

In that same disconnected part of her brain, Celeste knew it was probably an annular eclipse—it was dark, but not as dark as night. She only knew that because Elise had flown out West to watch one with Celeste when she was working out there. She knew that a ring of solar fire surrounded the moon's shadow now, but she would not risk her sight to see it.

Celeste felt Lorna tense up beside her. Something changed in the atmosphere and a bright, silvery light seeped out of the altar stone, growing in intensity as they watched.

A quiet rumble surrounded Celeste. A clacking of stone on stone grew as the summit started to tremble beneath her feet. First as a gentle vibration. Then it grew stronger, faster.

Celeste braced herself with both hands and leaned into Lorna's sturdy frame. Rocks dislodged themselves from the edge and tumbled down the mountainside; birds took flight from trees below the peak. The glow transformed into a pillar of light that burst from the altar stone and shot into the sky. It formed a direct line from the altar to the eclipsed sun that Celeste felt more than she saw.

Once it made contact, the world exploded.

Celeste was pulled to the ground by a force so great that

her bones should have broken. She watched as silver rain fell on the world, drenching her down to her soul, where it burned like acid. She wanted to cry out in pain as something wrapped around her insides, coiling like a snake that had slipped under her skin, but she was mute and paralyzed. The acid burned her bones and the snake curled tightly in her chest, squeezing all breath from her lungs in a soundless, wheezing cry.

The last of the air left her body, but she couldn't take another breath.

Celeste felt as the world around her changed. The ground beneath her heaved, the grass squirmed and vining plants grew over her still body as she stared unblinking at the sky where the moon had paused. Shadows blanketed the mountain and stars peeked out of the eternal void, their twinkling mixing with the silver rain as it continued to fall on Celeste, blisters forming on her skin with every drop.

Time had no meaning for Celeste while the world around her writhed and the snake coiled in her and the acid rained and the magic of Bloom Mountain was being bound again. She could feel the magic resist at first, not wanting to be contained. It wanted to be free, to wreak havoc, no matter who or what was caught up in it. It wanted to punish those who had confined it and all who had helped.

The spirit at the heart of the mountain was waking from its long slumber.

Celeste's mind filled with images of Milton in rubble, the sycamore forest burning, the golden deer and the wisps and the shadows and the serpentine giant hiding for fear of the mountain's wrath. Celeste felt the soul of the mountain, felt the anger and the pain and the hatred that it harbored there. It was like the Hangman's soul, but old, stronger, far more powerful.

The spirit was gathering the magic of the mountain to it, summoning the strength to awaken, to break through its physical and spiritual bounds and reclaim its place as ruler of The Valley.

Celeste watched and felt everything the spirit felt, yet she could do nothing to help. She couldn't call out to the raging soul around her. She was breathless. Squirming, yet paralyzed. The snake in her chest slithered, reaching out to the furthest corners of her being while the rain burned pathways in her soul and mind.

Celeste watched and felt as the spirit raged against its frayed bindings, the last remnants of the decade-old binding done by Selena. Celeste saw images of the old woman lying wounded on the Stairwell and the confusion the spirit felt. She watched as it sent Abram through secret pathways, jumping from shadow to shadow, and Ellie ran down the mountain with Lorna at her side and Berry on her shoulder. The protectors and the spirit caring for Selena when she needed it most.

The spirit dug into Celeste's own mind, ripped memories of the last few days to the fore. It watched as the baristas at Witch Peak smiled and laughed with each other, as Celeste and Marta ate pie together at Jed's. Saw Matches run screaming through the apartment. It followed them as they visited the Mennonites, looked at the ewes, at the Stormwalker handing its blessing to Celeste. It saw the farmhouse where Celeste grew up, the bedroom unchanged after 20 years.

The spirit tore her mind apart, bared her soul to itself. It dragged out each of Celeste's emotions. It saw the pain and wonder and fear and uncertainty. Caressed the tender feelings Celeste nurtured for Marta and Matches, her respect for old Selena. Felt her changing attitude towards Milton and its people. How she went from dismissive to protective in only a couple of days. How she was still hurting from the past, but hopeful about the future.

And that reminded the spirit of the old days, when it was

calm and peaceful, when it bestowed good luck and protection on those who lived in its shadow. It saw the images of its creatures hiding, dying at the hands of its magic, and paused. The spirit stopped fighting for a moment and looked and *remembered*. It searched through Celeste's memories again, saw what it had already done. And then it remembered that it had already hurt its people, killed people, driven them away from the mountain that called them its children.

And the spirit felt shame.

Celeste wasn't prepared for the soul-wrenching sob she felt ripple through the magics that made up the mountain, that caused the rocks on the summit to tremble even more. The spirit cried out in sorrow and shame. It shook the mountaintop and then calmed and shrank behind the bonds that were wrapping around it again, like a mother soothing a crying child.

It shrank further and further down into the heart of the mountain, feeling more calm and content, realizing that being bound was what it *wanted*, what it *needed* to thrive. It was strong, and powerful, and destructive. Without the bonds upon it, it would destroy everything in Yuback valley and be incapable of creating it again. The binding made it capable of creation, of caring, of love. And the spirit wanted something to tend, something to watch grow and thrive, something to love. And it wanted to feel that love in return.

Celeste felt that the spirit of Bloom Mountain was a deity of The Valley, tended to by Abram and Ellie and all the spirits that lived on and below it. A symbiotic relationship with the people of Milton let it thrive. And it knew that in being free, it would have had to die. And the death of Bloom Mountain would have broken cracks in the magic that protected The Valley from the Outside world.

Tears filled Celeste's unblinking eyes as the moon moved again, slipping off the sun, and light filled the world once again.

Celeste didn't see it, couldn't feel the warmth on her skin. She watched as the spirit of Bloom Mountain was bound once more by its own magic. And in the last moment of the ritual, when all the magic was drawn together, Celeste felt a tendril reach out to her, to the snake coiling in her breast. She felt the touch of the spirit of Bloom Mountain and serenity and love as the magic settled into her, rushing through her veins, filling her mind with visions of the verdant valley below, healed now by the magic that had threatened it.

Celeste was suddenly back on the peak, released from the spirit of the mountain and its magic.

She cried out as the pain blocked her vision and rocked her body. She spasmed and felt Lorna lay over her torso, trying to prevent her any further harm.

Celeste sank into slumber as the sun shined down upon her. The magic of Bloom Mountain rushed through her body, filling every hidden corner with love and power while the snake in her chest coiled itself tight into a ball and rested.

24

THE DESCENT

A ROUGH TONGUE ON HER HAND WOKE CELESTE. SHE opened her eyes to pastel colored clouds floating above in the cobalt sky. Lorna was beside her, a look of feline concern on her face that relaxed as Celeste stirred. She pulled herself up into a seated position and promptly vomited.

Her whole body was sore from the force that had pulled her to the ground and then rent her soul asunder. A ghost of the pain that had knocked her out remained. And the creeping feeling of *something* inside her lingered. It was under her skin, in her veins, crusted to her throat. Those feelings made her vomit again.

Her head felt clearer, the pain dimmed, and the feeling of the *snake* inside her body settled into an occasional, dull twitch. Celeste pushed herself back, away from where she'd been sick, and slowly stood up rubbing her head.

Ugh, that was one of the worst experiences of my life. Fuck, I really hope it doesn't feel like that every time.

"Wow," she gasped when she finally looked around.

The peak had undergone changes while Celeste lay paralyzed on the ground, wrapped up in the mind of the spirit of Bloom Mountain. The grass was now up to her knees and oversized sunflowers were abundant, their faces turned towards the uncovered sun.

Behind her saplings had grown near the far edge and the whole of the summit was overgrown, except for the area circled by stones.

The altar stone was clear once again; no ash from the straw doll remained, but something was in its place. Celeste waded through the tall grass to retrieve the item. It was a large, dark brown seed, the size of her thumb. It didn't look like any seed she had ever seen before but she picked it up and walked it over to the circles of stones.

The center was a bare patch of dark, almost black earth a foot across. Celeste knelt, Lorna peering over her shoulder, and shoved her free hand into the earth. It was soft and damp, giving easily to her scooping. She dug down six inches and then gently placed the seed in the hole and covered it with the dislodged soil.

"I don't know what you will grow into, but may you grow tall and strong."

Celeste stood and stretched, admiring the wild greenery around her. Her joints loosened but still held on to the sore-ness. She held out her hands to feel the tops of the plants as she walked to the edge of the summit and hopped down.

Below her the mountainside had taken on the garb of autumn. The grasses were fading and turning brown, the saplings wore red and gold and brown upon their brows, the wildflowers were wilting. The scent of falling leaves filled the air and one brushed against Celeste's shoulder and landed on Lorna's back. The lioness shook it off with dignity.

It's so quiet and empty now. Like everything is asleep.

They followed the trail back down Boulder Hill, seeing no

trolls on their way. Celeste had wanted to see them again, to admire their quiet strength and beauty, the seamless way that they fit into the landscape. But there would be other trips to the summit. For now, she needed to find her way down the mountain. Selena's instructions had said that there was an old back road down the mountain from near Ellie's cabin.

Celeste looked for the currents of magic, the trail that she had followed from the Old Oak Tree. It was barely a sparkle, a glint of light off falling leaves and pale, peeling bark.

Even the path is quiet, I can feel it but it's only a tingle in my brain. Like the mountain reclaimed the magic. Maybe it wasn't something in me after all. I don't know if that makes me feel better or worse.

They continued on, seeing no sign of life, but enjoying the chill in the air and the autumnal colors that had settled like a shroud on Bloom Mountain. They passed through the ancient sycamore grove and found the trees bare. Celeste placed a hand against a tree and felt it in a deep, restful sleep, preparing for the coming year.

Once they exited the grove, Lorna turned right and headed down the tree line. Celeste turned to follow, trusting that the lioness knew where she was going. The path sparkled along-side her, reassuring Celeste that the magic had not abandoned her with the binding of the mountain. They walked in silence, the quiet sounds of the slumbering forest a gentle companion. At the end of the sycamore trees, they found a battered metal sign with faded paint that said: *COAL MINE NO. 3.*

Lorna sat for a minute, breathing heavily. Celeste gently scratched the back of her neck. She set her pack down and pulled out the cup she'd used the previous day to drink at the giant's grave. It wasn't very large, but she filled it with water and offered it to Lorna. The lioness took her time sniffing the cup, but accepted the water in it.

"Sorry, Lorna, it's been kind of a morning for both of us."

The lioness looked up at her and slow blinked. "But it's almost over now. Just gotta get down the mountain and it's done."

She stared at the sign for a moment.

"I don't know what comes after that, but everyone should be safe for a year at least. And that means I have time to figure out what I'm going to do with my life."

And soon I will find out what, if anything, is between Marta and I. Will this little infatuation last longer than a week? A month? Will it blossom into something more?

Lorna stood and leaned into Celeste's leg while she was talking. Celeste drank some water as well and looked down at the lioness. The cup was empty and the lioness had water dripping down her face.

"Are you ready to go?"

Lorna snorted in response and leapt forward onto the old mine road down the mountain.

Step 12: Return down the mountain by the coal road and don't look back

THE ROAD WAS A WIDE, SMOOTH PATCH OF SOFT GRASS, hiding tracks where wagons once climbed to the peak. Stones from the summit had rolled down to rest on the road and fallen trunks were a common obstacle for them to climb over. But instead of being a chore, Celeste found it pleasant.

This is easier to deal with than magic and monsters. Even if my body feels like it fell down the mountain.

Celeste wondered, after only a few minutes walking, why there was a road for the mine up to the summit. Maybe at some point there had been an auxiliary entrance or exit for the mine on the summit. Or maybe there had been an easier route from the mine to the road down the mountain.

The road wound around to the left with a gentle slope. Celeste and Lorna made quick progress and soon were around the bend and skirting the south face of the mountain. In places the slope was steeper, but Lorna had no problems keeping her balance. Celeste had a little trouble with her knee. It shook and threatened to give out, but the poles mitigated most of Celeste's worries.

In a little under an hour they were looping around the eastern side of the mountain. Celeste started seeing birds and hearing animals in the surrounding woods. At one point, three of the golden deer, two does and one stag with large antlers, jumped across the path, heading up the mountain. One of the does stopped to stare at Lorna, and some sort of communication passed between the two animals because she was not afraid.

I wonder if that was the same group from last night…

Further along Celeste saw a blue heron wading in a small pond, looking for fish. It ignored the two of them in its quest for food.

It was a beautiful, sunny autumn day. The first of many to come. Celeste hummed as she walked and daydreamed about a long, hot bath and soft, clean clothes.

And then I need to start seriously thinking about the future.

Would she stay in DC and enjoy the benefits of city living as she had for the last five years? Sure, it had abundant stores, coffee shops, and restaurants serving every type of food imaginable. The Mall with the Smithsonian museums and the National Zoo were frequent haunts for her. It was nice to have all that so close, and she could just make the trek out to Milton every year for the binding. It wasn't very far.

But, then again, the city was loud and polluted and there

wasn't much in the way of nature or privacy. And there were so many people so devoted to the grind. And what if she couldn't find another job doing what she loved? She could probably find a contractor position somewhere else, but her mental state would probably just devolve further.

You forgot what silence sounded like after being in the city for so long. And you know you belong out here among tall trees and ancient mountains. Where people are fewer and further between and you can just breathe without worrying about getting everything right all the time. You can think without second guessing yourself.

And it was at this moment that Celeste realized she had finally broken out of the haze that had settled on her life. Out here with nature and mysteries to solve and people that might come to care for her, and not for what they thought she could do for them. Celeste was finally free of the malaise that had almost drowned her.

There is so much to consider, but I think I will do what I can to move out here, find some sort of stable job and do the Binding every year.

She placed a hand against her sternum, just over where the magic pooled. She could still feel it in her veins and deep in her bones, but she was starting to get used to the feeling. Bloom Mountain was now a part of her.

Celeste enjoyed the easy walk with Lorna's silent company. They passed over streams that gurgled down the mountain, across small fields of wildflowers, under trees covered with autumn foliage. She could feel the currents of magic all around them, could feel the spirits in the forest watch her as she passed. Soon enough she would have the chance to come up here and seek them out, meet them, learn their secrets.

Once they crossed back onto the north face of the mountain, Celeste saw the ruins of buildings on the slope in the distance. There were dozens of small wooden buildings set on a grid pattern with two larger stone buildings presiding over them. It looked like the mining camp or town for Coal Mine Number 3.

If it's for the mine, then why is it so far from the entrance? Were there more entrances before the collapse?

Celeste walked for ten more minutes before she reached the remnants of the wooden wall around the town. A section of the wall had fallen to allow her entrance.

There were wide wooden walkways between the houses and the two stone buildings to keep the residents out of the mud. Many of the beams were cracked or rotted now and Celeste had to pick her way carefully or risk falling through and hurting herself. Her ankle was still sore from being rolled yesterday and she didn't want to injure it further. Four rows of rotting houses stood on one side of pristine, green lawn that stretched across town from one stone building to the other. And another four rows were between the lawn and the far side of town.

There was a melancholy atmosphere to the ruins that was only emphasized by the pervasive smell of rot. The magic of the mountain was tainted here, like the farmstead and the Ledge, and Celeste could feel it like an oily film against her skin. The currents trickled through the town, along the walkways, but most had turned away at the gate, preferring to go around the perimeter.

Celeste and Lorna crossed town as quick as possible, avoiding stone buildings and wooden houses alike.

She was almost to the far fence when she felt the hairs on her arm stand on end and a creeping sensation down her spine. She stopped and focused, looking for the source. The last house before the fence sucked in the trickle of magic that wound through the town. Celeste stood, watching with whatever sense could see the magic and considered if she should investigate further.

You did say you wanted more mysteries to untangle.

Celeste sucked in a breath and concentrated harder. The magic was brighter to her vision, sparkling through the walls of the house. She could feel an absence of magic inside, despite it drawing the current inside. But it felt nothing like the ichor monster from the farm; it didn't feel like a creature, more like just a *thing* that happened and started to suck up the magic.

There must be some sort of…magic black hole in there. And that's why the rest of the currents are avoiding it. Like they are sentient or something.

Ah, yes, sentient magic. How far you've come in this last week.

"Whatever's in there, your time is coming to an end." She called out. "I don't have time for you today, but I'll be back soon." She stopped concentrating and rubbed her forehead where a headache was brewing.

I'll come back later with Ellie or an exorcist and some holy salt or water, or whatever works on magical voids. Then we can deal with it. Right now I just want a bath.

Her feet were reluctant to move at first and she could feel the void tugging at the magic in her veins. It was gentle, sweet, insidious, promising more if she just came closer, just crossed the threshold and allowed herself to be consumed. *There is infinite magic where I lead*, it sang to her. *Infinite magic and infinite understanding…*

"Stop that shit!" she yelled. The force that had kept her stationary released and Celeste almost fell over. "Gods, fuck this mountain. It needs a babysitter, not a Binder. Let's go, Lorna."

The building seemed to sulk as she passed by it and turned to follow the fence. They had to climb over fallen posts to get out of town. The road resumed by the rotted and ruined gate and carried on down the mountain.

Soon after, Celeste got her first view of the Bloom Farmstead. She was approaching the same slope she had climbed to start the trail. In the distance she could just glimpse the brilliant yellow of the birch trees that guarded the path. She picked up her pace and Lorna leapt ahead of her. A stretch of trees was all that stood between them and the start and end of the trail. They passed through them quickly; Celeste didn't stop to observe the variety or age of the trees or admire the colors they now wore.

I'm almost there…

They broke through the far side and Celeste stumbled down the slope. She slowed down, set her feet firmly on the ground and descended. Once at the bottom, Celeste stopped to catch her breath on the rock that marked the trail. While she rested, Lorna raced across the fields without her, causing birds to take flight and seek the safety of the trees. Celeste watched the lioness slow and come to a stop where two figures were standing by the ruins of the old barn.

25
THE THREE

ELLIE AND ABRAM STOOD BY THE FALLEN SYCAMORE TREE, their backs to Celeste, bickering. Abram's presence set her on edge—she didn't want to approach until she knew that he would not attack her again. He had done little to still her very rational fears.

How deep did his madness run?

Celeste stopped on the far side of the house to observe them. The shadows no longer held the same disgusting sensations of the previous morning. Nothing lurked in the ruins of the barn and the only creatures that she felt were animals. Birdsong filled the air and a squirrel stopped mid-run to place a little hand on Celeste's ragged boot. It focused on something in one of the small trees between the house and an ivy-covered shed. Its bushy brown tail twitched twice and then it ran off, chattering, and leapt onto the tree trunk.

"It's so quiet and yet so loud," Ellie commented. "I can feel dormant seeds waking in these fallow fields. The animals have returned and the descendant of the great groundhog has taken up her throne once again. That *creature* is well and truly gone."

"She was a child, Ellie. She had no concept of what was happening to her, what her father subjected her to. But now she is at peace. And the curse's hold has lessened, for the first time," Abram replied, his voice emotional and serious.

She peeked around the corner and saw that he stood side-by-side with Ellie, one arm in a sling while the other gently scratched Lorna's soft ears.

"This is a new era for Bloom Mountain, and for us, Abram." Ellie looked at him as she spoke.

"It is, Ellie. It really is," he responded, his voice soft.

Celeste got the distinct impression that she was overhearing a conversation not meant for human ears. Something passed between the two and Lorna looked over at Celeste and blinked slowly. A gentle wind rippled through the leaves of the fallen sycamore. A board broke loose from the ruins of the barn and fell to the ground with a *thunk*.

The *thunk* broke the spell of serenity.

Abram spoke again, his voice full of mock indignation and humor, sounding more like the Abram that Celeste had met on the slopes. "Blessed salt. Moon-blessed salt, Ellie. Do you know how long this will take to heal? I will feel the burning until I dig every last crystal out of my flesh!"

Ellie's voice was calm and amused. "If you hadn't held Celeste up, then you wouldn't have gotten an arm full of salt, Abram. This," she responded, pointing at his arm. "This is your fault."

"I was just having a bit of fun with her!"

Celeste crept out, feeling that the time was right to make her presence known. "I wasn't having any fun," she said aloud, startling the two.

Abram turned towards her, a broad smile on a youthful version of his now-familiar face. His hair was dark and thick. He wore the same nondescript clothing as when they first met and leaned on his walking stick. His left arm was in a sling. There was something different about him now, a feeling that Celeste had picked up in their first meeting, but still couldn't place. It was familiar but strange and confusing. Something that he had said the day before and she'd forgotten tickled at the back of her mind.

Ellie turned to face Celeste as well. Her dark skin and hair had a glow to them that hadn't been there only a few hours ago. Lorna too was vibrant, and in Ellie's arms Berry squeaked with newfound vitality. The grey hairs in the rat's coat were darker now and the film covering her eyes was less opaque than that morning. She squeaked happily at seeing Celeste.

Ellie stepped up beside Abram and together they bowed low to Celeste.

"What's this about?"

Together, Abram and Ellie held out their right hands. They started to glow and thin tendrils of light, brown for Abram and gold for Ellie, snaked out of their hands towards Celeste. She held still while her own torso started to glow a deep green, like pine needles in deep winter. The gold and brown and green twined together, wrapping themselves into a braid of light. It detached from their hands and sank into Celeste's chest. She felt nothing from the contact.

"Who *are* you two?"

Abram turned to Ellie, and something passed between the two. Celeste felt something in the atmosphere change, like a storm approaching. The world expanded and contracted and then righted itself again, all in the space of a breath.

Ellie turned back to Celeste. "We are spirits given flesh. Summoned out of the Lands Beyond to serve the spirit of Bloom Mountain."

Abram picked up where she left off. "We keep the people and creatures of Bloom Mountain safe. When the curse was laid on the mountain, and the binding ritual was necessary, we aided those who would keep the mountain content." His voice resumed that strange otherworldly quality that made Celeste's skin crawl.

Celeste rolled her eyes. "You have a funny idea of helping, Abram, God of the Mountain."

Abram's eyes went wide and he laughed. "It was not an incorrect statement, Celeste Foster. We *are* gods compared to the usual spirits of The Valley. In time, you will forgive me."

Celeste pursed her lips and raised an eyebrow. "I don't think that time will come soon." She turned to Ellie for her answer.

"Abram and I are two aspects of Bloom Mountain, and now you are the third. You are now as important to it and the health of the land as we are. You will feel the mountain in your soul until another binds themselves to the spirit, or you die. It will let you know when it needs something and in time you will understand it as well as you understand yourself."

That's assuming I understand myself a lot better than I do.

Celeste nodded. The explanation made sense to her now. She contained a measure of Bloom Mountain's power, a measure of its curse. Without the binder, the curse spread and the magic grew unstable. And when the magic was unstable, did that make the three of them unstable?

No, only Abram was unpredictable and dangerous. Ellie and Selena seemed perfectly normal, if strange, because of their magics. Something must have affected him more.

"I have a question."

Ellie turned towards the distant tree across the driveway. "I think we have time for that." She turned to Abram for confirmation, and he nodded.

"If you are both connected to the mountain, why did you seem less affected by the curse?"

Ellie looked to Abram, who shrugged with his good shoulder at something only the two of them understood.

"Ellie is more human and not as connected to the other spirits of the mountain as I am," Abram responded. "She is more like our warden. She keeps the spirits and creatures from harming the humans down in town. I am closer to the spirits and the creatures than I am to the humans. And that…*affects* me in ways that are unpredictable."

"So you didn't realize you were hunting down the person trying to make you sane again?" Celeste was still angry with Abram. And still scared of him.

"You might have avoided that by being a bit more open when we met," Abram countered, a smile on his face. "And by following the directions better."

Celeste opened her mouth to respond, but Ellie spoke first. "Well, now I think it's time for us to part ways."

Abram held out a small woven bag. "Take this," he said.

Celeste took the soft bag in her hands. There were two small, hard objects inside.

Ellie continued. "Find a private area and call one of us by name three times and we will come."

Abram chuckled. "Or the cat will come if we are busy."

Lorna looked up at him with a feline look of boredom. She stood and stretched and padded over to Celeste. Lorna butted her knee with her large head and Celeste scratched her ears with her empty hand. Lorna sat down heavily and started purring.

"It looks like you've made a friend," Abram said, his tone mild.

Celeste whipped her head up to look at him. His words were familiar, hauntingly so. But she couldn't place them.

Ellie smiled. "I think your ride is here, Celeste." She pointed towards the end of the drive. "As I said last night, sometime in the future bring Marta up the mountain and I'll tell you both everything. There is so much more than Selena ever wanted to know. Take Marta up the back way and Lorna will meet you."

Celeste stood, patted Lorna one more time, and looked where Ellie continued to point: a car had just pulled up and two people got out. One clearly was Marta, her pale skin and black hair highlighted in the sun. The other was hidden from view, but Celeste had a sudden feeling that she knew who it was.

"I have to go," she said, feeling tears welling up in her eyes.

Celeste slid between the two spirits or gods, not hearing their responses. She didn't say a further farewell to Lorna or Berry, but she hoped that they would forgive her.

The distance between the house and the fallen trunk felt like a mile as Celeste first walked and then picked up the pace to run, ignoring the aching in her body. Tears streamed down her face: from relief, from joy, from hope. The trunk grew larger and larger in her sight, her calves burning as she ran, her ankle groaning in its wrap, wiping a hand across her eyes every ten or twenty steps.

Celeste rounded the trunk and flew into her sister's waiting arms.

"Eellliiiiissssseeee" she cried, tears streaming down her face.

Elise was taller than Celeste, and she was used to wrapping her long arms around her younger, smaller sister. Celeste cried into Elise's shoulder, and Elise murmured as she ran the fingers of one hand through the hair on the top of Celeste's head.

Eventually the tears ran dry and Celeste backed away.

"What are you doing here, Elise? You should be in Charlottesville!"

"I got a call from Mom yesterday, saying that I needed to

meet her in Gainesville. That there was something we needed to discuss and that we had somewhere to go." Elise wiped tears from her own face. "Said it had to do with you and our grandparents and what happened when we were kids." She put one hand on Celeste's cheek. "And so I came for you, little sister."

They embraced again and Celeste saw Marta over Elise's shoulder. She gave Celeste a small, shy smile. There were shadows under her eyes and a tightness to the set of her mouth. She looked nervous.

Celeste smiled at Elise as she extracted herself from the hug. Elise winked at her, hidden from Marta's view.

Celeste walked around her and stopped in front of Marta. She reached out with her good arm for Marta, felt the soft, cool skin of her arm as she unwound it from her torso. A shy smile crossed her face. Suddenly Celeste felt awkward, didn't know what to say.

"Hey," Marta said.

"I came back down the mountain to you," Celeste said, the words tumbling out of her mouth before she had the chance to think them through.

"T-to me?" Marta asked.

"Thinking of you kept me going when…" She trailed off, unsure how much to share with Marta, or Elise. "Well, when it got rough." It sounded lame and Celeste felt herself flush with embarrassment. She didn't really know what to do to break the embarrassed silence that she and Marta had lapsed into.

Behind her, Celeste heard the car door open and Elise call out. "Just kiss already! We've got places to go."

Marta laughed and relaxed her stance, moving closer to Celeste.

Celeste's face burned. But she moved her hand up Marta's arm to her shoulder. She leaned in, still uncertain if Marta felt the same for her. Still uncertain if there was something there to go on in the future. Uncertain, even, what her own feelings were. But being near Marta was enough to lighten the burden of that uncertainty.

Marta smiled, a broader smile with a hint of something else. "Just kiss me already," she whispered.

And Celeste did just that.

26

FAMILY

Celeste sat in silence as Marta drove them away from the Bloom Farmstead. She was exhausted, but buzzing with anxiety and excitement.

I did it. I really did it; I bound Bloom Mountain.

In the front seats, Elise and Marta shared quiet words and occasionally glanced at Celeste.

Looks like they are already getting along well.

"Is there something on my face?" Celeste asked between mouthfuls of a sandwich Marta'd brought. The toasted bread had gone soggy after however long it'd sat steaming in the bag; ham, cheese, and spicy sauce were still good.

Elise turned to face Celeste. Her large, dark eyes and round face were still a sight for sore eyes. They had always been close, but Celeste felt warmth and love welling up in her heart now. She turned away from the eye contact and out the window. They were passing through the forest on the road that hugged the base of Bloom Mountain.

"People are waiting for us at the farm."

Celeste closed her eyes and took a deep breath. "I guess I

should've expected that. We were there a couple of days ago." She nodded her head to Marta in the seat in front of her. "Elise, did you know Mom has a twin?"

"I found out about the sister last night, but Mom didn't share any details. They wanted to wait…just to make sure. Selena sent us to retrieve you and go to the farm."

So Mom knew about the mountain, about what I was going to do.

Marta snaked an arm behind the driver's seat and shook her hand, getting Celeste's attention. Celeste reached out and Marta squeezed her hand when she found it. That little bit of contact reassured her, even though Marta hadn't said a word.

Celeste pulled out Abram and Ellie's parting gift: a bag made of loose, coarse fabric, closed with a living vine. The vine curled around Celeste's finger as she gently pried the bag open. Inside was a charm, two small stones drilled through and strung on thin cord. One side of each was carved.

An open eye.

A shining star.

Abram and Ellie.

Celeste slipped the cord over her wrist and marveled as it twisted closed. It clung close, but comfortable, against her left wrist, a tangible symbol of her connection to them and to the *Soul* of Bloom Mountain.

To her left, Celeste felt Bloom Mountain's immense presence: quiet, slumbering, content. Motherly. Fatherly. It felt like family, like warm nights surrounded by cicada calls; like cider sipped at the holidays; like digging in the soil, toiling beside kith and kin.

They continued in silence until they reached the shores of Lighthouse Lake. Celeste wondered if Elise would react the same way she had two days before.

Elise gasped, pressed herself against her window, stared out at the lake and the lighthouse. "Grandma used to take us to the shore to hunt for rocks and fossils. Sometimes she let me stargaze." Her voice was wistful, but Celeste heard the cracks in the veneer of her calm. Soon enough, they might shatter.

Elise hummed the first few bars of a tune that Celeste half-recalled and then stopped.

"Do you remember the night we saw the meteor shower? It must have been the Perseids because we were just about to go back to school. I must've been eleven or twelve. Grandma brought us out here so I could see the shooting stars. It was hot that night, but the sky was so clear and we could see everything.

"You fell asleep in one of the chairs we brought, cause it was really early in the morning. But Grandma stayed up with me." Elise fingered a necklace she'd had for ages, a pendant with a small chunk of meteorite that had been a present from Granddaddy. That had been more than a decade ago, and was the last time either of them had heard from him.

I wonder what happened to Granddaddy after Grandma died...

Elise looked back at Celeste, tears running down her cheeks. "But I don't remember anything else. I must have fallen asleep cause the next thing I remember is studying for my first test that year."

"I don't remember that night either," Celeste admitted. "It's fuzzy and confused."

Celeste could see Birch Branch ahead and soon they would turn down the familiar rural road that would bring them to the farmhouse where they had spent so much time as children.

And where they would finally get some answers.

THE FARMHOUSE WAS THE SAME AS A FEW DAYS PRIOR. BUT as Celeste exited the car, she felt tension in the air. She opened herself up to the new part of her that let her see and feel magical currents of the Valley. She still expected to not see any, but they were there, fainter than on the mountain, where the well of her new power slumbered under stone and moss and rich black earth.

Wisps of magic clung to the garden. It crept up the fence like vines and hung from trees like bats. It glowed under flowerbeds and in the ripened corn out back. There was a whistle in the wind, low and discordant, at odds with the bright sunshine and the gentle blues of the flowers in the garden. Small points of light glittered in meandering rows, showing the passing of some animal.

"Were Grandma's flowers always blue?" Elise asked as they crossed the periwinkle and sky blue dotted lawn.

"Only blue flowers grow here, that's why it's called Blue Mountain," Marta responded.

"Huh," Elise said.

Classic Elise. She's probably already accepted magic. I only do because I have seen it.

The three of them climbed the steps onto the covered porch and Celeste knocked on the door. They waited while people moved around indoors, each *thunk* and *clank* echoing through the old house. After a few minutes, Celeste knocked again.

The woman with straight brown hair answered. "Ah, Celeste, I thought maybe you would let yourself in again." She smiled as she spoke and there was a twinkle in her eyes.

Celeste's face burned. She didn't exactly regret breaking into her aunt's home, but it hadn't been polite. Beside her, Elise's mouth hung open.

The woman looked so much like their mother with her long brown hair, deep brown eyes, and straight nose. But the way she carried herself was different. She stood tall with her shoulders back, a self-confidence evident in her features that their mother didn't have.

Celeste and Elise's mother, Amanda Foster, was a shell of the woman before them. She went through life afraid of the world she lived in, looking over her shoulders in the dark when she thought that no one watched. She loved her husband and her daughters, but there had been a distance to her their whole life. Their father did many things because their mother *couldn't*, as he said. Visiting the farm had been one of those things.

I wonder if Mom will tell us what happened. Why she left the Valley when she was young. Why she never mentioned her twin.

Their aunt let the sisters gape for a moment before standing aside and letting them enter. Marta and Elise followed Celeste inside the familiar entryway and crowded in one corner, uncertain where to go or what to say. Soft voices came from the screened in porch at the back of the house.

Their aunt closed the door and smiled at the trio.

"I'm Alice, your aunt," she said, holding out a hand. Elise shook it but Celeste just nodded. "I can tell from your reactions that Mandy never mentioned me. But the reasons for that will be made clear soon enough."

Alice turned towards the porch. After a few seconds, Marta took Celeste's hand and followed, Elise a step behind them.

The mastiffs met them in the dining room, two large bodies standing in the way with their tails wagging. They allowed Alice to pass with just a pat, but they wanted to thoroughly sniff the sisters and Marta. One, a female with a beautiful coat of white and brown, took particular interest in Marta. After a few moments and several rounds of scratches, they turned and led the trio onto the back porch.

Celeste and Elise's parents sat on a wicker bench. Their mother sobbed as she looked up and saw Celeste. Alice stood near the door to the gardens and watched her sister cry. There was a strange look on her face, something between pained and amused. Certainly something had happened to damage the relationship between the two.

Their father, Jacob, squeezed his wife's shoulders and stood. Celeste let go of Marta's hand and let her father wrap his long arms around her. She'd inherited her dark hair and pale green eyes from him.

"I couldn't believe it when we got the call yesterday," he whispered and then let go. "I never expected you to end up *here.*"

Celeste didn't know how to respond. "I don't think I had much of a choice in the matter." Everything had lined up so nicely, so cleanly, and here she was after so much heartache, at the start of a new lease on life.

Maybe there is something to fate. Fate brought me here, gave me a task. I just have to make the decision to stay.

Her father frowned. "Yes, I'm afraid that's probably true. Your mother has been inconsolable since Alice called, saying that one of the girls was here. That she was going to attempt the Binding of Bloom Mountain."

In the background, her mother wailed with fresh tears.

Celeste scrunched her face in response. "What did they tell you?"

He sighed. "Alice explained some to us about the importance. *He* came and had more to say, but I'll let him share that with you. *He's* why your Mother is so distressed."

Granddaddy?

Celeste didn't have time to clarify who *he* was. Her mother rose from the bench and shambled towards her. She was in such a state of extreme distress that she almost fell into her husband's arms. That seemed to bring her back to herself, to the fact that her youngest daughter was alive and well, standing before her.

"I'm so sorry, Celeste, so sorry that I wasn't brave enough to be there for you that night. Sorry I didn't tell you about my home and my family and *everything*." She stumbled from her husband to Celeste and hugged her fiercely.

Celeste stood for several minutes while her mother mumbled continual apologies. For everything from not making breakfast right that one time to not doing enough to understand her strange youngest daughter. Celeste let her cry and apologize and knew that she needed the relief as much as Celeste had needed to see her room in this house.

Poor Mom, she's bottled things up for so long. Maybe my coming out here was the best for everyone. Maybe I can pay for all of us to get therapy.

When the crying and muttering had subsided, her mother pulled away.

"Can you ever forgive me, my darling?" Her eyes were full of fear, expecting that Celeste would never forgive her for things outside of her control.

"Of course, Mom." Celeste hugged her once more and then led her back to her seat.

Alice entered the porch with a glass of iced tea and a banana. She sat next to Celeste's mom and held them out. "Here, Mandy, this will help."

That led to another fit of crying, which Elise took over. She made sure that their mother drank her tea and ate her banana before she passed out from exertion.

Celeste turned back to her father. "Who is *he*?"

Jacob sighed and cast a long glance at his wife. "He's down by the barn. He doesn't get on with your mom, which is why she's stayed away for so long. She's...afraid of him."

"Granddaddy?"

He nodded. "Yes."

"Why?"

He only shrugged in response.

I guess I have to ask myself.

Celeste nodded and headed for the door, but stopped and turned around, looking for Marta. She stood to the side of the porch, trying hard not to stare at the cluster around Celeste's mother. She smiled when she noticed Celeste watching her, and walked over.

"Do you want to go for a walk? My Granddaddy is down by the barn and I want to talk to him."

"Do you want me to come with you?"

"I don't think I want to be far away from you for a long time." Celeste blushed as she said it but knew it was true.

Marta smothered a laugh behind her hand and nodded. "Of course."

They exited the covered porch into the back gardens. Bees and butterflies and dragonflies swarmed over the mounds of flowers along the fence. Rows of rose bushes, hydrangeas, and blue-tinted white azaleas dominated the garden closer to the house while squash and pumpkin patches took up space near the fence. Celeste led Marta to a gate at the back corner of the plot.

The grass between the garden and the tree line was long enough to let small blue wildflowers thrive, but not so long as to look overgrown and unkempt. The trees towered over them, a canopy of loblolly pine. Celeste wondered then if they were replanting that specific tree here in The Valley like they were out in Virginia and North Carolina. Or maybe The Valley didn't have the deforestation problems plaguing the Outside.

More questions to answer in time.

Despite the cheerful flowers and the sunshine, there was still a taint on the day.

Marta grabbed Celeste's hand as they emerged from the woods into untamed pastures where cows used to graze. The barn was a little ways down from the trees and they could see the silhouette of someone walking around the perimeter.

Celeste wanted to hurry down to the barn to see her Granddaddy again, but she remembered the way her father had spoken about him. How her mother was *scared* of her own father, and that made her pause.

She stopped and Marta noticed when their contact was broken.

"Celeste?" She looked confused. Concerned.

"Something my dad said has me…confused. He said mom was *afraid* of Granddaddy, but he didn't say why. I don't remember Granddaddy well. He was just a really tall, thin, old man who was happy and jolly and enjoyed playing with us. And he knew so much about trees, he told me exactly how old the trees were and where their seeds had come from, but I didn't believe him. Who could know where the seeds had come from?"

Something that had been bothering her, picking away at the back of her mind, clicked into place as she talked. She rubbed at her shoulder where the claw marks still burned with low-grade pain beneath soft bandages. She thought about the mountain lion who'd visited the farm, the very barn that they were looking at, and the responses her grandparents had given.

And how she'd heard the same response again, when petting Lorna earlier that day.

"It looks like you've made a friend," she whispered under her breath, horrified.

"What's wrong?" Marta stood before her, hands on Celeste's shoulders.

Celeste looked up into Marta's beautiful eyes and trembled. "Marta, I think my Granddaddy tried to kill me last night."

27
RECKONING

Several minutes of guided breathing later, Celeste successfully avoided a panic attack. Fingering the Stormwalker talisman, she wondered if it would continue to protect her. She had to confront *him*, needed to confirm her suspicions, needed to know the truth of her lost memories.

If she was right, Celeste understood her mother's fear.

If she saw anything like I did last night, I would be terrified too. I'm still scared of the bastard, even if he's "sane" once more.

Celeste stopped at the open barn doors, unwilling to go any further, not wanting to enter the darkness that was his abode. Sunlight streamed inside the opening.

A tall, gaunt shadow prowled around the interior walls, then stopped and looked back at them. They waited, Marta holding onto Celeste, keeping her grounded and calm. They watched as the shadow made one final circuit to stand just within the doors, sunlight bathing him in warmth.

The shadow was still tall and thin, with one arm in a sling, but he wore a face that was more familiar to Celeste. A person that was beloved for his knowledge and humor and the little toys he made for Celeste and Elise when they were kids.

"Celly, you've finally come home." The voice was familiar, but different, just like the man. Soft and musical, but dissonant like the call of a cicada.

Celeste breathed deeply, hoping to keep her voice calm. But her flight response fought with the image of her Granddaddy before her and the memory of Abram hunting her last night.

"Were you planning on telling me? Or did you want to surprise me again?" Celeste spoke through her teeth, keeping her emotions in check.

He laughed. Head thrown back, eyes closed. Then he straightened. "If you don't want to see the change, look away, little one." Marta turned and rested her forehead on Celeste's shoulder. Celeste snaked an arm around her back to hold her tight. She'd warned Marta about what Abram could do.

Here we go again.

Celeste watched as his face changed. The muscles twitched, melted together, eyes changing color, mouth widening, hair growing. It was enough to make Celeste queasy, but not enough to make her sick. The muscles and skin settled and Abram stood before them.

Celeste closed her eyes for a moment, holding back tears and emotions she didn't have time to work out. When she opened them again, she watched Abram shake his body, settling into the form she knew better now.

"So, dear granddaughter, what now?"

Marta's head left her shoulder and Celeste missed the pressure, the comfort of that one small gesture. She could've looked away or covered her eyes. Instead she used Celeste as her shield.

"Did you know when you met me on the slopes yesterday?"

He shook his head. "No, I didn't learn until earlier today."

Celeste sighed with relief.

I guess it's good he didn't knowingly hunt me down.

"The Soul of Bloom Mountain grew restless with its magic unbound. It started shifting more of its power to me to ease the burden on itself. It pushed me to great ends to protect the mountain, to keep the magic bound away, and that wore on my borrowed humanity." He sighed, the most *normal* thing he'd done. Celeste saw hints of Granddaddy Abner in the movement.

"Ellie told me after we parted at the farm. I should've known before, should've tasted the resemblance in your magic to my own. But I was delirious and overburdened by the curse."

"You should've helped her," Marta spat, anger in her voice.

Abram smiled, an honest one. "Back down, little Finch. I'm in my right mind now, old though it may be."

Marta flushed and Celeste squeezed her.

"I saw Celeste as a threat to the mountain. She was an intruder that didn't belong. I did what was in my nature."

"What did you do to terrify Mom?" Celeste blurted out.

Abram sighed again. "When the twins were born, I realized Amanda had inherited some of my powers. Some of my Spirit transferred to her, making her less human and me more. I didn't know what form those would take until she was a teenager. And by the time she started shapeshifting, it was too late to teach her how to come to it naturally. She had no control and changed in front of a friend. And he took it badly.

"I had hoped that she would take over the binding ritual when she was old enough, that we could keep it in the family down through the ages. But it was too late. She found out that I could shape shift and hadn't told her and she left as soon as she could. She said she never wanted to speak to me again." Pain etched his face, making him appear ancient. "The last thing I told her was that her powers would be suppressed by the Outside world and that was where she went. Alice stayed, but didn't have what the mountain needs. Her gifts lie elsewhere."

"Wait," Celeste interrupted. "So, you knew Mom had magic but you never told her? And then let her shape shift in front of someone else who didn't know?"

He nodded, eyes focused on the ground. "Yes, and when I showed her that I could also change my form, she didn't react well. Said I had neglected her, favored Alice instead. Then she left for college and never came back."

"What happened when we stopped visiting?"

If anything, Abram shrank in on himself more than he had. "There are times throughout the year where the natural magics of the Valley is stronger. I lose my ability to control the changes, and you saw me change. You and Elise saw me shift on the shore of Lighthouse Lake and it scared you.

"I had the Matron of Midnight's Ride burn the memories from you, but your mother had enough. She saw it as another of my failures."

Celeste exhaled through her nose. The truth didn't make it easier for her to remember.

Abram looked up at Celeste and there was pain in his alien eyes. "I can't make you see me the way you used to, Celly. But I am still your Granddaddy, and I love you as much as I am capable." Something caught his attention in the trees behind them.

Celeste looked over her shoulder and saw something large lurking in the shadows under the pines. Eyes peered out at them from the darkness.

"The eyes in the trees…" *Just like when I was little.*

"I'll do what I can to make sure your mother doesn't suffer more from my mistreatment of her. But only if she lets me."

Celeste nodded, only just realizing that she had been bargaining on her mother's behalf. She hoped that, given enough time, her mother might be less afraid.

"You and I, though. We will have to see each other often. You have powerful magics in you. But you need training."

Celeste swallowed hard. "I don't like the sound of that."

"No, you won't like it. It will be hard and it will hurt; your mind, body, and soul will be pushed to their limits. But I know you can do it. You have spirit blood running through your body, and that accounts for a lot."

"What the hell do you mean by that?"

"Time will show you, Celly. You just need to give it and me some time."

Abram motioned with his good arm towards the forest, where the eyes had been. He started walking, his long legs going at a slower, more sedate pace than the night before.

After a minute Celeste looked at Marta and the two of them followed, curious what would happen next.

Later that night, Celeste and Marta stayed joined at the hip while a celebration roared around them. It felt like half the Valley showed up to celebrate the successful binding of Bloom Mountain.

A field outside of town turned into a festival in the short hours since noon. Torches and lanterns and bonfires were lit, food cooked in great cauldrons and the scent of fresh bread somehow permeated everything. A troupe of musicians played on an impromptu stage and couples danced around them.

People watched from benches and camp chairs, plates laden with food on their laps and cups of alcohol in their hands. Jed and Sadie were set up with their pies. A broad smile covered his face as he doled out the appropriate pie to everyone who wanted some. He had a whole French silk pie boxed up for Celeste for later, and a promise for another every year after the binding was completed.

Everyone moved from Selena to Celeste, offering congratulations and heartfelt thanks for saving Milton. Some brought little gifts in baskets or wrapped in paper: books, jars of honey or preserves, fresh produce, bottles of cider and mead. It was overwhelming and Celeste was more than a little jealous of her family at the farmhouse. They got to sit this celebration out.

Her mother would need a long time to come to terms with what had happened, and there was no guarantee that they would ever be a complete family again. But, after the initial shock and fear subsided, she had shown that the Foster family stubbornness ran in her too.

Time, as Abram had said, would tell what happened to them all.

Celeste looked around at the people dancing and after eleven long years of anxiety and suffering. The future was bright for them, now that Celeste had come along and bound herself to Bloom Mountain and to Milton. They didn't know that she had already been bound to them by the accident of her birth, and it didn't really matter.

She felt the magic in her gut, twisting and turning to the rhythm of the music, flowing through her veins like the waters of the Nomini. It felt almost natural now, inevitable, like the slow procession of seasons and planets in the sky.

She watched as Marta laughed and bantered with her friends and played with their daughter. Celeste's heart was full and she knew she would one day fall in love with Marta. The trembling in her heart fought with the magic churning in her gut. And won when Marta turned back to her, eyes bright and a smile on her face.

"What now?" Celeste asked when Marta returned.

Marta thought for a moment, eyes wandering over the crowd. "It would be poor form for the Binder to not dance at their celebration."

"But, I don't know how to dance!"

Marta pulled Celeste in close. "The mountain must be bound every year, so there's plenty of time for me to teach you."

Celeste smiled. "I'd like that." And she leaned in to kiss Marta once more, knowing that there was a bright future ahead of her.

CHRISTMAS EVE.

Snow gently fell on Milton. Tiny flakes floated on
the wind, stuck to trees and eyelashes and hair.

Celeste watched from the overlook, fiddling with a small,
velvet-covered box in her coat pocket. The Camry hummed
behind her, keeping the interior warm. Christmas music played
on the radio.

It surprised her how similar the holidays were compared to
Outside. There was a certain pagan flavor to everything, but
there was just enough churn in residents to keep pace with
trends. Even Elf on the Shelf had a moment in The Valley.
Some of the more superstitious residents had been skeptical,
given the elven legends. But younger people, those who had
kids or a more worldly perspective, thought there was nothing
to it.

The biggest surprise was how often it snowed. Her first
winter they got 40 inches, the second 54, and forecasts
predicted even more this year. Something about weather
patterns in the Liminal Worlds and Lands Between made the
Valley get more snow than *Outside* in Shenandoah.

A *bzzzt* brought Celeste back to the world.

🖤Marta🖤: You back yet, babe?

Celeste: Yeah, just stopped to stretch
my knee.

🖤Marta🖤: Did you get that brandy
you wanted?

Celeste: Yep! Bought a couple of
bottles to share with Samone too.

🖤Marta🖤: Hurry home. I misssssss
you <3

Celeste: I'll be home soon enough ;) I
got you something too!

🖤Marta🖤: 👁️👄👁️

Celeste: That's what I'd expect from
Abram.

🖤Marta🖤: Ooo, that one stings.

🖤Marta🖤: Hurry up! Everyone will be
here soon!

Celeste chuckled and clutched the box.
I hope you like this, Marta.

Driving through town was a slow process. Not because the streets weren't plowed, they were. But because Christmas Eve was the traditional day to celebrate Solstice. Residents in coats and cloaks visited their neighbors with gifts of cookies, wine, and homemade goods.

Groups of carolers sang on corners, drawing crowds out of their warm homes into the snow. At one intersection in town, two groups alternated songs. One group did traditional carols from Outside, while the other performed darker, stranger carols to the gods of the Liminal Worlds. They sang of the dark of night, the shine of moonlight on claws, the gentle dripping of blood, sacrifices that must be made for the sun to return.

They finished a modified version of "Carol of the Bells" as Celeste pulled to a stop.

"On, on they send

On without end,
Their fearful tone,
To ev'ry home.
Ding, dong.
Diiiiing…
Donnnnnng."

THEY HELD THE LAST TWO NOTES UNCOMFORTABLY LONG.

The traditional group started up a cheery rendition of "God Rest Ye Merry Gentlemen" as the light turned. Celeste found most of the Valley carols unsettling, especially after her experiences with the soul of Bloom Mountain. And some of the darker creatures she helped hunt down over the last three years.

Let's not dwell on that. You've got plenty else to worry about right now.

Once she passed through town, the rest of the journey was quick and soon she parked in the driveway of her and Marta's new little bungalow.

💜Marta💜: I SEE YOU

💜Marta💜: Can you help bring in stuff from Samone's truck?

💜Marta💜: She's finishing up the cookies. 😊

Celeste waved to the three faces peering out from between the green plaid curtains she'd fought tooth and nail for. Marta had, of course, wanted black. But Celeste didn't want *everything* in their house to be black. Marta hadn't fought too hard.

Lights glittered in the snow-covered trees, reflecting off oversized ornaments and icicles. Warm firelight glowed within their neighbors' homes. Samone's truck sat next to the curb out front, the tailgate down. Celeste grabbed her bag of brandy bottles and a box from the truck.

Anna opened the door for Celeste and took the box from her hands before leaning in close.

"Marta's been anxious all day. I think she's figured you out." Her pale eyes were wide. "I didn't say a thing. Promise!"

"I know, Anna." Celeste looked over Anna's shoulder at Samone and Marta at the kitchen island. They giggled at something Samone said. Marta had frosting on her face and powdered sugar in her hair.

Celeste sat her bag on the couch and looked around the main living area.

Marta, Anna, and Samone had decorated in her absence. Wreaths hung from every door. Pine garlands wrapped with battery-operated lights decorated the walls. Another wrapped with plaid ribbon decorated the mantle, framing a portrait of Selena. The cat tree in the corner was tied with matching ribbons already torn to shreds. Candles dotted every table and more were piled into an old rocking chair by the fireplace.

Porridge leapt from his perch and trotted over to Celeste, meowing.

"Hey big guy, did you miss me?" He rubbed his big, cream-colored face against her cheek and purred.

Matches leaned against her leg and twitched her tail.

Celeste carried Porridge over to the kitchen.

"I see you two had some fun while I was gone."

"And you greeted your cat before greeting me," Marta countered with mock indignation.

Celeste turned so that Porridge was facing Marta. "Look. At. His. Little. Face!" She nuzzled him and kissed his nose. "Besides, he throws a fit if I greet anyone else first."

Marta reached over and scratched between Porridge's ears. "He's a very needy boy, and I really just don't measure up. Do I?"

Samone snorted. "You're just jealous that there's a cat that prefers someone else."

Marta pouted. "Yeah, a little."

Mrrroowwwwww!

Matches jumped onto the island and settled herself in a corner with a look of feline disdain.

"I think she's offended that you're offended, Marta." Celeste put Porridge down and circled the island to plant a kiss on Marta's cheek. "Or she's jealous that Porridge got attention and she didn't."

Celeste scooped up Matches. "Hello, little hell spawn alarm clock."

"I can hear her purring from over here," Samone called from the cookie sheet.

Matches leapt out of Celeste's arms and sauntered over to Porridge, who was sitting by the fire, cleaning himself.

The door slammed.

"Well, isn't this cheery!"

Celeste spun around in her spot, not believing her ears.

Elise stood in the doorway, taking off her long, dark brown wool coat and scarlet gloves, scarf, and hat.

"Elise!" She all but skipped over to her big sister and let herself be enveloped in a hug.

"Hello," Elise responded, her voice low and smooth like good brandy.

Celeste backed out of the hug. "Why are you here? Why aren't you at home with Mom and Dad?"

Someone knocked on the door. Celeste opened it and her jaw dropped.

"Mom? Dad?"

Her parents were there, dressed in their best clothing, holding wrapped presents. Best, and strangest of all, her mom had a broad smile on her face. Something that Celeste would never have believed after the events of three years previous. But therapy did wonders.

Celeste stood by in wonder as, over the next 20 minutes, more people arrived: Celeste's aunt, Ellie, Marta's parents, Jed and Sadie, and a few select friends. In total there were about 20 people at the house, and it started to feel crowded.

It was hot with the fire burning and the people milling about the living room, peeking into the other rooms if they hadn't been to the house yet, playing with the cats, tasting Samone and Anna's pastries and Marta's cooking.

Celeste stood out of the way, feeling the weight and heat of their presences. It was too much, far too many people for what she had planned for the night. And that was…upsetting. Too many people meant too many eyes watching Celeste, which was exactly what she didn't want.

Therapy had done wonders for Celeste, had helped her come to terms with her specific needs with relation to her autism. Crowds were easier to handle now, but she'd had a specific idea for the evening, something she really wanted to do, and now it felt like everything had been ruined. And that wasn't fair to Marta, who clearly wanted to surprise Celeste by inviting her family over for their first Christmas.

The heat and the lack of space and the change of plans started to build up. She could feel it in her stomach and her constricting throat.

"Air," she whispered to herself. "I need air."

Celeste smiled and excused herself as she waded through

the crowd towards the front door. No one seemed to notice as she grabbed her coat and slipped out the door.

The frigid air immediately enveloped Celeste. She put her coat on, but not before the shivering started. Somewhere down the street a group of carolers was singing, but she couldn't make out the tune. She trudged to the Camry and slid inside. It started up after a mild complaint and heat pumped out of the vents.

Celeste pulled the ring box out and flipped it open. A tarnished silver ring with three small, black stones sat nestled against the black velvet. It was vintage, but in excellent shape and had been professionally cleaned and resized for Marta. Anna thought she'd love it, and Celeste was hopeful. But she didn't know when she'd get another chance to do a memorable proposal. Maybe she was overthinking it, but the idea to do it on Christmas Eve in their new home had felt really important. And now she knew she wouldn't be able to do it.

A knock on the passenger window made Celeste yelp and snap the box shut.

She looked up to see Abram standing there, motioning for her to let him in.

"Of all the people…" she said under her breath. She hit the unlock and he slipped inside in that too-liquid way he moved when normal humans weren't watching.

"Evening, Celly." He settled himself and put his hands over the heater, though they were already rosy.

"Hi," she responded.

"Quite a party you have going on tonight." His voice was mild, as if he was commenting on the weather.

"Turned out to be bigger than I expected."

"Well, and is that a problem?"

Celeste sighed. "Yes. I don't think I can do this with all of *them* watching. Marta even convinced Mom and Dad to show up." Another sigh, though this one had more pain in it. "Mom even looks *happy* to be here."

Abram nodded, his alien eyes tinged with regret. "And yet, here you are, sitting in your car."

"I can't do it with all those people present."

Celeste had been in a weird mood the day she brought up proposing to Marta. She and Abram were tracking something with strange footprints through the woods on the western ridge that formed Yuback Valley. It had turned out to be a wounded deer, which Abram brought to Ellie. On their way back, Celeste had suddenly told him what she'd planned. She hadn't even told Anna at that point. But she found herself pouring out all her hopes and worries to Abram, of all *people*. And he'd taken it well, without his normal sarcasm.

For a moment they had a relationship reminiscent of grand-father and granddaughter again. Then Celeste erected the barriers that were normally there, just not as high as before.

"Why not take her into the backyard and propose in the snow? That would be memorable."

"I don't know…that's just not how I planned it." Celeste sniffed, tears threatening to fall. "What did you do with Grandma?"

Abram pursed his lips, an almost human reaction to her question. "I just kind of asked. She was halfway up the Stair-well and it just slipped out."

"Really? While she was climbing the Stairwell? You could've waited until she was done or at Coal Mine Number 3 or Giant's Mound. Anywhere but the Stairwell!"

He laughed. "She said something almost exactly the same. Once she got to the top and caught her breath." He paused. "But she did say yes first."

"Which will be harder: doing it differently but on the same night? Or not doing it at all?"

Celeste thought for a moment. "I don't know. I *think* not doing it would be worse, but it's so hard to have to change plans at the last minute. And now I'm hiding from people I love because I didn't expect them to be here."

Abram made a *hmmm* sound. "Why do you think Marta invited them as a surprise?"

Celeste sat up straighter. "I don't know. She's asked or told me ahead of time in the past..." She trailed off. Then she remembered that Marta had been acting a little strange lately, secretly making phone calls, giggling at things she wouldn't share, staring at Celeste when she thought Celeste was busy. And then she had gone out with Samone more often than normal.

Celeste slapped her forehead.

"I'm such an idiot. I was so worried about making sure that she didn't know what I was doing that I didn't pay attention to what *she* was doing."

Abram cocked his head, his usual halo of shadows quivering like they were giggling. "Oh?"

She glared at him. "Don't tell me she roped you into this, too."

"You are not the only one who knows how to call me when I am needed, Celly."

They sat in silence for a moment, only the far off sound of carolers broke through the crisp stillness of the night.

"You should go inside," he said. "You're wasting precious night."

He opened the door, slipped out, and dissipated into shadows before she could respond.

Celeste sat for another minute, turning the ring box over in her hands, before she turned off the Camry and got out.

A thin layer of snow clung to the sidewalk up to the front door. She stood there a while, listening to the sounds within:

voices happily talking, champagne bottles opening, Christmas carols on the speakers, the occasional *mrow* as a cat got in the way.

Celeste took one deep breath, and then another. Savoring the crisp, cool air in her lungs. Relishing the feeling before she opened the door and stepped back into the warmth.

No one noticed her return, or the black box she clutched in her hand as she hung up her coat.

"Celeste!" Her mother called from the couch where she sat with her husband and sister. She rose to embrace Celeste. "Your house is so cute! And I love what Marta's done with the wreaths. It's almost like what your Grandma would do when Alice and I were children."

Celeste swallowed hard. It was clear that her mother *had* gone to therapy over the last three years, had done her best to come to terms with her childhood and the reasons why she'd left The Valley. That she would come here and be happy, probably without knowing why she was invited, meant the world to Celeste.

Anna appeared at Celeste's elbow. "Where'd you go?"

Celeste looked over her shoulder. "I just needed to cool down."

"Literally or figuratively?"

"Both."

"You good now?"

Celeste nodded. "I think so."

Alright, time to do this. Or I never will.

Celeste scanned the room, looking for Marta. She wasn't there, so Celeste headed through to the hallway and found her talking to Ellie in the doorway to their joint study.

Ellie saw Celeste first and nodded to Marta.

Relief flooded Marta's face and she rushed down the hall.

"I'm so sorry Celeste, I didn't think this through very well."

Celeste pulled her into a hug. "It's okay. I didn't either."

Marta pulled back to search Celeste's face. "Didn't think what through?"

Celeste gulped down her panic and let go of Marta. The ring case was still clutched in her fist and she held it out on her palm to Marta.

Marta looked down, dumbstruck.

Celeste opened the box.

Marta squealed and leapt into Celeste's arms for a second, knocking her off balance. Then she ran off down the hall, yelling, "Wait a minute!" as she did.

Everything was silent until Marta returned, more composed than a minute previous. She held out a similar ring box, this one in green velvet. Her under eye makeup was smudged.

Celeste felt something bubble in her chest, threatening to climb her throat. She didn't know if it was joy or fear or apprehension. But she knew in an hour or so that she'd be in a haze of happiness.

Marta went a step further and knelt down on one knee.

The ring was a white gold branch that twisted around itself and was dotted with leaves. There wasn't a stone, but that was okay, cause Celeste would have had a hard time with that.

"Celeste, will you marry me?"

The tears started falling and all Celeste could do was nod.

Cheers erupted from the living room. Celeste turned to see that everyone was standing just on the other side of the entrance, watching the two of them.

Marta stood and the two of them fumbled with their respective rings, making sure they made it onto the appropriate finger of the appropriate hand. When they were done, Celeste stared at Marta in what she hoped was a loving way, despite the tears and sniffles. She had no idea what to do now.

"Just kiss already," someone in the crowd yelled.

Everyone laughed, Celeste and Marta included, and the tension was broken.

Celeste leaned in and kissed Marta softly.

More cheering.

When she pulled away, Marta brushed a tear from her cheek. "It's only the beginning for us, Celeste."

THE END

CHARACTER INDEX

Celeste Foster (she/her)

33 years old

Forester

Lesbian

Marta Finch (she/her)
34 years old
Alchemist/Barista
Bisexual

Abram Waite
God of the Mountain

'Shotgun' Ellie
Game Warden

Lorna
Familiar

Berry
Familiar

CAROL OF THE BELLS - THE VALLEY VERSION

Hark! how the bells,
    Dire warning bells
    All seem to say
    "Now start to pray."
    Solstice is here
    Bringing cold fear
    To young and old
    To hunters bold

Ding, dong, ding, dong
    That is their song
    With haunting ring
    All caroling
    One seems to hear
    Murmurs of fear
    From ev'rywhere
    Filling the air

Oh how they pound

Spirits o' th' mound
O'er hill and dale
Hunting the frail
Bloodcurdling screams
While people dream
Visions of fear
Solstice is here

Dreary, dreary, dreary, dreary Solstice
Eerie, eerie, eerie, eerie Solstice

On, on they send
On without end
Their fearful tone
To ev'ry home

(repeat)

Ding, dong, ding, dong

ACKNOWLEDGMENTS

The last time I wrote acknowledgements for *Bloom Mountain*, I went on a multi-page rant about how afab autistics are treated.

I'm not going to do that again.

I want to acknowledge all the people who made BOBM:DE possible.

First, to those who read and loved BOBM the first time around. And those who read it but had very reasonable criticisms of both the story content and writing. I wasn't happy with the book as it was published, but people loved it anyways. So while this book is for me, this edition is for everyone else.

Second, to the people who related to Celeste and *saw* themselves in a book for the first time. I wanted to show my experiences with autism through the lens of an afab person my age, in the part of the world I've spent most of my life.

Third, to my dearest friends: the SS Void Crew, the Little Dudes Chaos Chat, BARD, my Eruri friends. You are all the lights of my life. Without you this would never have happened. I cant possibly name you all individually, but *finger guns*.

Kara and Margherita, for the understanding and forgiveness.

Menoa and Kara, for being Bloom's biggest fans.

Freddie and Aria, for the sisterhood I missed growing up.

Mawce, Official Artist of BOBM and Mr. Doom's #1 Marta Artist.

Ronove, for the beautiful art for the prints and bookmarks.

Buttons, for reading the book then turning around and editing it. I owe you so many coffees.

Daneh, for everything. For our secret project.

Juniper, for the amazing cover, for the unrelenting support and encouragement, for being my skrunkle.

And lastly, Mike. None of this would have happened without you. I love you more than anything.

ABOUT THE AUTHOR

Vesper Doom (she/they) is a queer, disabled author of sci-fi, fantasy, and horror from the greater Washington, D.C. area. When they aren't writing, they enjoy reading, painting, collecting rocks and stickers, and inviting forgotten gods to coffee.

You can find them online @vesperdoom, vesperdoom.carrd.co, and contact them at vesperdoom@outlook.com.

ALSO BY VESPER DOOM

Broodmother - A Story of the Valley\
The Citadel of Ice (Winter 2024/2025)
Metropolis Down (2025)